STONE FRUIT

By

Dorothy Bunting Montgomery

COPYRIGHT ©2020

by Dorothy Marie Montgomery

Published by Transforming Perspectives, LLC

This is a work of fiction. Any references to historical events, real people, or real locales are used fictitiously. Other names, characters, places, and incidents either are the product of the author's imagination, and any resemblance to actual events or locales or persons, living or dead, is entirely coincidental.

ISBN: 9781074212841

DEDICATION

TO MY PARENTS, BARBARA AND RHINEHART
for giving me the wisdom to believe that anything is possible

AND TO BRIAN AND BRYN
for making everything possible

CHAPTER 1

New York City, 1990

"I'm looking at the picture right now." Patrice Powell squinted closely at the newspaper clipping in her hand, the phone pressed hard between her ear and shoulder.

"I thought she had died years ago." Patrice peered at the clock on the wall. It was approaching two o'clock, and she had too many deadlines and too much research to complete. She wasn't interested in taking an additional writing assignment.

Patrice's growing impatience was apparent as she tapped her foot. Glenn Collier, the editor of *European Art* magazine, was on the phone. He was Patrice's boss, and he was talking rapidly. Glenn had placed a newspaper clipping on her desk with a note stating he would call her. The note also said he had some exciting news.

"There isn't much to this story," Patrice insisted. "Yes, her brother was a famous artist and yes, she was a subject in his most famous painting. I don't think she did much with the rest of her life. There isn't more than a blurb to this story."

Patrice's chin fell to her chest, her blonde shoulder-length hair tumbled toward the phone that was cupped in her hand. She did not want to accept this assignment, but Glenn's voice was persistent. Patrice toyed with the thought of saying no to

Glenn, but she knew that would go over like a lead balloon.

"Yes, Glenn, I'm from their hometown, but that's not saying much. Yes, there's an art festival there once a year, but it's a very local event. *No ... big ... deal,*" she said, expelling her words.

Patrice swiveled her chair to find her coworker Brian looking at her from his cubicle. Patrice shot him a look of annoyance. Brian shot back a quizzical look. Patrice shrugged her shoulders and swiveled her chair with her back to Brian. *Concentrate*, she told herself. She grabbed a pen and started to write WYM on the note pad in front of her for "watch your mouth." Patrice had to remind herself that not only was Glenn the editor but most recently her former co-worker. Patrice pressed her lips tightly together as if sealing the door to her inner thoughts.

Glenn was not taking no for an answer, and the story was Patrice's.

"What was that all about," Brian asked when she had hung up the phone.

"Because I'm from quote, unquote "Grant Wood *country*," Patrice said, using her fingers to gesture quotes, "I have to do the story about his sister Nan's death. She's the face in his most notable painting *American Gothic* and, since I'm from their hometown in Iowa, Glenn thinks I'm the right person for this story. I wasn't impressed with Grant Wood's work growing up, and I'm not impressed with it now!" Patrice folded her arms across her chest. Patrice let her thoughts drift to a memory of a painting that had hung in her parents' home for as long as she could remember: Grant Wood's *Stone City*. It was a simple painting that she had made fun of over the years, believing a 12-year-old could have produced this painting. There was no sophistication in this work, just another boring landscape that didn't speak to the eye or the soul. The trees were too perfect; the swell of the hills looked like the belly of a pregnant woman. It was just an odd piece and, back in Iowa, the people she knew were not impressed with Grant Wood either, believing he was someone who put on airs and didn't earn a proper living like respectable hardworking Iowa folks.

"Get over yourself. Don't be knocking the guy who painted the most iconic painting in the United States," Brian shot back.

"Why doesn't Glenn give it to one of the junior writers, and why are we even doing a feature on Regional art? Our magazine focuses on European art and art collecting. This is an Americana story." Patrice was getting more disgusted by the minute just thinking about having to do the story.

"Then find the link of Nan's death to European art. Besides, this gives you a chance to go home, see family." Brian mimicked an upbeat smile as he swiveled back and forth in his chair. Patrice knew he was trying to make her feel better, but she was not in the mood to write *this story* or see her family.

She threw her pen at Brian, nearly hitting his face--not understanding why she was struggling with this so.

"Glenn wants the story for the November issue, so I have to leave tomorrow!"

The next day, Patrice was at LaGuardia promptly at 6:30 a.m., three hours before her scheduled flight. Coffee in hand, she sat down in one of the chairs near the gate. Taking a sip of her coffee, she was hoping to wake up, and shake off the loss of sleep the night before. She had been up late, finishing work assignments and packing. That's what she told herself any way, but the truth was she just couldn't sleep. The hand holding her coffee was shaking. *Get a grip, Patrice. You've traveled across the country and the world a million times!* She pulled a breakfast bar from her purse, took a big bite, and washed it down with her coffee. The coffee was comforting, as if someone had placed a sweater over her chilled shoulders. She started to relax and took a deep breath. A young mother sat across from her with a baby cradled in her arms, two bags dangling from the opposite arm, a purse and diaper bag. Patrice leaned forward in her seat to offer help, but the mother sat down easily and cradled her baby. *So not me,*

Patrice reflected on her life. It was simple, and she liked it that way. She rented a very small studio apartment on a noisy lower floor of a midtown Manhattan apartment complex. She could deal with the noise because she was usually at work. There were no pets to attend to and a few plants to water from time to time, to save them from dying. Her neighbors mirrored similar life-styles and left her alone. Simple.

Damn Glenn for his push on this story and the last-minute shove out the door. She had never felt this much anger toward him, and it would probably take the entire trip to cool down enough to forgive him. *What a waste of my talent and Glenn's. Maybe he wasn't the hot editor she thought he was. Maybe the caffeine will help me see things differently!*

"I don't think so," she complained under her breath. She sipped at the cup of coffee and looked at her watch. "I should be in Cedar Rapids by two. They'd better remove the hogs off the runway."

Patrice saw a newsstand in the distance and walked over, dodging the human sea of moving business apparel flowing toward her. Stepping inside, she grabbed *The New York Times*, flipping to the Arts and Entertainment section. Let's see if there's anything at all about Nan Wood Graham's death. There was not. No surprise there. The biggest story was the $82.5 million sale of van Gogh's *Portrait of Dr. Gachet*.

Patrice shook her head and walked away, muttering to herself about useless and totally inconvenient assignments that no one could care less about. Grabbing a bag of almonds and a packet of spearmint gum, she thought, *Well, at least this will give me some-thing to chew on between New York and Iowa.*

◆ ◆ ◆

As she stepped from the small plane, the Iowa humidity suffo-cated her. Beads of sweat started to form on her face and neck. Remembering days of detasseling corn by hand in her parents' cornfield, Patrice made a ponytail, tying a knot with her hair at the nape of her neck.

Cool air greeted her as she walked into the airport. She eyed a wall poster which read "Welcome to Cedar Rapids, Home of the World's Largest Cereal Company."

"You'd better love the smell of corn sweeteners and grain," she muttered as she followed the rest of the passengers toward the escalator that took her to the baggage claim. The walls to her left and right were adorned with posters of the University of Iowa campus and the Hawkeye football team in their black and gold uniforms. Education and food represented some of Iowa's best commodities and the airport's decor personified both.

As she approached Baggage Claim a conveyer made a sharp, honking noise like a security breach in a financial institution, and Patrice cupped her ears. The noise subsided once the luggage exposed itself from behind the plastic flaps that kept the passengers from seeing where their luggage came from. Patrice glanced at the people who were waiting for their luggage.

She became self-conscious about her outfit because she looked out of place here like someone who walked into K-Mart dressed for a cocktail party. She slipped her Ray-Ban sunglasses into her Gucci bag and shoved her bag behind her elbow. She pulled at her Gloria Vanderbilt tailored white slacks as if they were less than perfect and bent her knees slightly to cover up her Gucci pumps. She could hear the judgments of those she stood next to. *Who does she think she is? Doesn't she know you don't put on airs in Iowa.* Patrice listened to the exchange of vigorous conversation around her, realizing that she could almost "hear" the smiles as loved ones greeted each other. *Shoot--she forgot to call her parents!* Her regretful thoughts drowned out the sound of the obnoxious noise of the baggage conveyer.

Her suitcase felt heavy as she pulled it from the conveyer belt and toward the Avis counter. The young clerk greeted her, asked her name and adjusted his tie before presenting the paperwork to her. He raised an eyebrow when he saw the New York license she presented.

"Need a map of the local area?" he asked.

"No," she replied collecting the car rental paperwork.

She picked up the car keys for a silver Buick LeSabre off the counter and looked around for a phone booth. It was time to call her parents.

"Where's the nearest phone?"

The clerk pointed to a phone booth near the main area of the terminal.

"Thank you!" Whew. No one was in it. *What do I say to my parents after all this time! This is going to be awkward. Who forgets to call their parents? Me.*

Pulling her parents' phone number from a small address book she carried in her purse, she plugged in her coins and punched in her parents' number. The voice on the other side of the phone was her dad.

"Dad?"

"Patti? Renee, it's Patti."

He was the only one who ever called her Patti.

"Dad, could you take in an unexpected visitor today?"

"What? Well, I guess so," he replied with some trepidation. "Who's the visitor?"

"Me. I'm at the Cedar Rapids airport right now. I'm home for a work assignment for a couple of days. Sorry I didn't have time to call sooner."

"Renee, get on the phone, it's Patti and she's here in town!"

A second voice soon came on the line.

"Patrice? Is it really you?"

"Hi, Mom. Believe it or not, I'm in Cedar Rapids, at the airport."

"She's here in town for a story, Renee," her father breathed into the phone.

"A story? Are you staying with us? Have you eaten?" her mother quizzed her.

"Yes, to your first question, yes to your second question, and no to your third question--haven't had..."

Renee Powell cut off her daughter, "Oh my, we'll fix you something, and it will be ready when you get here."

"Do you need a ride?" her father asked.

"I've rented a car."

"See you in thirty minutes." Patrice heard a click on the other end.

"Bye," her father said, his voice trailing off. He hung up.

"Okay, bye," she chirped to the buzz of the dial tone.

Why did her voice rise two octaves whenever she talked to her parents? She was almost thirty for goodness sakes, but she still acted like little Patrice Powell in the presence of her parents. Were they surprised? Excited that she was in town? Patrice continued to examine her thoughts. It was hard to tell. Her father rarely showed emotion and her mother was more about taking action than showcasing her emotions.

She opened the door to the silver LeSabre and breathed in that new car smell—mmm, real leather. Placing her suitcase in the backseat she thought about the Avis clerk asking if she needed directions. *I know my way.* The Midwest was one of the easiest areas of the country to navigate if you knew how to follow directions, which Patrice excelled in. All roads ran north and south, or east and west. She didn't have far to go.

She pulled her Ray-Ban sunglasses from her purse and put them on as she drove off. The early June sun was intense and even the LeSabre's tinted windows did not dull the vivid colors of the Iowa countryside. Patrice looked out both sides of the car to see that she was surrounded by newly plowed earth as dark as the leather interior of the LeSabre. The grass bordering the fields shimmered an intense green against the sunlight, a sign that winter had been harsh in the Midwest.

It had been a long time since she'd seen this much grass or trees consistently. It was a bit overwhelming. Her surroundings in New York consisted of cement sidewalks and granite entryways. Both Iowa and New York could feel grimy and endless at times.

Over the next swell of a hill was Cedar Rapids, home of approximately 120,000 proud Iowans who enjoyed working at

Quaker Oats, Rockwell International, or one of the numerous insurance corporations. The alabaster skyline of downtown Cedar Rapids rose above the wide river that bordered its southern edge. Patrice remembered when Cedar Rapids looked so large to her. Compared to New York, it now looked modest and small. She wondered why her parents had never wanted to leave this place like she did.

The interstate started to shoulder the meandering Cedar River; together they propelled her through downtown and into the northwestern woods.

Fifteen minutes later, Patrice pulled in front of her parents' ranch-style home. The white frame house was adorned with black shutters. Blue bells and pink peonies were in bloom below the picture window at the front of the house. There was a flagpole twenty feet from the front door that Patrice had never seen before. It stood tall next to the Colorado Blue Spruce and Norwegian Maple in her parents' front yard. Other than the flagpole, not much had changed.

The front door opened and there were her parents, Renee and Martin Powell. Her mom extended both arms in welcome and Patrice awkwardly fell into her mother's embrace.

"Are you surprised to see me?" asked Patrice a little overwhelmed by the emotions she was feeling in the moment.

"Yes," her mother said, giving her a second hug. "It's been too long."

Patrice approached her dad to give him a hug. She felt his strong arms tighten around her as if he didn't want to let go. Patrice gave him a kiss on the cheek in response.

Patrice smelled something cooking on the stove as they entered the house and true to her word, her mom was preparing food.

"Mom, did you remember that I'm a vegetarian?" she inquired.

"I did. I just put some pea soup on the stove. I'll add ham for your dad after I serve yours plain."

"What brings you home?" her dad asked.

"I have an assignment to write about the death of Nan Wood Graham."

"Did that story hit the papers in New York?" Renee asked as she stirred the soup.

"I didn't see an article, but my manager saw one and he remembered that I'm from eastern Iowa. He put me on the assignment immediately." Patrice pouted. "I have to admit that I'm not too thrilled about doing this story. I've never been a great fan of Grant Wood. I just don't get the fuss over his work or over his sister. There's nothing interesting about it, just a bunch of cornfields, crops, farmers, and trees that any third grader could draw." Patrice's voice trailed off when she saw the disconcerting look on her parents' face. She was relieved when her mother asked the next question.

"What story will you seek?" asked her mother.

Patrice had forgotten that her mother could easily detect the dilemma she faced with a situation.

"That's a good question. The magazine wants to understand Iowa's reaction to her death, and I know most of her friends were here even though she lived and retired in California. I believe the story will find itself as I continue to collect the facts and talk to the few people who really knew her," Patrice added.

Patrice looked at the outline of her mother's face. She still had the same hairdo – dark coffee-colored hair that was always cut short, with subtle sideburns that ended at the middle of her ear. She had one curl that was allowed to dangle over her right manicured eyebrow. Her face still glowed, but her cheeks had grown pouches and the skin under her chin was starting to sag. Patrice was surprised to see her mother without makeup because she always saw her mother with it.

"Actually, I thought she had died a long time ago," Patrice said as she sat down at the table setting she knew was for her. Her mother and father for as long as she could remember always had designated places at the table. Her father sat at the end of the table closest to the radio and her mother sat on the other end near the stove. Few things had changed.

Patrice got up to add more ice from the freezer to her glass of water. She spotted numerous pictures of her older sister, Jenny, and her family on the refrigerator. School pictures of Jenny's daughter, Andrea and Andrea's older brother, Mitchell, smattered the top door of the refrigerator. A formal family picture of Jenny, the kids and her husband Tom was in the center.

"Wow, Jenny's kids are so grown up!" *Which you would know if you kept in contact more, Patrice.* The only trace of Patrice on the refrigerator was her senior picture and a magnet that said, "New York, The Big Apple." Patrice felt a twinge of jealousy toward her sister.

"I've never seen this picture of Jenny and her family before," Patrice said referring to the formal family picture of Jenny and her family.

As she talked to the pictures on the refrigerator, she missed the strained look between her mom and dad. A slight smile came across Patrice's face before she turned to face her parents. She didn't want them to see her jealousy nor the sadness on her face. She knew that Jenny's decision to raise a family, marry and live in Iowa was a very favorable thing to do in the eyes of her parents. Her choice to live and work in New York had upset them. They would never admit to it, but those feelings were displaced in other ways like not having a current picture of your youngest daughter on their refrigerator.

"Here's your soup," Renee said putting a hot bowl of split pea soup and crackers on the table.

The sliced bread on the table smelled warm and fresh. "Homemade, huh?"

"Of course," Renee replied. "Your father wouldn't have it any other way." Renee pulled up a chair to the table.

"You remember meeting Nan, don't you?" her mother said.

"No," Patrice said, keeping her attention on the hot soup.

Renee sat with her elbows on the table, her chin on her folded hands, and gazed at her daughter. "Remember the summer when you were eleven or twelve and you were working on your art bead for Camp Fire Girls?"

Patrice narrowed her eyes and shook her head slowly.

"You drew pictures from your troop hike to Stone City. You were so excited after you returned. You hiked to the mansion grounds where Grant Wood had painted."

Patrice was glad her mother was chattering so she could eat and relax. Her voice was soothing.

"You couldn't get that mansion out of your head," Renee added.

"I remember it vaguely," Patrice said between bites of cracker. "I remember drawing a fruit basket or something like that, but I don't remember why."

"It was the stone fruit basket that was on top of a pedestal at the foot of the mansion's front steps. Your Camp Fire leader, Ellen, decided that if you girls entered drawings in the *Grant Wood Art Festival,* you could earn your art beads."

"I believe we did earn our art beads from that art contest. What I can't remember is, did any of us win a prize?" Patrice asked.

She shifted her attention to her father, who was listening intently. Martin Powell was a man of few words and because of that he remained a mystery to Patrice. His glasses now magnified the wrinkles and puffiness around his eyes, and she wondered how long his eyes had looked that way. He was still tall, but his lankiness had been replaced by twenty pounds.

"No, but your drawing caught the eye of Nan Wood Graham who attended the festival that year," replied Renee. "While other kids drew flowers, houses, and pets, you drew a picture of that stone fruit basket. I'll never forget the look on Nan's face. It was as if she'd seen a ghost. She asked you about the picture and what inspired you to draw it. You replied that you had seen a stone pedestal with a fruit basket on it."

"I can remember Nan riding in the Grand Marshall's convertible in the parade and waving to people," Patrice replied.

"All I knew was that she was Grant Wood's sister. It wasn't until years later that I realized she was the woman in *American Gothic.* She seemed old to me then."

"She lived to be ninety," Martin said.

"Nan outlived Grant by fifty years and your drawing seemed to bring her back to the memory of the mansion, her brother, and the art colony," her mother shared.

"What was the art colony?"

"Grant decided to start an art colony in Stone City during the Depression," her father replied. "He liked drawing and painting the Iowa land and people. In his mind, Stone City had the perfect landscape for that as well as the perfect location to gather people together that wanted to learn to paint and sculpt. He used the old mansion in Stone City for classes and some of the artists stayed there too. Well, it burned down and that was pretty much the end of the colony."

"I didn't know that," Patrice said.

"Oh yes, people still talk about it," her mother said as she lifted her spoon and blew on the hot soup to cool it down. "Do you remember what Nan gave you?"

"No, should I?" Patrice asked over her shoulder as she walked to the sink to get more water.

"Nan asked who drew that picture and someone, I can't remember who it was, pointed to you. The Grand Marshal of the parade walked over to you and told you how much she loved your drawing and said you deserved a prize. I was standing next to you and saw her unveil a brooch placed in her hand. You said, "For me?" and she nodded. You asked her if she would pin it onto your Camp Fire vest and the look on her face told me that she knew you were someone special. I heard later that Nan felt you should have won first prize but she wasn't one of the judges so she couldn't influence that. You never took that brooch off your vest."

Patrice turned toward the table and leaned against the sink trying to remember this moment. The festival, the parade, and the carnival were memories an 11-year-old tucked away easily across the years. Why couldn't she remember this contest?

"Where is that vest or brooch now? Do you know, Mom?"

It's probably downstairs in the basement with the rest of

your things," Renee teased. "As the saying goes, it's not really an empty nest until the kids get their things out of the house."

CHAPTER 2

That night Patrice searched through the boxes downstairs, looking for her Camp Fire Girls keepsakes. Small talk was not her thing, so she was glad to have something to do. They made it easy, though, because they always centered the conversation on her. On the other hand, she asked very few questions about them. *I'm definitely my father's daughter*, she mused wryly. *Even with my parents, I just can't seem to do small talk, and the longer I'm gone, it seems the less I have to say to them.* Patrice felt a tiny pang of regret that her introversion kept her in her head, yet, it also allowed her to create different perspectives and realities that lead to writing great articles and stories.

She found the old chest of drawers pushed against a wall in the basement bedroom that doubled as a storage room. Boxes lined two walls at the floor level. Patrice peered into the first box and saw photos, old greeting cards, and letters. Her mother never threw away anything, and boxes were her way of keeping things tidy and out of sight.

That chest of drawers had been in the family as long as Patrice could remember. It had come to this house from her family's farm. It had been used for storage there, as well.

When she opened the top drawer, she realized it was now storage for her mementos. The top drawer had some of her school papers and a heart shaped box containing handkerchiefs she had received from both her grandmothers. The dresser had picked up the scents of dampness and warm heat, making its contents slightly musty smelling. That gave a nostalgic feel to the items. *Oh, here's that old mood ring. Boy, does that bring back memories.* She felt a smile creeping across her face. *Maybe I'll take it back with me and wear it to work telling the story to Brian of how I thought I was in love with a guy in high school chemistry class, just because every time I got near him, my mood ring turned purple, the color of love.* Patrice spied her old hair ribbons, a small Holly Hobbie booklet, and a yellow pen with an oval smiley face on the tip. In the next drawer she found some scratch paper and scribbled on it with the oval smiley face pen, but it didn't work. *It's been years since I've seen or touched any of these keepsakes.*

She found her Camp Fire mementos in the second drawer. Wrapped in plastic was the navy-blue vest and sewn to it were her beads and two patches. Above the upper left breast, she saw the brooch. Patrice removed the vest from the plastic cover and laid it down on the bed nearby. She traced the brooch with her fingertip. It felt thin and fragile, so she decided not to remove it. Every cameo represents the most intricate of art forms and the woman's face on this cameo appeared to be somewhat from the Edwardian era. The white cameo's face on the light caramel background had tiny scratches. Patrice gently lifted one side of the back of the pin and saw it had lost some of its silver colored coating. Though she didn't have a sense of its age, she did believe it held value other than sentimental value.

Just above the brooch was a horizon of eight green beads in the shape of small tube-like noodles. Patrice had sewn them on the vest herself when she was 11 years old. *My sewing's not much better now; good thing I've got my tailor on 32nd Street.* The disheveled stitches barely held the green beads in place; beads she had gotten for her art projects.

In the next drawer were old school papers and a handful of pictures. As she flipped through the pictures, a photo of eight girls caught her eye. It was her Camp Fire Girls troop. Patrice was standing in the back row sporting a pixie haircut and looking tall for her age. What a cute bunch they were in their blue skirts, short-sleeved white blouses, and knotted red scarves around their necks. She felt the knot she had made in the back of her hair remembering where she had learned this.

Patrice had no idea where these girls, now women, were. She had lost touch with them after high school. Her thoughts took her to scenes of her former friends probably marrying the boy next door, raising a family on an acreage or farm, and looking worn out from life. This was a life she never wanted.

Patrice had a sudden thought. *I wonder if that drawing Mom was talking about is here somewhere? I'd love to see it.* Sure enough, in the bottom drawer was a pad of drawing paper. She pulled it out and sat on the floor, her back resting against the bed. The loose drawings tucked inside the pad were those of a child and Patrice knew she had discovered the art she had worked on so long ago. There were numerous drawings and Patrice was impressed by the precision of each drawing. She had drawn them with different pressures of a pencil lead, giving the drawings shading and depth. *Did I want to be an artist not a writer?* Patrice searched her mind... *No*, she wanted to be a writer for as long as she could remember and then the tears started to fall. The blanket on the bed served as her Kleenex as she wiped the tears away. The love of writing began in Iowa and... *Stop.* The thoughts were soon tucked away to stop the tears.

Patrice found the drawing of the stone fruit basket, took a deep breath and flipped the drawing over and looked at the back. Her name was printed on the upper right corner and it was dated June 11, 1972. There were more pencil drawings. There was a drawing of a railroad track, a second drawing of the track disappearing behind a tree-lined bend, and a third drawing showing a cylindrically shaped stone tower on a hilltop. She could tell it was a stone tower because she had painfully drawn numerous rectangles representing stone encasing the cylinder-shaped building.

She felt sadness as she stood up and spread the pictures out on the double bed not really understanding why. Maybe it was nostalgia, missing New York or her boyfriend back in New York.

Who knew? She didn't quite know why either. She focused on the drawings before her and had a hunch these pictures represented the sequence of events from her hike to Stone City as a Camp Fire Girl. She started to remember and then the memory came tumbling back, taking her with it.

◆ ◆ ◆

Viola, Iowa 1972

Viola was one of many towns lost on the back roads of Iowa. There was no reason to go there unless you lived there. Snuggled against a hill to the east and tucked in by corn fields to the north, south and west, Viola's occupants enjoyed a tranquil life. Viola did not have a main street by definition, but it had a corner containing a small grocery store and a post office. Within a stone's throw was a Methodist church and to the west was a grade school, once a high school built in the 1920's. Houses filled in the rest of the town. Only one street was paved with the exception of the highway running north of town.

Viola boasted a library, which was in the basement of a local resident, Beryl Simmons. Beryl deemed herself the town librarian based on her extensive collection of books. A children's reading hour took place once a week, after school on Thursdays, and the children sat on a large oval rug listening to a story that Beryl selected herself. It was there that Patrice met Beryl's granddaughter, Carrie Simmons. It was there that Carrie's mother, Ellen, asked Patrice to become a member of the Camp Fire Girls.

In 1972, Viola had sixty families living in it. Patrice and her older sister Jenny grew up on a 40-acre farm south of Viola that her parents owned. Patrice could see the treetops of Viola and part of the grade school from her family's kitchen window when she was helping her mother with dishes. She didn't feel so lonely and isolated when she looked toward Viola.

Patrice and Jenny rode a bus to attend the elementary school in Viola which was part of a large school district that spanned almost a county. The school district was named after the largest town in the neighboring county, Anamosa.

Living on a farm, and living near a small town, Patrice had been fortunate to grow up with seven girls her own age within a two-mile radius. They all went to school together in Viola and all became members of Ellen's Camp Fire troop. Ellen had her hands full keeping the pubescent girls busy and focused on their projects. Many meetings started with the girls talking about boys, who they liked at school, or their heartthrobs on radio and television. Carrie played her 45's of Donny Osmond or The Jackson 5 with her friends, and often they danced to these records before Ellen reminded them, they had a project to work on. Patrice loved music but especially at the age of eleven when the words made even more sense because she had discovered boys. She wanted to play those sounds over and over again and think about her latest crushes.

As part of the Indian lore connected to Camp Fire Girls, the girls picked an Indian name for their troop. Each member also chose an Indian name for themselves. Patrice's Indian name was La Kon-nah Ko So, which meant believe, truth and merry-hearted.

As the girls completed individual projects, a parent, or Ellen, their troop leader, signed off on the completion of the project and the girls received beads in an honorary Camp Fire Girl ceremony. A red, white, and blue bead represented patriotic projects. Yellow beads were for business-oriented projects. Blue beads were for nature. Orange beads were for home economics. Brown were for outdoors. Red were for health and green beads were for hand crafts. Patrice's favorite bead was the red, white and blue bead as it matched the Camp Fire Girl colors and because of this she focused on earning these beads more than the others. By summer, Ellen had decided that the girls would earn their hand craft beads by entering drawings in the first annual

Grant Wood Art Festival in Anamosa.

The first day of June that year was a warm, sunny morning—a pleasant surprise after the rainy spring that had soaked the Iowa fields. School was over and Ellen scheduled Camp Fire meetings on Wednesday mornings. Patrice was always sad when school was over because it meant she wouldn't see her friends. She was relieved when Camp Fire Girls continued into the summer and she could stay in touch them.

Patrice was the first one to arrive at Ellen and Carrie's house on that bright June day. Carrie opened the door to the front porch with morning greetings. She was wearing dark blue shorts with a white blouse and her red Camp Fire scarf. She had a red, white and blue plastic slip knot holding her scarf in place. Patrice wore a similar outfit only she had tied her own knot. She had learned to tie knots from her Camp Fire Girl handbook.

Resting on Carrie's porch wall, Patrice gazed at Carrie's horse, Star in the pasture just east of the house. He was the color of iced tea with a white spot on his forehead in the shape of a star. His mane and tail were the color of cream.

"Have you ridden Star this summer?" Patrice asked.

"Yeah, a couple of times. I hope to ride him to your house again." Carrie had once ridden Star to Patrice's house which was over a mile south of town. Patrice wanted to be like Carrie, an only child, a house in town, grandparents two blocks away, and anything she wanted, including a horse. Patrice's father had his hands full raising pigs, cattle and crops. Patrice wished her father had a more glamorous job like Carrie's dad. Carrie's father, Steve, worked at a factory in a city thirty minutes away. Carrie said their vacations were paid for due to her father's job and because of that Carrie would vacation with her parents in places like Colorado and Texas. Patrice's family didn't take vacations. She had never been out of the state. Summers were for working the farm. Being in Camp Fire Girls was a diversion from the hard farm work that waited for Patrice.

The rest of the girls started to arrive and gathered on the porch. Patrice liked them all, but she was protective of her friendship with Carrie. They were becoming best friends and she wanted to keep it that way.

"We're hiking to Stone City today," Ellen explained. "That's why I asked you all to bring a sack lunch and your best walking shoes. I'm hoping this will give us some ideas for drawings to enter into the *Grant Wood Art Festival*."

"Who is Grant Wood?" Kim asked. Kim lived next door to Carrie.

"Grant Wood was an artist who was born in Anamosa and did a lot of his painting in Stone City. We're hiking to the place where he painted."

The girls buzzed with excitement.

"Shall we go?" Ellen said waving her arms for the girls to follow her.

Viola had no sidewalks, so the girls walked in pairs on the side of the road, heading east, toward the railroad tracks. Patrice paired up with Carrie. Carrie was taller than Patrice and Carrie's long legs were the envy of every girl in Viola. Patrice knew she'd have fun on the walk with Carrie who was known to do things the other girls couldn't get away with. Being an only child, Carrie had confidence that Patrice longed for. Carrie talked back to her parents and often got what she wanted. Patrice admired that because she could never talk back to her parents without consequences or loss of privileges.

The winter had been long and cold in eastern Iowa that year, so the warmth of that June day made Patrice skip and she was more talkative than usual. Her skipping helped her keep up with Carrie's long stride.

As they came upon the tracks, the girls ran up to the steel beams and balanced upon them, placing one foot in front of the other. Patrice had seen Olympic gymnasts on television prancing and cartwheeling on the balance beam. She imitated their prancing using one side of the railroad track as her balance beam bending forward on one leg and holding the other leg back behind her with her arms outstretched.

"Come on Olga Korbut, you're going to be left behind," Carrie teased.

Soon the small houses of Viola were behind them, seen only through occasional clearings in the trees. Patrice could hear the winding creek keep pace as it babbled across rocks and tree roots. It was dark, like coffee, and barely visible behind the oak, sycamore, and pine trees that shaded its banks.

"What's the name of the stream?" Patrice asked.

No one knew. It was just the creek near Viola.

"I've been back here before," Carrie confided in Patrice. "Mom would kill me if she knew I walked the railroad tracks alone."

"Same with my mom," Patrice agreed. "She always worries that convicts from the Anamosa Reformatory follow these tracks when they escape." The two girls cringed at the thought.

The sun poured through, as trees became few. A grassland waved in upon them. And the little creek which was barely visible now appeared. The wildflowers and grasses were fragrant, something Patrice had missed throughout the long Iowa winter. This renewal made Patrice wished the walk would never end.

As they rounded a bend, they realized they were passing through someone's property when the overgrown grassland appeared to be mowed and a stone building came into view.

Ellen said, "Girls, we're behind what's left of Green Mansion which means we're almost to Stone City. The mansion burned down in the early thirties."

"Is this where Grant Wood painted?" Lorri asked.

"Yes, this is it!"

A few of the girls started running up the hill toward a stone cylinder tower including Carrie.

Patrice stopped Lorri and asked her about the large bandage on her left knee.

"What happened?"

"I fell off my bike yesterday and tore my knee up pretty good."

"Does it hurt?"

"It did when we started the hike. It's feeling better now."

"Come on girls," Ellen called from the top of the hill.

Patrice paced herself with Lorri who didn't run very fast due to her bandaged knee.

Ellen answered questions about who now owned the property. "A farmer bought the land. He left the foundation of the mansion and what was left of the buildings on the property in their original form. Oh, yes, and there was once a stone palace on the edge of the grounds."

Patrice listened with wonderment and interest.

"The stone palace was like a grand hotel," Ellen continued. "It was built at the turn of the century and it also had a theater inside."

"Look at that!" Ellen pointed to the west, near the lower slope of the hill. Through the prairie grasses and flowers, a decaying house made of stone could be seen.

"That's the carriage house. That's where they put their carriages and horses."

"Was the owner so rich that he had other houses on the property?" Amy asked.

Ellen admitted that she did not know much more about the property except that the original owner had wealth and the property was once a working acreage complete with servant quarters, ice house, water tower, blacksmith shop, and a carriage house.

Patrice did not know much about this property. She found it hard to believe that excessive wealth actually once existed here. None of the girls came from wealthy parents. Carrie's grandmother was probably the richest person in Viola, and she held the honor by having the town library in her basement.

Patrice heard more questions from her friends. "What did they do to become so rich? "Did they really have servants? How did the mansion burn down?"

Terri pointed to the cylinder-shaped tower at the top of the hill. "What's that?"

"It's the mansion's original water tower," Ellen replied.

"There was also an ice house where they stored the ice that the servants carved from the snowy river. The ice house was insulated, so the ice stayed cold during the summer months."

"They must have kept a lot of ice," Kathy said.

"They probably used it for the palace, too," Ellen replied.

Patrice wanted to know where the river was. She was always fascinated with rivers. They had a personality all their own. Rivers were sometimes peaceful, turbulent, and swift as they headed to the Mississippi River. She was taught to respect rivers because there were currents and whirlpools that would carry you far and down into the depths of the cold water. She was forgiving of these wild waters because they brought cool air that sliced through the immense summer heat radiating off the land they passed.

"The river is on the other side of the road, just behind us."

They started climbing the hill towards the water tower and soon discovered they were coming toward the foundation of the mansion. The girls jumped onto the foundation and traced its perimeter with their footsteps. Partial walls remained with the outline of a fireplace.

"Evidently, the mansion had seven fireplaces on the first and second floors to heat the rooms. This is all that is remaining," Ellen said.

The steps at the front of the house were still there and a few of the girls raced up and down them, laughing. At the foot of the stairs was a stone pedestal. On the top of the pedestal was a stone configuration of a fruit basket.

"Cool, what is that?" said Lorri, observing the stone design.

"It's a sculpture of some kind, see how it was chiseled into these different fruit shapes—remember rich people lived here once," Patrice commented. She thought the stone fruit basket was the most interesting thing she had ever seen and stepped closer to examine the carved stone. Placing her hand on top of her head, Patrice moved her hand from the tip of her head to the very tip of the fruit basket. They were exactly the same height. The stone had darkened with time and age, but Patrice could see the traces of apples, pears, grapes and bananas. She touched a banana, as if expecting to remove it from the basket.

Patrice thought about the years this pedestal had stood in the sun, endured the rain, and withstood the cold and snowy winter months of Iowa. It had seen more life then she had. This thinking made her shiver for she feared her life would never take her far from the toil of a farm. She quickly removed her hand from the top of the stone fruit basket and looked around. The other girls were now racing up and down the steps near the pedestal. Patrice decided to join them as they tried to see how fast they could ascend and descend the stairs. She jumped across the last six steps and onto the grass below. She made the jump but fell forward to her knees. As she lifted herself up, she caught a breathtaking view before her. She was near the crest of a large hill that overlooked a tiny town lying in the valley below. Every house and every building were made of the same stone as the remnants of Green Mansion. The town was edged from the north and east with a quarry whose stone hills were the same warm color as the houses. From where Patrice stood, a stone church was down and to the left and a gravel road was beyond the church. The road curved eastward and became the main street of the town, meeting the stone houses along its way. A river passed underneath the road at the center of town. The main street continued straight until it disappeared behind a bend and trees. Patrice had never seen colors more alive—the rich black earth in the fields next to Stone City, the greens from the sprouting corn, the gold from the dusty quarries dotting the valley, and the dark blue river splitting the town in half.

Ellen walked up, stood next to her, and said, "That's Stone City."

CHAPTER 3

The next morning, in her rental car, Patrice thought of Glenn and her nostrils flared. She was feeling pressure about this story of Nan Wood Graham's death and she blamed him. He didn't take any work off her plate and expected her to squeeze in this story with everything else she had to do. There wasn't a lot written on Nan Wood Graham. *She was born, she lived, she was in a famous painting and she died.* Patrice calmed her thoughts thinking about what Nan had done for her. Children weren't doted on back in 1972 as they are today. That was a special moment, and Patrice now realized she wanted to learn more about this woman, i.e. what did she do for a living, how will the people of Iowa remember her; Patrice's gut told her the answer would be through the stories and memories of those who knew her at the start and end of her life. Anamosa was as good a place as any to begin. Locations drew ideas for Patrice, and she was desperate for some inspiration.

Patrice hadn't driven for some time. Did anyone drive in New York besides taxi drivers and misguided tourists? Still, the skill had returned instantly the day before when she stepped into the Buick. Turning the knob to defrost, Patrice flipped the air conditioner on to remove the fog collecting on the windshield. Even her Ray-Bans didn't provide a clear view of the highway.

She had dressed in khaki slacks, navy pumps, a navy-blue sleeveless top, and a camel colored sweater around her shoulders. She knew she was overdressed in the Iowa countryside, but these were the only clothes she owned.

It was still early, but she was sweating. The cool air blowing on her skin felt great.

She turned on the radio and paused at the first soft rock station. The song playing had been a hit when she was in high school. She continued her search, hoping for an edgy rock station. She found another radio station, but the music was a decade old. In frustration, she settled for a news station airing the national and local news.

Patrice had invited her parents along, but they declined saying they had work to do around the house. She knew they were being kind, letting her have her day to research. She also realized that this was their home, so riding around the county didn't present any point of interest for them. In some ways she was sorry they had not come along. If they had, maybe they would have found some things to talk about.

As Patrice was leaving her parents' house, the neighbor next door was out in front of her house shaking rugs in her bathrobe, slippers and curlers dangling low around her face. The neighbor didn't seem to care that her bathrobe string was loosening around her middle and revealing a big gut and loose flabby skin.

"No one needs to see that!" Patrice grimaced backing her car out of the driveway and making a disgusted face. Patrice peered back at the neighbor. As if hearing Patrice's words, the woman started to shake her rug in Patrice's direction with gumption.

Patrice drove by the neighbor, waving cordially and rolled her eyes when she was safely past the neighbor's view.

The previous day now seemed surreal—leaving the familiarity of New York, flying home, showing up at her parents' house unexpectedly, and being deposited into a world she had left so long ago. She let out a long breath and knotted her hair into a ponytail at the first stop sign she encountered on the highway.

It had been a long time since she had been home and, for some reason she imagined there would be a lot of catching up to do. Unfortunately, it was the opposite. She felt awkward with her parents, as if she owed them an explanation or was waiting for theirs. She searched her mind for why she did not come home more often. The answer wasn't coming.

She thought about her college years in New York, receiving her Journalism degree and a minor in Art History. Becoming a writer had been her dream. It had taken her almost ten years to be where she wanted to be professionally, but she was happy now and there was no turning back. That dream had pushed aside any want for marriage and a family. It took all her focus to become a magazine writer, let alone an art magazine writer in New York.

Consumed in her thoughts, she had driven five miles before she was conscious of the countryside around her. She drew in a deep breath and straightened her back. Her anxiety rose as the next stretch of road and land would present the farm where she grew up. The neighboring farms still had the same shapes and colors she remembered. Trees had replaced saplings in some farmyards, but the countryside was almost exactly as she had left it. Soon she saw the outline of the bulky oak trees bordering the west and south corners of the farm. Their leaves hid the overall view of the farm. The corn south of the farmhouse was young and therefore not very tall. She could peer across, catching glimpses of the house and barn while watching the highway. The corn rows represented multiple entry points into the farmstead. Patrice soon found herself drifting across the center line of the highway relieved there was no traffic around her. She opened her eyes wide and decided she had seen enough for the time being.

She was now entering Jones County, marked by a large billboard that read "Stone City" in very large letters with an arrow underneath and the words "two miles." That billboard had been there as long as Patrice could remember. It had advertised *The Great Jones County Fair* every summer before Patrice left for New York.

"Yes, one thing has changed!" she exclaimed passing the updated billboard.

She would have to make a point of driving through Stone City on the way back to Cedar Rapids. She wanted to learn more about the art colony. Why would someone have an art colony during the Great Depression in the middle of cornfields? This did not make sense to Patrice.

Patrice's eyes fixed on the Williams' place coming up on the right. The long gravel lane led to a circle drive that passed in front of the house, barn, and airplane hangar before re-directing the driver back toward the highway. The hangar housed the small airplanes owned by Jack Williams and behind the hangar was a runway that ended at a cornfield. Growing up, Patrice had been fascinated by the fact that their neighbors housed a miniature airport in the back of their farm. Jack and Mary Williams belonged to a group called The Flying Farmers, a special society of farmers who enjoyed flying to and from each other's property. Patrice remembered her fear as a little girl when the Williams flew low over her father's farm. She thought they were being attacked by Russians until her parents recognized their neighbors' plane and started waving at the airplane.

The flat landscape was becoming hilly. The hazy sky and lasting terrain ahead blended into mixtures of green, black, and gray. She missed the protection of a New York skyline. Here she felt vulnerable and exposed.

The driver of an oncoming Ford truck gripping his steering wheel raised his index finger at Patrice. Patrice thought he had flipped her off and began to swear in disgust. Then the next car's driver passed by and displayed the same gesture.

"What?" she said tensely. Then she placed her hand on her forehead as she remembered the local custom of gesturing hello with one's forefinger lifted off the steering wheel.

"I forgot there's *no* stranger in Iowa," she said to herself, aloud, smiling.

The Buick started the descent into Anamosa. Patrice tapped on the car's brakes, taking in the natural invitation that the town extended to all visitors. A forest at the edge of a state park was to her right. A rocky bluff bordered the left side of the road and loomed larger as the car descended into the valley. This hill drew a sense of expectation until the bridge at the bottom of the hill was in sight and Patrice could see the Wapsipinicon River. A sign caught Patrice's eye that read "Welcome to Anamosa, Grant Wood Country."

The river was high, nearly spilling over its banks. Every local paid attention to the swell of that river. If it crested over its banks, it would flood the low roads of the state park to the south, the baseball fields to the north, and some of the local businesses located on the north shore. Rivers in Eastern Iowa were never small. They were strong arms of the mighty Mississippi River and this area of Iowa was only forty-five minutes from that great river. The Wapsipinicon was wide and swift.

The cemetery was on the northern edge of the river. Patrice could not remember the water rising high enough to flood the cemetery. Grave sites were not positioned near the water and the purposeful hills of the cemetery provided that added protection. As the LeSabre crossed the Wapsipinicon, Patrice turned left into the cemetery's entrance. The small city of Anamosa lay just beyond.

Patrice smiled. She loved this cemetery if it was possible to love cemeteries. It was inviting. Just like the state park across the river, the cemetery was a scenic excursion. Patrice's shoulders relaxed as if she was receiving a backrub that released all tension. She entered the cemetery and drove on the single lane pavement, surrounded by sloping grassy hills, burr oaks, and elm trees. Out of sight were two river basins to the south and west, but she knew they were there.

As Patrice drove upward to the crest of the first hill, she looked at the names on the headstones. This was a special section of the cemetery. Those buried on this hill had experienced sudden and tragic deaths: the homecoming queen who died in a car crash the night of prom, a grade school friend who died from playing with a gun, a teenage boy who lost his life the last day of school from a fall, and a beloved choir teacher who died of cancer. Small towns never forget those heartbreaks. Patrice's Uncle Robert was also on that hill. He died in the war serving his country. All she knew of him was pictures she had seen in her parents' home. Why this particular hill seemed to hold these tragic memories she did not know. It served as a reminder to Patrice that all life is precious.

Numerous graves were decorated because Memorial Day weekend had just passed. Patrice's parents came to this cemetery every Memorial Day to pay their respects and place flowers on the graves of loved ones. She unclenched her hand, which was against her heart, and continued to drive through the cemetery.

Jones County residents never forget where Grant Wood is buried, and neither did Patrice. Grant's grave was near a white granite gravestone with a large stone lion lying majestically across the top. Not many gravestones in this Iowa cemetery were as grand as this one. Beneath the stone lion were the letters that spelled "Wood." If the visitor did not get out of their car and walk up to the lion, they would easily assume it was Grant's grave. It was not. The lion marked the area of the Wood family plot.

Patrice pulled the car over to the side of the cemetery road, parked, and walked up to Grant's grave at the midpoint of the hill. Grant's modest gravestone was approximately five steps from the stone lion. His granite marker was an amethyst colored rectangle about twelve by twenty-four inches. With only his name, year of birth, and year of death, his stone looked very small relative to the gravestones next to it except for one. She noticed the fresh dirt next to Grant's grave and found it was Nan's resting place. The newspaper article that her boss, Glenn had shared with her had stated Nan's final resting place was here next to her brother. Nan's marker mirrored Grant's in size and simplicity and read, "Nan Wood Graham, 1899-1990."

Patrice stood staring at the simple gravestone for a long time.

She said softly, "I don't understand why there's no reference to *American Gothic*. In the art world, her face is as famous as the *Mona Lisa* and *Whistler's Mother*." Patrice was surprised and disappointed by the frugal markings. Both Grant and Nan's tombstones were small and simple.

Patrice started to think about Nan's generosity that June day in 1972. Nan's gift of a brooch to an eleven-year-old girl was extremely kind-hearted. Patrice remember that her mom made a big deal out of that gift and wanted Patrice to send a thank you note, but no one seemed to know where Nan lived or had her address.

Patrice's lips formed the words *thank you* as she gazed at Nan's grave. It was her way of paying homage to Nan and Nan's generosity. Patrice was barely aware that it was starting to rain. The earth underneath her feet was softening. She turned and went back to the car. She sat and watched the rain drops plop on the front windshield and dribble downward into slivers of liquid. It was starting to make sense why she was back here to write this story yet instead of feeling confident, she was feeling unsure about it. It was one thing to report on a story for 200,000 subscribers of *European Art* magazine from behind your desk organizing facts and information. It was a different matter to realize you may be writing a story that has familiarity with your own life.

"And what if you found that *your* life, your story has no meaning or significance?" Patrice said out loud. She didn't think she could live with that.

CHAPTER 4

The dark red brick on the nineteenth century buildings of Anamosa's main street looked worn more than she had remembered. Many of the shops were gone. The once vibrant storefronts were faded, and letters were missing from some of the signs. The farm crisis in the early 1980s and the new Wal-Mart had forced several shop owners to close their doors. Antique stores and offices replaced the once thriving heart of Anamosa's mercantile district.

The Grant Wood Store was on the north side of Main Street in the center of town. The rain had gone from sprinkles to downpour and Patrice dashed across the street with her sweater over her head once she had parked. Part of her hoped no one would recognize her. She had only been home once in the ten years since she'd been in New York and that was five years ago. She had gone into the local café for breakfast with her nephew and niece and found a morning crowd of locals who called her by name as if she had never left. Patrice had recognized the waitress as someone she had gone to Sunday school with. She had greeted Patrice by name, and when Patrice asked how she had remembered her, the woman replied, "Oh, you still look the same." Patrice had changed. Her hair color was lightened to blonde and she had shed fifteen pounds, yet the local people still knew who she was. It had bothered her to be recognized so easily then and she did not understand why. She still didn't.

Patrice opened the shop door and a bell tinkled overhead. The store had once been a gift shop where she had purchased her favorite perfume as a teenager whenever she had money from babysitting. Patrice was quickly brought back to the moment when she noticed the Grant Wood prints lining the walls and folksy memories of the town's history. The famous portrait of Nan and the farmer was on the back wall.

"May I help you?" she heard an older voice say. A woman appeared from the back room of the shop and appeared to be in her early seventies.

"Actually, I'm just browsing for now," Patrice said, shaking the rain from her sweater on the floor rug.

"Please sign our guestbook while you're here, dear," the woman said as she walked toward the front of the store.

The clerk's pin said "Anna." Patrice realized that the woman took her for a tourist.

"Thank you. I will do that before I leave." She was not ready to reveal her name, where she was from, and who she was related to. That would lead to another conversation and she wanted to get some work done.

She decided to play shopper and browsed at the prints. She looked through brochures highlighting places of local interest and peered through the glass counter at small pewter trinkets of an artist's palette and paintbrushes.

On the west wall were black and white photos of Grant Wood. The pictures were dated from the late 1920s and early 1930s. There was also a photo of Grant in a field with his palette and another image of Grant at the stone mansion.

"The stone mansion," Patrice said out loud.

"Have you heard about the art colony he formed in Stone City?" asked Anna, who was poised to capitalize on Patrice's interest.

"Yes, well, a little," Patrice said.

"Grant Wood started an art colony at Green Mansion in Stone City, just four miles west of here, in the summer of 1932. These pictures were taken that summer. This print here," Anna said pointing, "is a picture of the faculty that taught at the art school."

Patrice could not take her eyes off the picture of the artist with his faculty and peers. Wood wore overalls in the picture with black and white dress shoes. The rest of the group wore summer dress clothing. They all looked to be around thirty years of age. Grant looked slightly older. To Grant Wood's left was the stone fruit sculpture sitting on top of a stone pedestal. Patrice realized the picture was taken in front of the mansion and made a small gasp. The picture was titled, *The Stone City Art Colony Faculty*.

"We're asking local citizens to help us identify the names of the people in this picture," Anna said not hearing Patrice's gasp.

Patrice looked down to the counter in front of her, collecting her thoughts, and found a piece of ruled paper with names written in pencil. Some names were scratched out and new names replaced them. Some of the lines were blank. Half of the faculty had yet to be identified.

"Why would people come to rural Iowa to paint during the Depression?" asked Patrice.

"Grant Wood was regionally known by that time as an artist," said Anna. "He had studied art in Germany and France. People at that time believed that the finer artists came only from Europe. Just the fact that he had lived and studied there for about four years was enough to intrigue people to come to the colony to see what he was about."

"What do you know about his sister, Nan? Was she at the art school that summer?" The words spilled out of Patrice's mouth in a burst of enthusiasm.

"Yes," replied Anna. "She was at the art school that summer. I think she posed for paintings more than she created anything. She just died. Did you hear about that?"

"Yes," Patrice replied. "Tell me more if you can. I'm fascinated by her."

"She retired in California with her husband and only came back for our art festivals. We are having one in about two weeks. She was frail her final years, so we haven't seen her at a festival since 1987. People always think she posed as a farmer's wife in *American Gothic*, but the painting is really about a farmer and his daughter during the Depression. Nan was only thirty or thirty-one when it was painted."

Anna and Patrice walked toward the print of the famous painting. The print had a cream-colored matt and distressed wood frame in browns and blue. The frame brought forth the detail of the farmer's hand and the blue threading in his shirt under his jacket.

Anna gestured to another print, "Did you know that *Woman with Plants* is a portrait of Grant and Nan's mother? She is wearing the same rickrack across the apron that her daughter is in *American Gothic*."

"Oh, yes I can see that now," said Patrice, studying both works of art.

"They're also wearing the same cameo brooch. That's how we know it's mother and daughter."

"Brooch? "

"Why, yes, dear. Take a look at both prints. Nan has said that Grant gave that brooch to his mother because the cameo face looked so much like Nan."

"Do you know what happened to the brooch?" Patrice asked.

"No. I imagine that it's part of Nan's estate," said Anna. "Nan didn't have any children so I'm sure it stayed with her estate."

Patrice found herself breathing rapidly and tried to draw in long breaths to calm herself.

"Can I get you some water? You look a little flushed," Anna said, studying Patrice's face.

Patrice fanned herself with her hand. "Oh, no. I'm fine. I think it's the humidity. Wh-what more can you tell me about the art colony?" Patrice regained her thoughts as she and Anna walked toward the front counter.

"People came from all over to spend the summer at the art colony. There were approximately ninety-two students and ten instructors that first summer. The classes were held in the mansion itself. They offered oil painting, sculpting, frame making . . . about anything you can image. Grant took them across the countryside to find the perfect settings to paint. I was a small girl at the time, but I remember seeing them out in the middle of a field, painting whatever caught their eye.

Patrice looked through the prints of *American Gothic*, *Woman with Plants*, and *Stone City*. She also saw a reproduction photograph of *The Stone City Art Colony Faculty*. In postcard form was a painting of a beautiful young woman in a yellow and black polka dot dress, holding a baby chick in her hand. She had never seen this before. It was titled *Portrait of Nan*.

Patrice asked, "What's this?" holding up the postcard.

Anna peered over the counter at the postcard as she was ringing up Patrice's purchases. "Oh, that's Nan. Nan didn't like the attention she got for *American Gothic.* People and the national media teased her about looking like an old spinster. Grant felt bad about that and painted this portrait to show how beautiful his sister really was."

As Patrice was pulling her credit card out of her purse, she looked at Anna and said, "Would you know a student at the art colony or even a faculty member who is still living?"

"Not many are alive, but there is one person left in the local area that I'm aware of. Her name is Rose Boston. She lives in Davenport and has an art shop there named *Rose Boston*."

"Thank you for your help."

Anna nodded and Patrice was out the door like a young girl who could barely hold in a new secret.

She now had a lead. Maybe she would find a story yet.

CHAPTER 5

"Fill her up?"

Patrice was startled by the question but nodded a yes.

The man started to turn, then turned back and said, "Patrice? Patrice Powell?"

Patrice looked him in the face and said, "Brad? Brad Holloway, how are you?"

Brad shook his head in disbelief. "I haven't seen you for so long, how are you?"

"I'm doing well. I'm home visiting the folks."

"I heard they had moved to Cedar Rapids."

"Yes, they retired from farming a few years ago and seem to enjoy it."

Brad pumped gas into her car. "You'll have to stop by and see Terri."

"Terri?"

"Yes, I married Terri Barrett. She was in our class at school."

"Yes, I remember Terri."

"We live just behind the station here. She's home if you'd like to stop and say hello."

"I might do that."

"Great. That will be $3.25. Your car didn't need much gas."

Her face was flushed when she handed him her company credit card. She felt like an idiot only purchasing $3.25 worth of gas. Brad probably thought their class valedictorian had grown stupid in the last ten years. In actuality Patrice realized she was startled by seeing a guy she used to have a crush on.

Their home was easy to find. It was behind the gas station, just as Brad had said. She had not anticipated visits with old friends, but she and Terri had been close childhood friends and had been in Camp Fire Girls together. She felt it was the polite thing to do but planned to stay only a few minutes.

Through the crack of an opened window, she could hear a baby crying and someone using a kitchen mixer. Patrice opened the screen door and knocked on the front door loudly. She heard footsteps, the door opened, and there stood Terri with a toddler in her arms. Terri's hair was short and darker brown than Patrice remembered, and it was styled in a crop cut that framed her face. She was without makeup and wore jean cutoffs and a yellow colored shirt that had food stains on it.

Terri started to say, "Can I help you?" and then recognition slowly came to her face. "Patrice? Patrice Powell?"

"Yes." Patrice grinned. She realized how happy she was to see Terri.

"What are you doing in Ana-mosa? Come on in."

Terri moved away from the door so Patrice could enter. They passed through a small tiled foyer and into the small living room, which was covered in baby toys and smelled like scented diapers. The living room had a long couch and two recliner chairs in dark dusty blue with specks of mauve woven in. The carpet at Patrice's feet carried the same mauve and blue colors. She had seen this décor often in the Midwest.

"I'm just visiting. Is this your daughter?" Patrice said, touching the toes of the pink-socked little girl that Terri was holding.

"Yes, this is Emily."

"She's cute."

Terri led the way into the kitchen and gestured for Patrice to follow her and take a seat at the kitchen table.

"Sorry my house is a mess," Terri said as she placed an unwilling Emily in a high-chair and put a bowl of cake batter from the table into the refrigerator.

"Not to worry. I'm just glad to see you. How long has it been?"

"I think since high school. I haven't seen you at our class reunions." Terri was now facing Patrice.

"That's probably right. I don't get home much."

"Where do you live now? Did I hear you live in New York?" Patrice noticed that Terri was appraising her from head to toe. Patrice slid her hand guardedly over her Christian Dior watch, a gift to herself after receiving a bonus at work.

"Yes, I got my masters at Columbia University and ended up working and living in New York."

"I bet your folks are glad to see you. How are they?" Patrice noticed that Terri didn't want to know about Patrice's life in New York; it was easier to talk about things more local.

"They're good. They moved from the farm into Cedar Rapids, so they are enjoying life in town," Patrice responded realizing a lot had changed in ten years.

"I think my mom told me your parents had moved after she saw your mom and dad at some church event or other," Terri cocked her head as if trying to remember that conversation, "and make sure you take your mom to our sidewalk sales over on Main Street. They're having the best sales. I just bought Emily an adorable pink tractor. It's a scooter she can use in a year or two."

"I probably won't be able to do that with my mom. I'm actually home on a brief work assignment and will be heading back to New York soon."

Terri paused for a moment then asked, "How did you find where I live?" as if this thought had just popped into her mind.

"I stopped for gas and saw Brad. He suggested I stop in and say hello."

"Oh. Did you say you are home on a work assignment?"

"Yes, to write about the death of Nan Wood Graham."

"Who?"

"Nan Wood."

"Oh, Nan Wood. Yes, we were sad to hear about it, but we haven't seen her around here for so long, I sort of forgot about her."

Emily started to squirm and wanted out of her high-chair so Terri put her on the floor and placed some toys in front of her.

"How long have you and Brad been married?" Patrice saw that Terri was distracted and continued to keep the conversation simple.

"About nine years now. We started dating after high school. Brad's dad worked at the gas station for many years so that's how Brad got the job. I worked at the credit union up-town but quit my job once Emily was born. Are you married or just a workin gal?"

"No, not married. I've been dating the same guy for about four years now."

"Sounds like it's time to tie the knot don't you think?" Terri had a tone that implied Patrice had neglected something.

Patrice and Terri fixed their eyes on Emily as she played and there was silence between them for a time. Then Terri looked up and smiled shyly. "Can I get you anything to drink? Are you thirsty?"

"No, I'm fine." Patrice started to say something but hesitated.

Terri caught it. "What?"

"Nothing."

"What?"

"Do you enjoy living in Anamosa?"

"Yeah," Terri said nodding her head slowly and hesitantly at first, but then more confidently. "I do. Our family is here, and Emily is surrounded by family. There are times I guess I get bored, but we find things to do. We shop in Cedar Rapids, or Brad and I go to his annual bowling tournament in Des Moines."

Patrice thought of where her life had taken her. She lived in New York City and had a wealthy boyfriend who lived in the Village. Her job often provided perks like travel overseas and meeting affluent people. Patrice began to feel the familiar feelings of judging this modest way of life. She watched Terri swing Emily up and down in the air and smiled as they giggled at their own frolicking.

"Terri, do you remember Camp Fire Girls?"

"Yes, I do."

"Do you remember a hike we took along the railroad tracks between Viola and Stone City?"

"Not really. Why? Do you remember something about it?"

"Just that we found the site where the *Stone City Art Colony* was."

"Wow, I don't remember that at all," Terri said shaking her head. "I just remember things like camps and some of the bead ceremonies. Do you remember when we went to Camp Hitaga and the horses we were riding stepped into a snake nest? My pony had a fit and almost bucked me off."

"Yes, I wanted to ride a pony, but the only horse left was a horse named Sun. He was so huge it was scary just to get on and off that horse. Luckily, he remained steady in that situation. Do you remember we were on the side of a ravine? If we would have fallen off our horses, we would have rolled down that steep hill."

Emily looked up with a broad grin at the sight of the two older women giggling.

"You seem very happy with your house, your baby, and living near Brad's work."

"It fits us. We've made a life here and will do the same for Emily."

The conversation with Terri was getting more comfortable and Patrice found herself confiding in her. "So why didn't I choose this life for me?" Patrice asked reverently, not looking into Terri's face.

Terri shook one of Emily's rattles to keep her entertained and then she turned to Patrice and her face got serious. "Patrice, this wasn't enough for you. With all your accomplishments in school, everybody believed you could do more, and you did too. In many ways, you didn't fit here—a small town, everybody knowing everybody's business, the haves and have nots, the popular and the unpopular. Small towns define who we are or are not. You probably were afraid of being stuck here and determined long ago, that your life would not be here."

Patrice was surprised by how quickly Terri had summarized a lifetime of feelings. It was as if they were sitting in Terri's bedroom once again as teenagers talking about school, boys, and their futures.

Patrice remained silent. What could she say? Terri had nailed it.

CHAPTER 6

As she drove back to her parents' home in Cedar Rapids, Patrice thought about what Terri had said. Patrice had known her as far back as she could remember. They attended grade school, junior high and high school together. They weren't best friends all those years, but they were in the same circle of friends, so Patrice gave credibility to Terri's comments. At the age of twenty-nine, Patrice felt she had accomplished much for a small-town girl, yet in a simple conversation, a friend from the past had given her a real glimpse of who she believed she was inside – a farmer's daughter from rural Iowa who didn't feel like she'd find the life she wanted here. She had felt the urge to leave home and those she loved because of it. Patrice felt an overwhelming sadness come over her and like the weather, her thoughts had turned gray. The sky opened and the rain came down hard and so did her tears.

The car was approaching the next small town of Springville. Patrice decided to pull into town and gather her thoughts about the weather. Familiarity surrounded her as she recognized this township well. The farm she grew up on was only two miles behind her. Time had only ensured that the trees were taller, and the stand-alone car wash was out of business.

The main district of town had numerous parking places and she quickly picked one. Patrice put the car in park and looked out the side window. It was no longer raining. She was confused. Her slacks and top had drops of water on them. She peered at herself in the rear-view mirror and saw that her eyes were red and puffy. She took Kleenex out of her purse and wiped the tears. Through the tissue she saw she was in front of a restaurant called The Cozy Café. She felt the hunger pangs of the day. She took a deep breath, and grabbed her purse and briefcase, and walked into the refuge of the small restaurant. She jerked when she heard a strong voice yell across the room, "Seat yourself."

Patrice sat at a table that gave her a window view of the sidewalk and main street.

"Can I get you some coffee honey?" said the young waitress approaching her with a coffee pot in one hand and a cup in the other hand. The waitress' name tag said "Darlene."

"Actually, tea would be a good start, do you have iced tea?"

"We sure do. Here's a menu, I'll be right back."

Patrice looked around the room. The restaurant had booths lining one side of the café. Numerous tables seating four a piece was spread across the rest of the room. The plastic tablecloths were white and black checked. Patrice imagined the locals playing chess on the tablecloths. That image started to lift her spirits. The café was almost vacant except for two farmers sitting near the café's counter. Patrice watched them as they conversed over slices of pie. The forks were barely visible in the grasp of the large hands of the men. Patrice then peered at the waitress who was filling a glass of iced tea for her near the kitchen. Beyond the waitress was a view into the kitchen. Patrice saw an elderly woman hunched over a grill cleaning it.

She opened the menu before her. There were not many choices for a vegetarian which made her selection easy.

"Have you decided?" the waitress said placing the iced tea in front of her and silverware rolled up in a paper napkin.

"Yes, I would like a small garden salad with vinegar and oil."

"We don't have vinegar and oil. We have French salad dressing, Thousand Island, and Ranch?"

"Uh, I'll have the French, but could I have it on the side?"

"Sure. That's all you want? That's not enough to feed a mouse."

"We have some fresh rolls coming out of the oven, and cherry pie made this morning."

"Thanks, I'm going to pass."

"Okay, but you don't know what you're missing!"

Patrice pulled a notebook out of her briefcase and with pen in hand started to write down notes from the day. It was a comfort to write and it took her mind off the conversation with Terri.

The salad arrived in a small bowl, accompanied with the French salad dressing poured into a small saucer. The waitress also placed a small plate with a slice of cherry pie in front of Patrice.

"I said I didn't want the pie."

"I know. Honey--it's on the house. Once you try it, you'll come back to The Cozy Café for more." The waitress turned away before Patrice could protest.

Darlene was right. As Patrice finished the last sentence in her notebook, the salad was devoured along with the cherry pie and the check was resting near her iced tea. The farmers had left, and Darlene and the cook were putting chairs on the tables as if they were closing for the day.

Patrice caught Darlene's attention, "What time do you close?"

"At 5:00," came the response.

Patrice looked at her watch, and it was 4:50 p.m. She walked up to Darlene and handed her the check and her credit card.

"Why do you close so early?"

"We just don't have the dinner crowd like we used to. The new bypass south of town takes people onto Marion and Cedar Rapids for dinner."

"I'm sorry to hear that."

"Did you like the cherry pie?"

"Yes – yes I did. Thank you."

"You'll have to come back."

Patrice walked to her table and left Darlene a generous tip.

◆ ◆ ◆

Sunlight pushed through the rain clouds. The heaviness in Patrice's heart started to lift upon seeing a radiant sunset splash its rays across the gray clouds. The New York City skyline hid a view like this. Patrice followed the sun to Marion. *Not again!* Her parents' next-door neighbor was outside once more only this time instead of shaking rugs, she was down on her hands and knees pulling weeds from the flowers in front of her house. She's wearing the same bathrobe and slippers! Patrice looked away before she saw too much.

Patrice parked next to a maroon Ford Taurus sitting in her parents' driveway. Someone bolted out of the front door and Patrice recognized her sister Jenny.

"Patrice!" Jenny called out as she ran toward her little sister and gave her a hug. "I'm so glad to see you. Mom and Dad told me you had made an unexpected visit. How long are you here for?"

Patrice looked into her sister's beautiful face and said, "A week." Patrice thought Jenny was the better looking of the two sisters. Jenny was well proportioned with the leanness of an athlete's build, unlike Patrice who was often told as a child she could lose a couple of pounds. Like Patrice, Jenny had added highlights to her hair, so the two sisters looked similar, but Jenny's highlights brought out her brown eyes and tanned skin.

"Did you come all the way from Davenport today?" Patrice asked when she released their hug.

"I did. The kids are in a summer camp program and Tom offered to pick them up tonight so I could travel here to see you."

"How are the kids?" Patrice asked.

"Growing. Mitch plays all kinds of sports and Andrea acts as if she's a teenager."

Patrice smiled as she had always envied how mature Jenny

was at such a young age and now like mother, like daughter.

"I'm so happy to see you and so are Mom and Dad," Jenny said opening her eyes to look at her sister again. "You've lost weight!"

"Some."

They continued to talk outside until their mother poked her head out the front door.

"Are you coming in?"

"Sorry mom," Jenny answered.

Jenny turned and walked toward the front door and Patrice captured her arm.

"What?" Jenny said.

"Who's the neighbor?" Patrice gestured toward the woman now digging in the dirt next door and glancing in the direction of the sisters.

Jenny motioned Patrice toward the front door and opened it, "That's Mrs. Kroft. She's lived in this neighborhood probably before the streets were paved."

"Why would she be pulling weeds in her bathrobe and slippers especially after a rain?"

"Maybe she wants to give the petunias a thrill. I don't know. Let's just say she's a little off." Jenny pointed to the side of her brain. "Don't you see people like that every day in New York?" Patrice heard the glib tone in her sister's voice.

They joined their parents in the glassed-in porch at the back of the house. Her parents were enjoying some coffee.

"We wondered what happened to you two girls," their mother said, beaming at her two daughters.

"I headed back to the kitchen for coffee when I saw Patrice pull in. I went out to greet her and we started quickly catching up," Jenny said putting her arm around her sister.

"Patrice, do you want coffee?" her mother asked.

"No, I'm good. I grabbed a late lunch."

"Have a seat," her father offered. Patrice walked over to a padded wicker love seat opposite her parents. Her parents sat in separate chairs and a long wooden chest separated them. Patrice assumed they both rarely sat in the wicker love seat.

"Mom said you went to Anamosa today. Now catch me up on why you're home and what you were doing in Anamosa? Wait before you answer that, I want to grab my coffee mug from the kitchen and I don't want to miss a word you say," Jenny said hustling out of the room.

"It's cool out here on the porch, aren't you two cold?" Patrice said making small talk with her parents.

"We got some good rain around the noon hour, but it started to feel muggy in the house. It feels better out here. There's a blanket in the chest, do you want that?"

"Yes, that would be great."

Renee Powell opened the lid to the chest and pulled out a thin blanket and draped it over her daughter. The blanket had an outline of Lake Okoboji.

"You still have this?"

"Yes, it's in good shape. Remember that summer we went up to Lake Okoboji and bought it in a gift shop."

"I do. I haven't seen it for so long."

"Well if you came home once in a while you could see it." Jenny said entering the room and sitting next to her sister.

"Give me some of that blanket," Jenny said tugging at the corner of the blanket.

"When you two are together, it's as if time stood still," Renee Powell said.

"It's hard not to pick on my little sister especially when I rarely see her. So, tell us what you did today, Patrice?"

"I'm home to write about the death of Nan Wood Graham," Patrice said catching up her sister. "I wanted some inspiration for my story, so I went into Anamosa. I stopped at the cemetery to find Nan Wood Graham's grave and then I found the Grant Wood Store and spent some time there."

"Did you find Nan's grave?"

"Yes, she's buried right next to Grant. There were some lovely flowers on the grave, but I was surprised at how small the gravestone was. Grant's too."

"What did you expect?" Jenny said.

"That's actually a good question. I guess I thought the grave-stones would be bigger to capture more information than the year they were born and the year they died. Gravestones here are usually larger and include month, date, year of birth, and death, as well as some scripture. I also expected to find numerous bouquets of flowers laying everywhere. There were probably four small bouquets."

"There wasn't very much about her funeral in the local paper other than a small article," her mother said.

"I just find this a little odd after years of the *Grant Wood Art Festival* and her support for the festival. I thought people here would make a bigger deal of her funeral."

"She hasn't been in the best of health for the last ten years and didn't get back very often," her mother added.

"Plus, some people here didn't think much of Grant Wood. Artisans did but hard-working folk did not," her father advised.

"We used to laugh at some of his paintings Patrice, remember? We thought his trees were shaped funny and wondered why anyone would paint Stone City!" Jenny snickered.

Listening to her family, Patrice now understood where she had gotten her opinions about Grant Wood and had transposed those feelings onto the assignment of writing about Nan Wood Graham's death.

"True, but people outside of here see it differently like my manager, Glenn, who saw the article of Nan's death in *The New York Times*. He finds it to be a big deal. Maybe that's why I'm conflicted about doing this story. This conversation just confirmed it --- it's not a big deal here."

"Well, like your dad said, it is important to some and to others it's not. People who volunteer at the Grant Wood Store must have found it a big deal. Who was working today?" her mother asked.

"The clerk's name was Anna."

"Oh, that's Anna Richardson. She was the librarian at the Anamosa Library for many years. Did you ask her about Nan's death?"

Patrice looked at her mother's hands. Whenever her mother was deep into a conversation, her fingers were laced together, and her right thumb traced the outer rim of the palm of her left hand. Patrice had found herself doing this same ritual.

"I should have but we started to talk about the – "

"Isn't that Randy Richardson's grandmother?" Jenny interrupted.

"Yes."

"Randy went to school with Patrice."

"Randy Richardson was actually a year older than me." Patrice replied.

"Didn't you date him in high school?" Jenny said.

"Barely. We didn't last long."

It'd been a long time since Patrice had thought about Randy Richardson. He was a cute guy who she had a crush on long before he noticed her. She would find ways to walk by his locker and say hello to him between classes. She didn't have the nerve to tell him she liked him. She asked her best friend, Beth, at the time to tell him that she had a crush on him. That worked and they soon started dating but when school let out at the end of May, Randy broke up with her.

"Why not?" Jenny asked.

"Just didn't work out," Patrice answered.

What she didn't say was that he broke up with her because she was a country girl. He wanted to date someone in town who he could see every day that summer. She didn't want to share this information with her family because they wouldn't understand how painful that was for her. She had really liked Randy but evidently, he hadn't liked her enough. Patrice had a strong urge to bite her nail, but she resisted.

"Mom, do you mind if we order pizza? I'm starving," Jenny said.

"Did you drink too much coffee? You're bouncing off the walls."

"I'm just excited to have you home. You should try it more

often you know," Jenny said looking at Patrice as she rose to her feet and headed for the kitchen phone.

"Make sure you order half cheese for Patrice," her mother said.

Patrice knew she was never going to hear the end to Jenny's ribbing about leaving home. She decided to be patient with her sister even though it was getting annoying.

"How long has Jenny been here?"

"She pulled in about 2:00. I called her this morning after you left for Anamosa."

"So, you had some time to visit before I got home?" Patrice said.

"We did. We weren't quite sure what time you'd be coming back from Anamosa so we've been chatting."

"Sorry about that. I meant to get home sooner but when I refueled my car in Anamosa, I ran into an old school friend and then realized I hadn't eaten all day, so I grabbed some late lunch."

"We know you're working so do what you need to do." Patrice's mother had always been so understanding of her kids, never placing demands on them like most parents did to their adult children. "What's on your agenda for tomorrow?"

"Anna talked about the *Stone City Art Colony* and Grant and Nan's presence there. When I asked her if there were any students from the art colony still living, she mentioned a Rose Boston from Davenport. I'm thinking I could do research on both the *Stone City Art Colony* and Rose Boston."

"Who did you say?" Jenny said gliding into the room.

"Rose Boston."

"Rose Boston?"

"Yes, do you know her?"

"Everyone in Davenport knows her. She's a big deal there. She's a local artisan and has her own shop in the art village."

"Davenport has an art village?"

"I knew you were going to say that. Yes, Davenport has an art village. You're surprised, huh?"

Patrice ignored her sister's comment. "Can you give me directions to her shop?"

"Sure, but what does this have to do with your story?"

"Anna Richardson told me that Rose is one of the last living students from the *Stone City Art Colony*. Maybe she remembers Nan and can give me some insight into who she was."

"Does that mean you're going to Davenport?"

"Yes, it means I'm going to Davenport."

"Did you ever think you'd be writing a story about Iowa?"

Patrice returned the sarcasm, "No, not in a million years."

Patrice got to work on her notes the following morning. She was thankful she had her laptop along. It was a bit heavy to lug around, but its portability allowed her to type her notes instead of writing them up. She'd made the dining room table her temporary desk. Her mother was doing laundry and her dad had left for work at the grain elevator.

"What time are you leaving?"

"I think I'll leave in about forty-five minutes," Patrice said starting to shut her laptop down.

"What is that?"

"This?" Patrice said pointing at the laptop.

"It's a laptop computer. We have them at work in case we need to travel for a story. I'm still a little clunky at it, but it's great. I can plug this in anywhere I go and start typing." Patrice demonstrated the use of the laptop for her mother by typing a few sentences. "It's much better than a typewriter because I can correct my mistakes by typing over my mistake or erasing it."

"I think I'll stick with my typewriter," Renee Powell said. As a young girl Patrice watched her mother type letters to members of the family that lived out of state. Renee Powell had been a secretary in a government office during WWII and pounded the keyboard faster than anyone Patrice had ever seen. Between Renee Powell's keyboarding talent and a high school typing class, Patrice had mastered the keyboard with the same precision and speed as her mother.

◆ ◆ ◆

"Mom, I didn't mention this last night, but yesterday I realized how important that brooch is that Nan gave me. I'm very sure it's the one depicted in *American Gothic*."

"What?"

"I'm sure of it." Patrice felt the certainty in her chest. "It's got to be priceless."

Patrice peered at her mother's surprised face.

"I'm not sure what I should do, or if I'm ready to tell anyone I have it. Who knows what could come from that?"

Patrice had her Camp Fire vest lying next to her on the dining room table. She carried it carefully over to the entryway. Almost every house in the area had a print of *American Gothic*, including Patrice's family. Their's was a small print in the front entry hallway facing the front door. Her mom followed her. They compared the brooch on the vest with the brooch in the painting.

"Well I'll be," Patrice's mom said shaking her head. "I can't believe it!"

"Neither can I. Please don't say anything until I figure out what I'm going to do with it. I may find out that it's not the same one."

In her heart, she knew it was.

"I've decided to go to Davenport today. I called the *Cedar Rapids Museum of Art* this morning and they mentioned that the art museum in Davenport has some additional drawings and most of Grant's personal belongings. Not only will I schedule some time there, but I want to look up this Rose Boston and visit her. I think I'll call Jenny and see if I can't stay overnight with her, Tom, and the kids."

Patrice carefully laid her Camp Fire vest back on the dining room table and covered it with the dry-cleaning bag it had been stored in.

Patrice hugged her mother goodbye and left for Davenport to

talk with the last surviving member of the *Stone City Art Colony*. Her mother had declined the offer to go with her, saying she wanted the two sisters to have their time together and that she would stay and look after their father.

Patrice pulled out of the driveway and drove by Mrs. Kroft's house on her way to Davenport.

"She's staying in this morning. Oh, I'm wrong about that," Patrice said catching Mrs. Kroft spying at her from her front window.

"Good morning, Mrs. Kroft," Patrice said from the car as she waved cordially to the old woman and pushed the gas pedal.

It was eleven-thirty by the time Patrice arrived in Davenport, and she was starting to get hungry. She had directions in hand for both the *Davenport Museum of Art* and to her sister's house, which Jenny had left for her the night before.

Patrice found the city of Davenport easy to get around. Situated on the western bank of the Mississippi River, all roads in Davenport lead downward toward the river's edge. The art museum was on the top of a steep bluff a half a mile up from the river bank. It was a one story building so Patrice didn't see it until she reached the crest of the street. The parking lot was large, and Patrice found a parking place easily. No charge for parking. *That's what I like about the Midwest. No clamoring for parking with outrageous prices*, she thought as she left her car.

She decided to call Jenny to say she was in town and found a pay phone just off the museum foyer. Jenny quickly answered and told her sister that Glenn had called her parents' house asking that Patrice call him back.

Patrice had given Glenn her parents' phone number but had hoped he wouldn't check in with her. She wondered what was up and returned the call right away.

"Glenn, it's Patrice," she said when he answered.

"Hi, how are you?" he replied.

"Fine."

"How's the story going? You have less than a week to turn it in you know."

"I know. I appreciate the reminder and the fact that you sent me here."

"Really? I'm not buying that," he replied with a friendly laugh.

He had her on that, and she knew it. She was silent for a moment and then got back to business.

"I'm on my way into the *Davenport Museum of Art.* I called ahead to schedule time to review some of the Wood's estate that is stored here."

"How did you know about that?"

"I called the *Cedar Rapids Museum of Art* and they referred me to Davenport. I'm not sure why most of this estate is in Davenport, but I'm hoping this will provide some history about Nan through her brother Grant. Remind me how this story relates to our magazine?" Patrice was sure Glenn could hear the sarcasm in her voice.

"I've decided to change the November issue to reflect European influence on American art. Christine is working on a Regionalist piece and your story will complement that."

Christine was one of the junior writers at the magazine.

Patrice bit her lip.

"I'll let you review her piece and you can share any findings with her based on your research on Nan and Grant."

"Okay. Wish me good luck. Better go."

"Of course. Good luck. And will you call me later and let me know your progress?"

"Will do." Patrice was holding fast onto her patience.

"Bye."

"Bye," Patrice echoed. Whew...she was not ready to talk in any detail to Glenn. She still had not forgiven him for giving her this assignment, when it should have gone to a junior writer to complete.

"Thanks Glenn!" she fussed in a whisper. Patrice caught her reflection in the floor to ceiling window. Her white sun dress and short pink sweater looked nice, but her makeup was drooping under the humidity. She pulled her lipstick and blush out of her purse and made the needed repairs utilizing the reflection of the window.

She stepped into the museum and approached the security guard at the information desk. He gave her a knowing smile that said he had been watching her repair her face. His name tag read "Scott," and while he looked to be only forty, he had a receding hairline and just enough extra weight on him that she hoped he would never have to run down an art thief.

As she approached, he yelled "Stela!" Evidently, he was covering the information desk while Stela was working in the gift shop.

Patrice wondered why he could not help her and give Stela a break.

Stela walked toward Patrice, ignored Scott, and said, "How may I help you?" Stela was petite with locks of curly golden red hair and Patrice thought she looked very pretty in her bright green dress with matching sandals.

"I have an appointment to view some of the Grant Wood and Nan Wood Graham artifacts."

"Oh, you must be that woman from New York. I'll tell Sheila you're here."

Scott, Stela, Sheila—was it a pre-requisite that your name had to start with an S to work at this museum? Patrice met Scott's gaze, wondering if he was eyeing her because he knew she wasn't a local. Out-of-staters were a novelty in Iowa and curiosity followed.

"What brings you to Iowa?" Scott cooed.

"I'm writing a story about Nan Wood Graham," Patrice replied, smiling but avoiding eye contact. She was relieved when Sheila appeared at the doorway to her right.

"Hi. Come with me." Sheila said crisply, her tone all business. She led Patrice to the basement room without saying a word. No small talk, no questions, just brisk efficiency. Sheila had the Wood drawings and artifacts already displayed in the room. She gestured for Patrice to sit down at the table.

"Your call didn't give us much notice to pull this all together, but everything is here," Sheila informed her.

"Thank you."

"You can take as long as you want. Just remember not to touch anything with the exception of the scrapbooks. We have security cameras in this room and Scott will be outside the room if you need anything. We close at 5:00 p.m. May I ask why you are interested in all this?" Sheila asked, gesturing the expanse of the room with her hands.

"I write for an art magazine and I'm doing a story on Nan's death. I wanted to learn more about her and Grant. There's not a lot of information out there about Nan so you could say that I'm getting to know the woman through her brother. I hear they were very close." Patrice looked down at the display and took a breath. "I didn't realize Grant Wood did pencil drawings."

"Yes, the Regionalists designed affordable art whether it was sketches, pencil drawings, or black-and-white lithographs. It allowed more Americans to purchase art in the '30s and '40s. What I do know is that lithographs represent Wood's last creative work. I'm sure you're familiar with the *Stone City Art Colony*."

"Yes..."

"He brought Francis Chapin, from *The Art Institute of Chicago*, to teach lithography at the art colony. At that time Grant had not even dabbled in it. It wasn't until a few years later that Grant delved into this form of work. Wood executed twice as many lithography prints as oil compositions. He even had Nan and her husband working on lithographs, which brought in some added income for their household."

Sheila's forced commentary was coming off more like a monologue than a dialogue. Patrice found herself wanting dialogue with a kindred spirit who loved art like she did. She wasn't going to find it in Sheila. Patrice noticed that Sheila barely looked at her as she spoke.

"Over the years she kept scrapbooks that followed her brother's career and she gave them to the museum before her death. These are the scrapbooks I have here on the table for you." Sheila glanced over her shoulder at Patrice.

"The museum will receive the rest of Nan's estate. What I'm really hoping for is that the remaining estate will include the brooch she wore in *American Gothic*."

This was Patrice's segue into the conversation that Sheila was having with herself. "How do you know it even exists? Couldn't Grant have just added it to the portrait?"

Sheila turned and looked Patrice squarely in the eye. "Old newspaper clippings talk about the brooch belonging to his mother and being passed on to his sister."

Sheila changed the subject as if she didn't want to talk about the brooch any further. "We're making plans to build a new museum. I hope to ship all of this to *The Art Institute of Chicago* before the new museum opens here. They're interested," Sheila sniffed.

"Why would Davenport do that—allow Grant and Nan's estate to leave Iowa?" Patrice asked in bewilderment.

"No one really cares about this stuff. It doesn't attract a lot of visitors. They want to see *American Gothic* and Chicago isn't allowing us to borrow that right now. I agree with the visitors, I'm not really interested in this stuff myself."

"What kind of art are you interested in?"

"Nineteenth century British painters."

Patrice was now starting to understand Sheila's mood and even though this woman was entitled to her opinion about art, Patrice felt she was the wrong curator for this art museum. Patrice recognized those feelings of being enamored by European artists but giving away a state's legacy was carrying it a bit too far. She felt protective and it showed as she clenched her fists underneath the table.

"How about asking the other Iowa museums if they want these artifacts first?" Before she could receive an answer, Sheila had already left the room.

Patrice pushed back her chair and stood up and then sat down in a huff. She had to collect her feelings if she was going to get through this information before 5:00. She couldn't get Sheila's attitude out of her mind. Nothing bothered her more than a curator who didn't appreciate the art they were responsible for. It was like a mother who didn't love one of her children.

Still fuming, Patrice pulled her chair back up to the table and grabbed a scrapbook. There were two. She opened one that was red with black swirls. Both scrapbooks were almost two feet in length and connected by what appeared to be shoe strings. The scrapbooks were full of newspaper clippings depicting Grant's career, mainly through the eyes of the local and Midwestern media. There was a brochure from 1933 that caught Patrice's eye. It described the art colony's purpose.

In Grant's own words, it read on the brochure, "Join us in working together toward the development of an indigenous expression . . . a stimulating exchange of ideas, a cooperation of a variety of points of view. If American art is to be elevated to the stature of a true cultural expression, it cannot remain a mere reflection of foreign painting. A national expression . . . must take group form from the more genuine and less spectacular regions. It is our belief that a true art expression must grow up from the environment itself. Then an American art will arrive through the fusion of various regional expressions based on thorough analysis of what is significant to these regions. Stone City Colony has this for its objective."

Patrice felt this was one of the best descriptions of Regionalism and it was in Grant's own words.

She searched the rest of the brochure which listed the fees for the colony. Tuition was $15 for two weeks, $26 for four, $30 for six, and $36 for eight weeks. Rooms were $1.50 per week, but only $1.00 per week if paid in advance for three weeks. Linens were not furnished at those prices. Rooms in town were listed as $2.00 and up per week and campsites were a relative bargain at fifty cents per week. At $8.50 per week, board was stated to be comprised of "excellent cuisine" under "expert supervision." Patrice marveled at the last statement.

She read that the three-story mansion had been vacated for over three decades. There were seven Italian marble fireplaces and no electricity before Grant rented it for the art colony's use. He added plumbing to the mansion with showers in the basement and converted the top floor into a dormitory for the women.

For the men, he had purchased ice wagons as sleeping quarters. Grant traded fourteen ice wagons from the owner of the Hubbard Ice Company in Cedar Rapids in exchange for giving away a scholarship to the *Stone City Art Colony*. Grant got permission to move the ice wagons down the roadways overnight so as not to disturb travelers. The wagons had awakened local citizens because their iron banded wooden wheels had clanked against the road's pavement.

The men using the ice wagons could leave them on the mansion's property or pull them down to the river in order to bathe and wash their clothes, she read. As part of an art project, they were asked to decorate the ice wagons with paint, artifacts, or awnings. Patrice saw a picture of Edward Rowan, one of the colony's founding members with his white colored ice wagon. It had hanging flower pots on the front and false windows, complete with curtains.

"The wagons appeared to be four tall panels long on each side from wheel to wheel. The front had a seat that extended the width of the ice wagon and designed to be drawn by horses. The very front panel was carved on the upper half in a half moon shape so the traveler sitting on the front seat could look at the countryside from side to side," she read out-loud to break the silence in the room.

A picture showed Grant painting his ice wagon with a mountain motif. The article stated that he had painted his interior with aluminum paint and had placed screened windows on the front and back so he could see the landscapes surrounding him.

Patrice smiled and mused that the screens also kept out both flies and mosquitoes. He also had a folding bed inside his ice wagon.

Other students stayed at a mansion once occupied by a quarry magnate with the last name of Ronen. That mansion was on an opposing hill, across the Wapsipinicon in Stone City. The article also talked about how desolate Stone City became after cement had been introduced at the turn of the century. The need for limestone rock diminished and therefore the town.

Patrice continued to pour through the scrapbooks, fascinated that so much of the art colony happened in her own backyard but no one ever spoke about it. The scrapbooks appeared to have captured every detail about the art colony. Patrice sensed that Nan had to be part of the colony but how?

Another article from *The Gazette* talked about how the art colony was financed, the start date, and the local companies that sponsored the art colony. It stated there were thirteen faculty members from area universities and *The Art Institute of Chicago*. Their talents were diverse. Some taught fine art and others taught framing or life drawing. One taught sculpture. There was a newspaper picture of the faculty dressed in summer clothes and sitting on the front steps of the mansion. Grant Wood was dressed in overalls sitting on the top step and Patrice noted he was wearing his dapper dress shoes of the time period. The group looked approachable though some looked uneasy.

"Must have been the heat," Patrice muttered to herself.

In-between the faculty members was the pedestal with the stone fruit basket on top. This picture was similar to the one in the Grant Wood Store in Anamosa. She wrote down the information so she could take it back to Anna, the clerk at the Grant Wood Store. All of this validated for Patrice that those memories of playing on the mansion's bare floor and front steps were indeed true. She stared at the stone fruit basket pedestal. There was something about that fruit basket that she felt strangely connected to, but she couldn't put her finger on it.

Patrice sat back thinking about Grant returning to Iowa, visualizing this dream of an art colony, acting as a mentor, teacher, and sharing his talent. Yet, he did even more. He had exposed the students to art through natural landscapes and practical precise functionality. In some ways, he had shown them that art was all around them even in the midst of a little town, surrounding cornfields, and dusty roads.

Another article from the *The Des Moines Register* entitled: *Fools Rush in Where Angels Fear to Tread* blasted the vision for the start of the 1932 art colony. There were words scribbled in pencil next to the article. Patrice assumed it was Nan's writing, that said, "Who's the fool?"

Patrice chuckled and reached for the second scrapbook. This scrapbook had more photos of Grant with his sister, Nan. A newspaper article talked about Nan's visits to the art colony and how she helped with preparing meals, doing bookkeeping or running errands. Every Sunday evening, Nan joined the students and faculty for an outdoor chicken dinner. This was a Sunday ritual, gathering for a feast of vegetables, breads, and pies that were locally donated. Patrice read that large tables were joined together and covered with red checked tablecloths, plates, and silverware to accommodate all the eaters. Local citizens joined them as special guests to meet the students and support the art colony. If local citizens did not make a reservation for the chicken dinner, they could buy hot dogs from students who made money as food vendors. Patrice further read that the colony pulled in over one thousand people on those summer nights, and students' paintings were auctioned off as well. The article closed by saying that Grant gave away some of his paintings for free that summer.

Patrice closed the scrapbook for a minute, using her index and middle fingers to hold her page. She absorbed what she read, surprised to read about the local support for the art colony. She grew up hearing stories that sensible men and women during the Depression found this to be a waste of time and resources during a very difficult economy.

Patrice re-opened the scrapbook and read another article entitled: *Stone City Art Colony Offers Saturday Night Dances Featuring Master of Ceremonies Jay Sigmund.* Patrice learned that Jay lived in the neighboring town of Waubeek. The article said he enjoyed the presence of the art colony and volunteered to announce local singers and bands at the Saturday night dances. He played records on the phonograph when there was no live talent. His volunteer efforts were actually paid for handsomely by a savory chicken dinner on Sunday nights at the colony. Patrice smiled about the simplicity of it all.

To play off the Jay Sigmund piece of the article, there was an associated story about the families from Waubeek who had come to this part of Iowa from New England. Many were descendants of sea captains who honored their heritage by hanging anchors, ship ornaments, oars, and other shipping gear on their houses and garages. *That astonished Patrice.* She had thought Jones County was mainly German, Irish, and Danish descendants that migrated directly into Iowa in the late nineteenth century. Waubeek was unique and Patrice was learning a lot about the area she grew up in.

"How did I not know all of this?"

Scott, looked into the room, with a bored expression on this face, "Did you say something?"

"No, I'm good."

The final pages of the scrapbook were of Nan participating in the *Grant Wood Art Festival* in Anamosa, an event that started in 1972. Then married and living in Riverside, California, she often returned to Iowa to celebrate her brother's legacy with the citizens of Jones County.

Patrice heard a closing bell and knew it was time to go. She peered at the other artifacts remembering Sheila's admonishment not to touch them. She had visited enough museums to know to leave the room as it was. She was not sure of the way out and Scott was nowhere to be found. She took a staircase that lead to a room just off the front entrance. She could see Scott standing by the information desk. *So much for museum security.* As she walked toward the door, a floor-to-ceiling mural caught her eye. It was a painting of farmers threshing hay. It was signed by a Ben Boston. *Was this artist related to Rose Boston?* She decided to ask.

The gift shop was dark, so she assumed Stela had gone home. Scott saw her advancing and she asked, "Is the artist of that mural related to Rose Boston?"

"Yes, Ben is her husband. He's a local artist." Scott turned, said good night in a tone that suggested he was glad it was closing time, and shut off the lights.

Patrice followed him out to the parking lot and jumped into her car. She would be glad to see Jenny.

◆ ◆ ◆

Patrice had never visited Jenny at her home and had only seen pictures of the house. It was a beautiful two-storied house on the outskirts of Davenport. Painted a soft bird egg blue, the house had a large porch that wrapped around the front and west side of the house. The porch and windows were trimmed in white. Patrice drove up a slight incline of a driveway and saw Jenny's Taurus parked outside the double garage. She was surprised to see two horses in the field east of the driveway. She never knew Jenny and Tom owned horses. As Patrice got out of the car Jenny came from the back of the house and greeted her.

Jenny, always the first to hug, caught Patrice in an embrace. "I get to see you twice in one week. How lucky is that?"

"This is nice," Patrice said with a smile. "I didn't realize you had horses."

"Actually, we acquired the horses when we bought the house. The owner was going to get rid of them—if you know what I mean—because they're too old to ride. We couldn't bear to think of that and offered to keep them."

Patrice could see the interstate in the far distance. "You are at the edge of town, among cornfields. I pictured you in a suburban area."

"As you know, we don't farm any of this. Our neighbor to the west does. I still like it, though. Our view looks like a Grant Wood painting wouldn't you agree?"

"Yes, it does," Patrice said scanning the rolling hills that surrounded Jenny's house.

"Wait until you see the sunset. It's beautiful and we see it every evening when we sit down for dinner." Then, turning and waving toward the house, Jenny said, "Come on in but look out for Baxter!"

As Jenny opened the back door, a large chocolate lab bounced out the door and jumped right onto Patrice. Jenny grabbed hold of the dog's collar and pulled him off Patrice and back toward the house. "Sorry about that. Baxter is only a year old and hasn't learned to control himself."

Jenny blocked Baxter so Patrice could enter the house. They walked into a comfortable family room just off the kitchen which had a large television and comfortable plaid sofa and chairs. "Would you like a tour?"

"Definitely," Patrice said.

"Don't' worry about Baxter. He'll calm down once you've been here awhile."

Baxter followed them around the house sniffing at Patrice. Patrice brushed Baxter away from her keeping her distance. It had been a long time since she had to deal with dog slobber and dog hair.

Noticing her sister's discomfort, Jenny grabbed Baxter's collar and took him down to the basement, promising to be right back.

When she rejoined Patrice, Jenny took her toward a wide foyer where a large staircase led to the second floor.

"We have more room than we need, but we love having a large house, especially with the kids," Jenny said.

Patrice listened idly to her sister while looking out the front door at the Grant Wood-style landscape before her. The front door framed the blanket of rich earth across the road which was dotted with row after row of sprouting green corn. The ground swelled and dipped as if mother earth had shaken the earthy blanket but never smoothed out its ripples.

"Do you want to see where you're sleeping?" Jenny had started up the stairs.

"Let me get my overnight bag out of the car first."

"Okay, we can do that later."

Patrice entered a large dining room, just off the foyer, where there were two fireplaces, on opposite sides of the room and large windows looking out to the western sky. Patrice spotted Jenny's collection of blueish-green figurines on the western fireplace mainly angels, and some figurines that were little girls in different poses.

"You collect these too? I saw a few in mom's house," Patrice said.

"Yes, there's hardly a person in eastern Iowa who doesn't have these. The figurines you saw at mom's house I gave to her," Jenny replied. "Do you want some iced tea?" Patrice noticed that Jenny was high strung moving from one thing to the next. She had forgotten this idiosyncrasy about her sister.

"Love some. Who's the artist?"

"Rose Boston." Jenny said from the kitchen area. I receive them as Christmas presents from Tom, and some are from Tom's mom and dad.

Patrice could hear Jenny adding ice to the glasses as she made the connection to Rose Boston.

"Really?" Patrice said, raising her voice so Jenny could hear. Patrice had lifted a figure from the mantel and was looking at it.

"Look underneath each figurine and you'll see Rose Boston's signature." Jenny returned to the room and handed Patrice a large glass of iced tea with a lemon wedge on the glass's rim.

"How interesting that you're collecting her work. Why didn't you say so last night?"

"It didn't occur to me. We were talking about so many things so fast I didn't think about it."

"What do you know about Rose Boston?"

"Not much really," Jenny said, taking a sip of her iced tea. "Her art is very popular around here and I love her angel collection. I have a brochure around here somewhere about her art. I believe it has her bio in it. Did you look at the bottom of the figurines?"

Patrice looked again.

"You'll find the year the mold was made and Rose's signature. They're similar to Precious Moments in that they are collectibles and some figurines are retired."

"Are any of these retired?"

"Yes, about half," Jenny said. "Drink up."

Patrice nodded her head and took a sip.

"I've decided to go to the store tomorrow. Maybe she would take a few minutes to talk with me if she's there. Do you want to go?"

"I'm volunteering tomorrow at a church garage sale at ten. I don't think I can make it, even though I'd love to go. Any excuse to visit her shop is worth it."

Patrice continued to look at the other figurines.

"Do you think you'll learn anything about Nan Wood?"

"I hope so. I didn't learn as much about her as I'd hoped at the art museum today. They have her scrapbooks, which are mainly newspaper articles about Grant's achievements and the art colony. I do know that Nan visited the art colony and maybe Rose could give me glimpses of her and her relationship with her brother. Did you hear me say that Rose is one of the last survivors of the *Stone City Art Colony*?"

Jenny nodded her head.

"Grant also left his estate to Nan, who gave it to the *Davenport Museum of Art*. Why the *Davenport Museum of Art*? Why not Cedar Rapids? He was connected more with that community than any other. I'm hoping that Rose can tell me more about all of this. It's just a hunch, but I feel I can learn a lot from her."

"Did you ask the *Davenport Museum of Art* people why Nan had given them her estate?"

"I forgot. The curator was less than friendly and doesn't really care about the estate." Patrice added her lemon wedge to her iced tea and took another drink.

"We've lived in this area all our lives and I've never heard about Rose Boston. I also saw a large mural by Ben Boston at the museum today. The mural had a Grant Wood feel to it. The security guard told me Ben Boston was Rose Boston's husband."

"Yes, that's true," Jenny replied.

"To be honest, I'm surprised by all the artists I'm uncovering in Iowa. I never think of this state as being interested in anything but farming and hard work."

"We're more than that. You know that," Jenny scolded. "Do you remember that Aunt Louise used to paint?"

"Yes."

"And my friend Elisabeth, her mother did those paint-by-number pictures."

"Yes, and didn't we call Elisabeth "Elise"? I loved her name. I remember her mother doing that, but that's not really the type of art I'm talking about," Patrice chuckled.

"And Aunt Patsy."

Now Patrice was laughing so hard she was clutching her stomach. "Yes," Patrice clucked. "She painted on furniture and farm tools, but that was more arts and crafts just like Elise's mom doing the paint-by-number pictures. What's your point?"

Jenny did not see what was so funny. "My point is that Aunt Patsy ended up becoming a painter and eventually belonged to the Paint 'n Palette Club in Anamosa. There were, and still are, many locals who belong to that club and enter their paintings into local, state, and national art competitions. The interest in art has *always* been around this area. It probably rubbed off on you, you just didn't know it."

"You're talking about that little building we went by every Sunday on our way to church on Highway 64?" Patrice said, trying to control her laughter.

"Yes, there were summer art sessions there. The building was next to the one-room schoolhouse that Grant and Nan Wood attended. The Paint 'n Palette Club aligned their festivities with the *Grant Wood Art Festival* every June."

"I never thought that local painting mattered. It was more hobby-oriented to me. I remember going home after school with Donna Ridgeway, and her mother also had a paint-by-numbers kit. She was painting flowers or something. I thought that was kind of hokey."

"There was a lot more to it. Always has been, but you looked at it through the eyes of a child."

"Maybe. I just think great art is what we see in the major art museums around the world such as those in New York and Paris."

"It must start somewhere, right, Patrice? Why not Iowa? You're writing for an art magazine in New York but you're from here. You know, you have a real bias toward the Midwest," Jenny said. "You're stuck-up!"

"What? I don't think so!" Patrice denied.

Jenny cut off her sister. "Yes, you are! "

"Who uses the word stuck-up. I haven't heard that term since 1973."

"You couldn't wait to leave here, thinking life was better somewhere else—like running off to New York. Why is that, Patrice? You thought you were better than everyone else. Where did you get that? And why did you have to leave to prove that to everyone?"

Patrice glared at Jenny. Jenny turned and went into the kitchen. Patrice followed right behind her like she was fifteen again. Jenny removed skillets from her cupboard and set them on the counter, then went to the refrigerator and pulled out a pan of marinated steak.

Patrice placed her hand on the countertop next to where Jenny was working. "Where is this coming from? What's wrong with wanting to see places and wanting to live somewhere else?"

Jenny was fuming and turned her back even more ignoring her sister.

"Yes, I'll admit, I couldn't understand why people wanted to stay here and never venture outside of the state line. I thought *that* was pompous. To think you have paradise here when you haven't even ventured out to see the world and compare the two. That's where I placed the arrogance. Your words are the living example of that. You think I'm wrong or selfish for wanting to leave. That's what I always heard growing up when I talked about it. People did not want to hear that. It upset them. Why? Why is it a sin to want to live elsewhere than precious Iowa?"

At this point, Patrice knew her feelings were taking over, and she was not going to stop. She continued her rant. "You take it as a snub. Maybe that's what I was rebelling against—conventionality. Jenny, this isn't about you. It's about me. I didn't think I'd find what I wanted here. Iowa didn't offer me my dreams. Iowa didn't expose me to a lot of different people or different ways of thinking. I felt it offered me a life sentence of passionless work with no hope of getting ahead, yet I was supposed to act grateful for that. Maybe I think people stay because they're afraid—or just plain stubborn to try something new."

Jenny stopped what she was doing, turned to look at Patrice, and put her hand on her hip as she opened her mouth to reply. But Patrice didn't let her have a word.

"I didn't believe that was forward thinking and I didn't want anything to hold me back. So why does it anger you that I left? You just said you think I believe I'm better than you, everyone else. Is that it? Why can't you see that it was about unmet dreams and personal survival? You found a way to survive here. I didn't think I could."

In that moment, realization set in. Patrice had never had this conversation with her family. It had been avoided. She made sure of that. She had been home once in the last ten years for a friend's wedding. She had done all the functionary things like send Christmas cards and presents, remembered her niece's and nephew's birthdays every year and called her parents on their birthdays and key holidays. The most she had ever done for Jenny and Tom was a Christmas gift and a birthday card every year. She had not been involved in their lives.

The sisters stood in silence.

Jenny broke the silence but did not look Patrice in the eye. "I didn't want to start a fight. Maybe . . . maybe when you left home," Jenny stammered, "you made the rest of us take a hard look at why we stayed."

"Are you happy, Jenny?" Patrice asked with a sigh, genuinely concerned.

"I suppose so, yes." Jenny nodded shaking her beautiful blonde mane.

"You look like you have everything."

"We do. Tom wants to start his own veterinarian business here on the acreage and quit working for Mason. We've got the kids and that keeps us busy." Jenny paused and looked at her sister. "I suppose I'd like to have what you have from a material sense. You're very successful at what you do."

"I'm not married though," Patrice said, knowing this would make her sister feel better.

"You could be. Are you dating anyone?"

Patrice recognized she had not told Jenny or her parents about her four-year relationship. She looked her sister in the face. "I'm dating a guy at work."

"Really?"

"Yes, for about four years." Patrice did not look directly into Jenny's face but just past her face, toward the microwave over the stove.

"You've been dating someone for four years and haven't mentioned it to me? Do Mom and Dad know?" Jenny asked, incredulous.

"No." Patrice continued to stare at the microwave.

Jenny stopped what she was doing and composed herself. "Why don't you share these things with us, Patrice?"

Patrice didn't know the answer herself. "It's just starting to get serious."

"What's his name? Spill."

"His name is Glenn Collier. We met at the magazine and we were peers."

"Go on," Jenny wasn't missing a thing.

"He was promoted to editor about six months ago and he's now my boss."

"Whoa."

"Our former editor took a job in Europe. We've kept our relationship low key, but it's becoming increasingly difficult to keep it under wraps from the employees."

"How have you kept your relationship low key with people

you work with every day?"

"Because we're professionals and we don't live together. I'm sure some suspect we're dating, but we're both workaholics and rarely in the office at the same time. Glenn wanted to move in together, but I said no. I'm not ready to become the 'little woman.'"

"What's he look like?" Jenny was now pulling lettuce and vegetables out of the refrigerator to start a lettuce salad.

"He's very good looking. He's about six feet tall, brownish-blonde hair, with piercing brown eyes. Dresses very nice. He grew up on Long Island. His mom is an interior designer and his dad works for a publishing company." Patrice spilled just like Jenny asked.

"Do you have a picture?"

"Not with me." Patrice pulled up a chair at the kitchen table getting ready for more questions.

"So, if you don't want to become the little woman, where is this relationship going?"

"Now that he's my boss, he's pushing for a change in our relationship. I guess I'm concerned that we don't want the same things, especially within the context of marriage. I sense he'll want me to stay home, have kids, and leave my career behind. I'm not ready to give that up yet."

"But you do want kids, don't you?"

"I suppose so, yes."

"Time is running out, Patrice."

"I know." It was hard taking advice from her older sister, but Jenny was always forthright.

Jenny stared at her a moment. Then, as if returning to focus from a daydream, looked at the clock. "Well, it's time to pick up the kids from camp and Tom won't be home until late tonight so he'll miss dinner with us. I'll finish prepping for dinner when I return, won't take me long. Uh, do you want to ride along?"

"Sure."

Patrice was happy that the subject of Glenn did not come up again that evening. Mentioning him at all was more than she had planned. She wanted to keep the detail of their relationship out of conversation. She was never completely sure how she felt about Glenn—or him about her, for that matter—and she did not want to further complicate the matter by sharing their relationship with her family. Dinner was polite and strained, considering how little she had seen her sister and her sister's family over the past years. She talked mainly with her niece and nephew with great interest, trying to conceal that she had regrets over missing the start of their lives. Mitch and Andrea asked her lots of questions about her life in New York and what she did when she wasn't working. That was a hard question to answer because she was always working. The ambiance of the evening matched her somber mood. She took that mood to bed with her yet tossed and turned all night thinking about why she had turned her back on her family. The reason wasn't clear, but she wanted to do better. Jenny had been a good sport about it overall. She was more forgiving about things than Patrice. With that thought in mind, Patrice finally fell asleep.

◆ ◆ ◆

Patrice awoke to bright sunshine streaming through the guest room window. Her thoughts turned to the sunset she had witnessed the night before, its raspberry hues cascading across a deep blue and marmalade sky. Jenny had been right, it was spectacular. She tried to remember the last time she had seen a sunset like that. She glanced at the clock and saw that it was already 8:30. She heard the garage door opening and knew Jenny was returning from taking Mitch and Andrea to summer camp. Patrice had slept late, not simply for the sheer luxury of it, but also because she wanted to give her nephew and niece ample time to use the bathroom and kitchen before another day of camp.

She showered and draped a lemon-yellow sleeveless dress

over herself and placed a white sweater across her shoulders. She pulled her hair back into a ponytail and put it in place against her neck with an antique silver pendant that once held a scarf in place. It had topaz at the center which complemented her dress and her pale hair. She put on the diamond necklace Glenn had given her as a Valentine's Day present, thinking how relieved she had been that the gift was a necklace and not a ring. She'd had time to think about their relationship on the way to Iowa and she did not feel ready for a lasting commitment. Not now anyway.

Jenny had a mug of coffee and some scones waiting for her when she came downstairs.

Jenny hugged her good morning and said, "I hope there are no hard feelings."

"No, no hard feelings," Patrice hugged her sister tightly. She scanned her sister's face when they released the hug. "Evidently this was something that needed to be said by both of us."

Jenny hugged her again. "I love you. Call me after your visit with Rose."

"I will. Can I take the mug of coffee and a scone with me?"

"Yes, and by the way you need to gain some weight!"

Patrice took a big bite out of her scone as Jenny walked her outside to the rental car.

"Mitch and Andrea wanted to stay home today and be with you. I told them you had your appointment and then needed to head back to Cedar Rapids. Tom is sorry he missed you. He didn't get home until after midnight and was out the door by six this morning."

"Give them all my love. I enjoyed catching up with them last night. Thank Tom, too, for his hospitality."

Patrice backed out of the driveway and drove down the driveway to the road that would take her toward Davenport. She glanced back at her sister and put her arm out the opened window and waved. Patrice thought Jenny looked somber and wondered if there was something missing from Jenny's life. Or was there really something missing from her own?

CHAPTER 7

The Art Village in Davenport was only a block from the Mississippi River. It had been a long time since she had seen this magnificent river. There was a white riverboat anchored on the shoreline not far from the Art Village. Red, white, and blue bunting hung from two tiers of the boat. Patrice loved the Iowa rivers and their large expanse. Like most things in Iowa, there was abundance—an abundance of land, water, soil, and crops. It was mind-boggling when one thought about it.

The Village was four spacious blocks of art stores, intermixed with trendy restaurants, in a quaint area of town. Patrice followed Jenny's directions and circled the block to find a place to park. She parked in front of a small house that had been converted into an art store. She followed the sidewalk and rounded the corner. It was a warm day and Patrice could smell the scent of lilac in the air.

"Mmm, lilac." Patrice took a deep whiff noticing yet another thing she loved about Iowa, all the smells of the flowers.

The sidewalk started to slant, following the decline of a small hill. Ahead of her at the bottom of the hill was a line of women. It was only 9:30 and there were ten to twelve women of all ages and sizes waiting, one behind the other. Patrice's eyes scanned beyond the front of the line. They were in line for Rose Boston's store.

She took a place in line and asked the woman in front of her,

"Why are you standing in line?"

"I have a figurine whose hand has fallen off," the woman said. She opened her dark blue plastic sack to let Patrice peer into the sack. "The shop fixes things like this for free."

"Why do you think the other women are in line?"

"Oh, for dozens of reasons. Most are collectors and want to see what's new, what's been retired. I'm sure many are from out of town and want to make sure they get into the shop before it gets too busy."

Patrice's curiosity was piqued. What was it about this store that had a line of women standing out in front of it thirty minutes before it opened? Patrice took out her notebook and started making notes.

There were six more women standing behind her when a woman peered from the front door window at 10:00. She flipped the door sign from "closed" to "open," unlocked the door, and greeted each customer as they entered the store. Patrice followed the assembled line of women. The store was also a converted small home, with 3-4 small rooms whose doors and entryways were removed so it opened into two large narrow rooms. Displays of molded clay figurines in pale aqua greens adorned the rooms, and when the sun shone on them, they had a copper cast. There were animals, angels, children, and various forms of nature in different sizes. Rose Boston certainly had signature designs. Every figurine had rounded features and resembled the Sistine Madonna Cherubs. There was also a display of sculptured baskets, bowls and vases. Displays were cleverly done matching the charm of the old house. There were large knick knack shelves on the walls holding figurines, circular tables with white linen table clothes with lace edging, and antique china cabinets housing the retired pieces. Patrice loved the craftsmanship of the figurines and could see why they were so popular in Davenport and beyond. Patrice made note of 3-4 designs she wanted to buy but first things first.

Patrice looked toward the back of the store, where the customer service counter was, and saw that a few women were already standing in line with returns or purchases. She moved toward this counter and could see a back room containing row upon row of various figurines. She heard women conversing about what figurines were new and which were soon to be retired. Patrice continued to browse, wanting to understand Rose's business before she asked about Rose's whereabouts.

On a wall, above a display, was a small chalkboard that caught Patrice's attention. There was a local phone number written in chalk on it. No words, just the phone number. *This is odd.* She rummaged through her purse for a slip of paper and pen, found both, and wrote down the number. She had a hunch. She looked toward the customer service counter and when no one was in line, she walked up to the clerk and explained that she was from out of town and wanted to learn more about the business and Rose. Very efficiently, the clerk opened a brochure and handed it to Patrice.

"Read through this and you'll learn all about her."

Patrice accepted the brochure and, as if reading her mind, the clerk said, "You can keep that."

"Is Rose here today?" Patrice asked.

The clerk smiled. "No, she sold the business about five years ago, even though it still carries her name. Rose is now in her eighties and lives up the street, about one block from here." She pointed to her left, which Patrice knew was north.

Patrice asked if she could have the specific street address and surprisingly, the clerk provided it for her on a small piece of scratch paper. Patrice, still surprised at the ease of the exchange, thanked the clerk and took the brochure to browse through it.

She found a lonely corner and continued to thumb through the brochure. Toward the back, she found a young picture of Rose with members of the *Stone City Art Colony*. Her face among the crowd of students was circled. Grant Wood was in the picture and was easily identifiable with his round-rimmed glasses and overalls. Patrice did not see anyone who resembled Nan.

She continued to walk the store and found two small paintings that had Ben Boston's signature on them. One was a painting of a bridge that crossed the Mississippi River connecting Davenport to Rock Island, and the other was a boy sitting on a riverbank, looking at the river. The paintings were very good, and she was now very interested in learning more about the Bostons.

Patrice left the shop and headed to her car. She decided to find a pay phone and drove to a gas station she had seen two blocks down. She parked and pulled out the phone number from her purse that she had taken off the chalkboard. Patrice found a pay phone in the gas station and dialed the number.

The voice on the other end answered, "Boston residence."

Patrice was elated that her hunch was right, yet caught herself, embarrassed to be calling from a pay phone.

She blurted, "Is Rose there?"

The female voice on the other end asked, "Who's calling?"

Collecting herself and pulling up her best professional tone, Patrice said, "I'm Patrice Powell. I'm a writer for *European Art* magazine and I'm interested in talking to Rose about her life's work."

The voice on the other end of the line was now muffled and Patrice guessed this person was probably talking with Rose. The voice came back to the line. "Rose cannot come to the phone right now but thank you for calling."

Patrice said politely, "I'd like to schedule time to meet with her to talk about the *Stone City Art Colony*."

Patrice once again heard a muffled voice. The voice came back on the phone, stronger this time, and said, "She can see you today at one o'clock."

"I'll be there," Patrice replied. Then she confirmed the address and thanked the person on the other end of the line.

Patrice decided to call Jenny and left a message on her answering machine to say she had made an appointment with Rose. Jenny was probably already at the church, working the garage sale. Patrice had expected to talk with Rose in her store or set up a phone call for later in the week. While she had expected

Rose to be in her eighties, she had not anticipated needing to employ any formal protocol to talk with her. She now realized that this had been a mistake. She had put an Iowa stereotype on a very progressive woman. She didn't plan on making that mistake with Rose again.

Patrice heard her stomach rumble and decided to stop at a restaurant in the village for lunch. Patrice chose a restaurant that resembled an old colonial inn. Inside, light streaming from eastern facing windows provided the only natural light in the otherwise dark restaurant. It smelled smoky and she followed the scent to a woman sitting at the counter having coffee and smoking her cigarette. Patrice took a seat at one of the tables by the window; the furthest table from the smoke. The menu, wedged between the ketchup and mustard, did not offer much for a vegetarian so she asked the waitress for a grilled cheese sandwich and some iced tea. The waitress talked her into some home fries which Patrice hadn't had for years.

She had brought her briefcase, which contained her notebook and tape recorder, and pulled out the notebook to prepare questions for her meeting with Rose. She had a standard set of questions that she used for most interviews and started to scratch those questions into her notebook. She felt the pressure of pulling a viable story together but was confident Rose was the answer to so many unknowns.

Patrice took a deep breath and another one and then relaxed. She heard a boat in the distance tooting its horn and smiled. There really was life outside New York and she was going to enjoy this moment and this simple lunch.

Upon finishing, Patrice allowed herself plenty of time to find the Bostons' address. True to the clerk's word, it was one block up from the shop and across from a park that rested near the Mississippi River. Rose and Ben's house had a direct view to the river and the state of Illinois, just on the other side. The street was a row of two-storied houses that appeared to be built at the turn of the twentieth century. They were truly American looking with their white picket fences, and flags still flying from the

Memorial Day holiday. Most of the homes were white or beige in color, the dark charcoal gray color of Rose Boston's house beckoned. Patrice stood on the sidewalk looking at it. *Why so gray?* The murky colored house seemed ominous looking like the kind of houses that looked frightful to a kid on a cold Halloween night. Patrice slowly walked up to the front door and rang the doorbell. She didn't know what to expect now. A woman of about sixty wearing a light blue housedress answered the door and said her name was Dora. Patrice introduced herself and extended her hand. The housekeeper shook it awkwardly and brushed a gray curl from her forehead while showing Patrice in. Patrice was surprised to see Rose immediately to her left in a front sun room whose windows drew in the park and the river. Rose was in a wheelchair and Patrice saw her pale white skin and shaking left hand. Rose seemed frail.

"Rose has another visitor at 2:00 and you'll need to leave by then," Dora said curtly. *Nice to meet you too* Patrice thought sarcastically to herself.

Patrice thanked Dora for this information. Dora walked her over to Rose and introduced Patrice, gesturing for Patrice to sit across from the aging artist on a small chair with a white seat cushion that was embroidered with red roses. Patrice eyed Rose's skin that seemed to be as translucent and fragile as a Dresden china figurine. Even though Rose was now much older, Patrice could see a resemblance of the younger Rose from the picture in the brochure at the shop. Beyond Rose toward the back of the sitting room was a large living area with a wide wooden staircase that lined the south side of the room. Artwork and pictures of her family followed the staircase up to the second floor. The first floor of the house appeared to be separated in half by a long wall that started behind the staircase and extended to the north wall of the house. At its base was three to four feet of dark brown wood topped with cream-colored paint over drywall. There were three wooden doors and Patrice wondered what was behind all three.

"You're here to talk about the art colony," Rose said with a voice that kept pace with her nodding head.

"Yes, yes I am. I'm writing an article for an art magazine in New York City, but I was born in Anamosa. Actually, I was raised near Stone City. Unfortunately, I'm back home to write about Nan Wood's death."

Rose was silent and Patrice continued respectfully.

"I was told you were a student at the *Stone City Art Colony*."

"Yes . . . in '32 and '33," Rose continued slowly.

"How did you hear about it?"

"I had seen an advertisement about it in the local newspaper. After begging my parents to attend the colony, my father gave his approval." Rose drew in a breath. "I was eighteen years old. My father knew he could no longer discourage my love of art and financed my trip."

Patrice felt Dora's presence in the adjoining room. Patrice glanced at her and Dora turned away.

"What do you remember about the art colony?"

Rose, who had been sitting in the chair somewhat despondent, perked up. "It was a magical place, magical time. That's where I met Ben."

Dora added from the next room, "Ben is her husband and a local artist."

Rose did not turn her head toward Dora but nodded at the comment.

Rose added, "Grant Wood knew of Ben and invited him to attend the art colony. When Ben said he couldn't afford it, Grant gave Ben a job as groundskeeper." Rose paused and looked up and to her left for a moment, as if remembering a better time and place. She took a deep breath and slowly started again. "Ben would often talk to me because I usually sat outside sculpting limestone that I had brought back from visiting the quarry. I was making a mess and Ben knew he'd have to clean up after me."

Patrice said in surprise, "They allowed you down in the quarry?"

Rose nodded. "They knew we were art students and they

didn't mind if I grabbed some stone to carve. One of the workers would help me carry a block back up the hill to the mansion."

"What did you carve?"

"All kinds of things; statues mostly."

"How did you come up with your ideas?"

"When I was little, after a rainstorm, I would go outside and look for puddles. I would squat down and look into them and I would see faces and figures in the water. I've never forgotten those faces and tried to carve them. Most of them you see today in my shop. Have you been to my shop?"

"Oh yes, that is how I found you. I especially liked your use of river rock as eyes and other decorative design."

"My father sometimes took us to the backwaters of the Mississippi for picnics. My brother and I would wade into the water and pull these rocks from the muddy bottom."

"Were you born here?"

Rose reached for her water glass with careful hands and Patrice found herself on guard ready to help in case Rose spilled.

Dora came over and gently took the glass from Rose's hand once she had taken a drink, then dabbed the corners of Rose's mouth with a handkerchief.

"No, I'm from Indiana. My parents moved here when I was young. I left when I was seventeen to work in a dress shop in Chicago, but I just wasn't interested in the city or the life of a shop girl. I quickly returned home and that's when my father realized I wasn't going to give up my pursuit of being an artist."

"So that's when you left for the art colony?"

"Yes."

"What do you remember about Grant Wood?"

"It was a magical place." Rose repeated.

She smiled at the elderly woman politely, wondering if Rose was stretching her own truth.

Dora had retreated toward the back of the room.

A flush of a toilet drew Patrice out of concentration, and she heard a door open. An elderly man appeared into the living room.

"Would you like to meet Ben?" Dora said with little expression in her voice.

Ben was holding a walker before him and stretched out his hand for Patrice to shake. She got up, walked toward him, and shook his hand. It was wet, as if he had washed his hands but not dried them. He asked her who she was. She politely gave her name and dried her hand against her skirt. With Patrice's presence forgotten, he clomped across the living room with his walker, put it aside to stretch out on a daybed near the window, and fell asleep.

Patrice looked at Dora who gave her a look that said, *do not ask.*

Patrice rejoined Rose but kept glancing over at Ben who was sleeping contently on the daybed.

"He's not well," Rose announced.

Patrice nodded her head in understanding.

"I want to hear more about you. You were raised near Stone City but live in New York?"

"Yes, I live and work in New York City."

"What took you so far away from home?"

"I got a writing scholarship to Columbia University, in New York and got a job there after graduation."

"At the magazine?"

"Yes."

"What magazine did you say you write for?

"*European Art.* It focuses mainly on European art of today."

"Why are you writing about Nan Wood and asking about the art colony?"

"Good question. The article I'm doing on Nan will be part of a new series we're launching on the European influence on American art and culture." Patrice was half making this up for Rose, but she now suspected that Glenn was considering the same.

"I want you to see the Russian icons I collected when Christian artifacts were being removed from Russian churches. Dora?"

Dora motioned to Patrice and said, "Come with me." Dora did as she was told and guided Patrice to the stairwell. A few artifacts were at the staircase landing. Patrice gazed upon the crucifixes and crosses made of wood, brass, stone and copper. She gazed further up the staircase and saw the pictures of Rose's three sons. They were mounted near the top steps of the staircase as if to lend privacy to family matters.

A hand grabbed her elbow and Dora led her to a back room filled with more artifacts. Now she knew what was behind two of three doors, a bathroom and now this room full of art. Patrice's mouth dropped open as her eyes fixed on paintings of Christ, paintings of the Madonna and baby Jesus, and other biblical figures with halos above their heads. The paintings were all about the same size, 16" x 20", and were in vivid golds, dark browns, stunning azures, and brilliant reds. Patrice wanted to touch the clunky wooden and gold-leafed frames that outlined this beautiful art. Her eyes took in over twenty paintings and artifacts. Patrice peered behind the paintings and noticed most were applied to wood panels. She turned to face Dora.

"This is amazing."

Dora nodded her head in agreement.

Patrice continued to look at Dora, wondering if she grasped the worth of this artwork.

"Some of this art may date back to the fifteenth century, before Peter the Great opened Russia to western influences. This tells me that Rose could have collected this as far back as the late '30s when the Great Purge took place in Russia."

Dora did not bat an eye. Patrice stared at her, speechless, and took the cue to be escorted back to Rose. Patrice contained her enthusiasm when she saw Rose dozing off in her wheelchair. Dora patted Rose's hand, waking her up. Patrice nodded her thanks to Rose for sharing this exquisite artwork.

"Do you have children?" Patrice asked.

"Yes, two are in the local area and one lives in Kentucky."

Patrice looked at Rose in silence. She realized this was not her format for an interview, but under the circumstances, this was the best she could do based on Rose's health issues. She had also decided not to record the conversation. She again asked Rose what she remembered about Grant.

A voice from the daybed said, "Who? Grant Wood? Nice fellow." Ben had wakened from his nap, but slowly drifted back to sleep.

Rose added, "Well, he sat at the head of the dinner table every night and started our evening conversations. I looked up to him like a father."

"Did Nan participate at the art colony or join you for dinners?"

The doorbell rang and Rose's two o'clock appointment had arrived early.

Dora was at the door and greeted her warmly.

"Hello, Kate."

"Hello," returned the cheery reply from the front porch. A beautiful young woman about Patrice's age stepped into the house. She was dressed for the hot weather in long khaki shorts and a deep pink polo shirt with the sleeves rolled up to her elbows. Her sunglasses were perched on the neckline of her polo and her blonde hair was swept up in a bun. Kate spotted Patrice sitting across from Rose.

"Hello, I'm Kate Garvey and you are . . .?

Patrice stood up and extended her hand to Kate, "Patrice Powell."

Kate clasped Patrice's hand with a squeeze more than a handshake.

"How do you know Rose?"

"I just met her. I came here to talk with her about the *Stone City Art Colony*."

"Oh, we'll have to talk," Kate answered. "I'm writing a book about her life and I'd love to hear about the art colony. Here's my card. Call me and we'll talk more." Kate moved past Patrice and sat in Patrice's place on the chair with the embroidered cushion. Kate talked with Rose like a niece talking with her elder aunt. Patrice realized Rose reminded her of some of her aunts, especially her Aunt Patsy who had passed away a couple of years ago. Patrice felt a pang of melancholy, the kind of melancholy of being pushed out, moved away from something she loved.

Patrice spotted Dora leaving the room, evidently more comfortable with Kate's presence than Patrice's. Kate was already chattering with Rose.

Patrice interrupted and extended her appreciation and thanks to her gracious host. She said goodbye to Kate and asked Rose if she could say goodbye to Dora. Rose nodded. Patrice peered over at Ben who was still asleep on the daybed by a large window. He would have been a great interview as well, but he appeared to be in no better health than Rose.

Patrice surprised herself by saying she wanted to say goodbye to Dora. Something propelled her to do so, call it writer's instinct, so she decided the least she could do was to let Dora know she was leaving. *She'll probably cheer the moment I say goodbye and slam the door behind me.* Patrice poked her head through the door Dora had disappeared into, and found the housekeeper in a small kitchen polishing silver at the table.

"Dora, I'm leaving. I wanted to thank you for your hospitality today and for allowing my impromptu visit."

Patrice was surprised when Dora told her to sit for a cup of coffee.

"Why yes, thank you," she said obeying and taking a seat. Her curiosity had gotten the best of her. Maybe the two could pump one another for information. Besides, housekeepers always knew the details of the family they worked for.

The small woman was quick to her feet and poured a hot cup of coffee in a china cup with a blue and white Currier and Ives motif with a matching saucer. Dora put the coffee down in front of Patrice and sat down opposite of her. She continued to polish the silver while she began to share the Bostons' current situation.

"I appreciate your tactfulness with their health. Ben is now eighty-seven and his mind wonders a lot. Rose is eighty-four years of age and has Parkinson's."

"Oh, I'm sorry to hear that," Patrice replied.

Dora eyed Patrice as she continued, "They have their good days and not so good days, and I try to protect that. Kate, who you met, is writing a book about Rose's life. Rose has had an incredible life, but so has Ben. Ben is the last of the Regional artists." Patrice didn't know if she should be more surprised that Ben was one of the last of the Regional artists or how strong Dora was at polishing silver.

"Rose was correct in saying that Grant Wood knew of Ben, having seen his work in local art exhibits. Grant gave him a job both summers at the colony. Ben became something of a protégé to Grant."

This was new information and it piqued Patrice's interest.

"Dora, would you mind if I asked you some questions and took some notes?" Patrice said.

"I'm okay with that. I know you didn't get to finish your interview, but I can help you with some of the answers to the questions you asked. I want to make sure you write well about the Bostons, they deserve that."

"How long have you been with the Bostons?"

"I've been with them since about 1960, but I never get bored of the stories they share. I'm hoping to hear something I haven't heard before."

"Please continue with what you were saying about Ben being a protégé of Grant Wood's."

"After the art colony closed, Ben and Rose got married and lived in Tipton, just outside Davenport. Ben's first mural is in a post office west of here in a town called Freemont. They moved to Davenport to raise their family and that's when Rose started her business at Ben's urging. He continued painting and taking small jobs to help raise their family."

"I saw his mural at the art museum here in Davenport and some of his paintings down at the store."

"They're all over Davenport. He is highly respected and knows so many people. It's a pity that he can't remember things because he could tell you so many stories."

Dora continued the tête-à-tête in rhythm to shining the silverware. "Rose started her business from her basement. She told you how she liked to carve figurines and found a way to make them out of an inexpensive concoction of cement, water and sand. As she worked on molding this cement concoction, she'd often looked out her basement window, keeping an eye on her children playing in the backyard. Their playing was the inspiration for many of her figurines—children tumbling, children smelling flowers or playing with their favorite pet. At one time, Rose even had her own television show for children, teaching them art through storytelling. Her show lasted three years on our local Channel 6."

"My mother and sister collect her figurines. I didn't know about her until just this week," Patrice said, realizing she had not taken a sip of her coffee.

Two sips later Patrice asked, "Did Ben or Rose see Nan or Grant again after the art colony closed?"

"They did correspond for many years. Rose had a fondness for Nan."

"How so?"

"Well, they met at the art colony and they became close. She said that Nan was there almost every day. Men in those days had more opportunity to attend an art colony than women did. I'm sure their closeness had to do with being among the few women in a male dominated profession."

"I've heard that Nan has willed her remaining estate to the art museum here in Davenport. I wondered why she didn't consider the *Cedar Rapids Museum of Art*. She, Grant, and their mother lived in Cedar Rapids most of their lives."

"Rose and Ben were both on the museum board. That may have had something to do with it. Do you want me to warm your coffee?" Dora asked once again.

"No thanks, I'm fine," Patrice said holding her hand over the china cup.

"So, you went to New York to pursue writing and now you're back home; isn't that ironic?"

Patrice raised her eyebrows. *Nothing like hitting me straight between the eyes, just when I thought we were becoming friends.*

"My editor heard about Nan's death and knowing I was from this area, sent me on 'special' assignment to do the story. I have to admit, I was surprised because we don't really write about Midwestern art. The better story for our magazine would be to cover Nan's relationship to Grant and connect that with his schooling overseas and how it influenced his art." Patrice's words trailed off as she watched how hard Dora polished the silverware.

"I'm a little frustrated about doing this story because there isn't a lot of information about Nan. Rose was a wonderful find because I was hoping she could tell me about both Nan and Grant. Nan married, but never raised a family. Grant never had kids, so there are really no relatives to talk to. In my arrogance, I thought I could write a simplified story from New York about Nan. You know, she was born, she lived, she had a well-known brother, and she died. Believe me, that's not my preferred style of writing but I didn't see the necessity to come home to write this story. I wasn't too happy when my editor sent me here to write it."

"Smart editor. What's his ... or her name?"

Patrice looked Dora in the eye and Dora returned her gaze.

"His name is Glenn."

"Ahh, nice masculine name." Dora grinned and then her face grew serious as she followed her thoughts. "So, why don't you want to write the story?"

Patrice's thoughts raced toward confusion. She knew Dora would not like her answer. She did not want to undermine the progress she had made with this woman and admonished herself for getting too familiar with her. But she also had to admit that there was something comfortable and homey—minus the expectations of family—in sitting with Dora, having a cup of coffee, and chatting. She wanted to give Dora an honest answer but, in some ways, she did not quite know the full answer to Dora's question.

What she did know and didn't want to blurt out was that Grant Wood's art brought her embarrassment, of the people she knew and the area she came from. Other than *American Gothic*, the rest of Grant Wood's art seemed simple and amateurish to her. He drew landscapes of round trees, overly dramatic and swollen farm hills with crops and clouds. To add insult to injury, Patrice felt his painting of farm scenes and people with toiling faces and stocky looking farm animals were not charming or appealing. *His paintings did nothing for the people of Iowa except stereotype them.* They were stereotypes she didn't want to be associated with. Whenever she told people she was from Iowa, the jokes would start about pigs and farmers—and sometimes potatoes from those who confused Iowa with Idaho. She was tired of defending who she was, a farmer's daughter in a world that now placed little value on this class of people. When she wrote this story for the magazine the joking would begin again. Her peers would find ways to tease her about this sister-artist connection and remind her how, once again, nothing great ever came from Iowa. She was turning her back on it again. Yesterday she realized she had turned her back on her family. Now the two thoughts converged.

She spilled her betraying thoughts. "I'm not proud of where I come from and maybe I'm afraid this story will remind me of that." She looked away as tears formed in her eyes.

The Dora who appeared to be unsympathetic handed a napkin over to Patrice and said, "You know both Grant and Nan left the state like you did. One returned and settled here and one did not. Nan was the one who did not. You may find you have something in common. Start with that."

Patrice wiped her eyes on the napkin and looked into the cup of coffee that was now cold. She finished it out of politeness and respect for the generosity Dora was showing her.

"Maybe I'll find something behind the sourpuss face Nan has in *American Gothic*," Patrice said looking for some humor in her outburst of emotion.

"I bet you might."

"Well, I've taken more of your time than I expected to. You've been a gracious host, Dora. Thank you." Patrice reached into her purse. "Here's my business card should you have any need to call me or think of anything that might help me with my story. I'll write my parents' phone number on the back. I'll be here for another three days." Patrice pulled a pen from her purse and wrote down her parents' phone number and handed the business card to Dora.

Dora offered Patrice a way out of the house through the kitchen door. Patrice was grateful because her face was red and puffy from tears that she didn't want to share with Kate and Rose.

Patrice started the car but sat clutching the steering wheel, thinking, just thinking. Dora had unnerved her asking why she hesitated to write this story. The tears begin to flow again, and Patrice put her head against the steering wheel. The afternoon sun beat down on the crown of her scalp. The mighty river in the distance shimmered in the same warm afternoon sun and Patrice looked beyond the river at Rock Island, Illinois. The river separated Iowa from Illinois and Patrice felt that same split in her heart. Her thoughts returned to Dora's question, *why did Patrice resist coming home to write this story*?

Patrice had buried these feelings for so long that they were not easy to evoke here and now. She put her sunglasses over her eyes. Her hands were shaking.

CHAPTER 8

Thirteen people were in line for the tour and Patrice was at the head of the line. She decided to be practical and had worn some fashionable looking jean shorts and a gold tank top. It was to be a scorcher-with temperatures rising into the upper nineties and humidity to match. She had applied sunscreen to her exposed skin and pulled her hair back into the familiar ponytail. Socks and tennis shoes, instead of flimsy fashion sandals, made her ready for anything that came her way.

It was Friday and this was Patrice's fourth full day in Iowa. Her mother had read in *The Gazette* that the *Cedar Rapids Museum of Art* was offering a tour of area locations where Grant Wood and Marvin Cone had painted. Marvin Cone had been a high school friend of Wood's and an art professor at Coe College. Marvin had also been an instructor at the *Stone City Art Colony*. Patrice signed up readily.

She stepped into the small bus, happy to feel the air-conditioning. She took a window seat in the second row. The other tourists entering the bus were of all ages, genders, and hairdos. Patrice wondered what their interest was in taking the tour. The tour guide was the last to enter the bus and introduced herself as Natalie Murray, a third-year art student at Coe College, and the intern who had, in fact, designed the tour. Natalie didn't look old enough to be an intern, Patrice thought. Maybe it had something to do with her long brown frizzy hair that needed styling. Natalie explained they would be visiting all local points where Marvin Cone and Grant Wood spent time painting.

"The tour will take us across two rivers and two counties in total today," Natalie conveyed.

Patrice was looking forward to the tour because the longest stop was a one-hour visit at Stone City. When Natalie was finished with the day's itinerary, the driver shut the door and Natalie took a seat next to Patrice.

The Linn County destinations were the first stops and mainly represented the painting locations that Marvin Cone liked to frequent. Marvin Cone, like Grant Wood, learned his technique mainly in Europe. Marvin spent most of his time in France and Belgium.

"How many of you are familiar with Mr. Cone's work?" Natalie surveyed the small smattering of raised hands and continued "Like Wood, he returned to Iowa, his home, to paint the panoramas within his local area."

The bus stopped for only a few minutes at each location, allowing the passengers to get out and stretch their legs. Everyone had been given brochures highlighting the painting created at each stop, along with historic anecdotes from the date the work was painted and what had inspired the artist. The text included where each painting currently resided.

An hour and a half into the tour, the bus was heading to Jones County on Highway 151. Patrice knew it was not long before they would be in Stone City. To her surprise, the bus turned onto the road where she grew up.

"What's down this road?" Patrice asked Natalie.

"I'm about to explain that," Natalie said with a smile that showed she knew the answer and rose to talk to the tour group. She braced one hand on the seat and the bus slowed down.

"In the summers of 1932 and 1933, Grant Wood opened his art colony in Stone City. He liked to comb the countryside with his art students, always looking for choice vistas that would stretch each student's imagination and talent. You might wonder how Iowa corn or bean fields do such a thing. Think about having to paint row after row of thick, lush corn or beans. It would require a meticulous hand, much like Grant Wood's, to learn this craft. This road to Viola is two miles from Stone City. Imagine you were a local resident that lived here. You would often see a group of students at the side of the road or in the field painting." She chuckled and added, "The students even asked a local farmer to pose—which meant that he would miss a day of work as he stood out in his field being captured on canvas by the students."

When Natalie sat down, Patrice said excitedly, "I grew up on that farm right over there."

Natalie followed Patrice's pointing finger and a big grin came over her face as she turned to look at Patrice more directly, "No kidding. Did you know your farm appears in one of Wood's prints?"

"What do you mean?" Patrice said trying to understand where Natalie was going with this.

"Grant Wood did a lithograph called *Seed Time and Harvest.* Our records show that he traced that drawing from this farm."

Patrice's heart pounded as she thought about this artist, and how he felt about his home. He didn't apologize for who he was, or what he did. In fact, he was inspired by it. She looked out the window at the familiar farms and houses. They were homes of former neighbors. Some houses sat near the graveled road and some sat back almost a quarter mile. No farm appeared to look the same in structure or layout. What they had in common were the crops they grew, either corn or soybeans. Patrice leaned forward taking in the scene in front of her, the farms were clean, and the lawns and ditches were mowed. Farmers seemed to have an abundance of everything, field crops, large gardens, pets, livestock, numerous farm buildings and machinery yet everything was impeccably organized.

Now she looked upon this expanse with great wonder. She thought of Grant and his martinet ways for his art. Traits such as thoroughness, pride, and resolve were ingrained in the people of Iowa and his work reflected this.

The bus took a right on the county highway and the terrain

started to become hilly. She recognized the large hill before them. She had seen the pencil drawing of this hill in Davenport. Sheila had laid out this drawing on the table, not knowing that Patrice grew up near this hill. It still felt steep after all these years. People often thought Iowa was flat but what they did not know was geography. *Any land among numerous rivers would be nothing but hilly.* The bus turned onto a gravel road heading north toward Stone City. Beautiful new houses appeared on either side of the road, bordered by a large expanse of woods. Patrice remembered when it was nothing but trees on either side of the road.

It was not long before the bus descended into the Stone City valley. Patrice knew that the mansion would be to her upper left, but it could not be seen from the road's lower embankment. She had chosen her seat deliberately, so she could look off to her right and see the Stone City valley. The bus went past the bullion-colored stone Catholic Church that clung to the hillside. She followed the view out the window of the bus seeing the other stone houses and buildings that defined the lower river road.

The bus turned into a parking lot next to the old general store. Natalie said they had an hour in Stone City to eat, wander, or catch a tour ride on a tractor-trailer visible through the window. It was a guided tour of Stone City and lasted about forty-five minutes. Patrice followed Natalie out of the bus and saw a tractor pull up to the bus with a long trailer behind it with seats covered with an awning to shade the tourists from the sun. The driver took off his cap and waved hello to Natalie.

"Hi Bud, how's your day?" Natalie responded. Patrice didn't hear his reply because the tractor-trailer's motor was too noisy. She figured she would go on the wagon tour first and then eat the sack lunch she had brought with her. She stuffed her sack lunch into her purse.

The tractor-trailer outing was included in the cost of the tour, so Patrice and her fellow passengers climbed aboard. Patrice took the very back seat and figured she would have a good view from there. Bud, the driver had a microphone so she was sure she would not miss out on any information. She was wrong. As the tractor-trailer engine started up, the noise drowned out the speaker. Fortunately, Stone City had not changed much. She could probably have given the tour herself.

The tractor-trailer slowed down at the foot of the hill leading up to the mansion and pulled off to the side of the road. Bud cut the engine, and this allowed her and the other passengers to hear him provide the history of the mansion, John A. Green's nineteenth century home. Patrice knew that the tour would continue to the quarries to the west and north of the mansion, and the tractor-trailer would then circle back toward the parked bus. The tractor-trailer started up again, sending its bitter diesel smell back to the passenger's noses. Patrice looked over to the hill leading up the mansion. There was no fence and she figured she could easily walk up that hill unseen. She made a quick decision and slipped off the seat, then stood behind the slow-moving wagon. The back board of the trailer was high enough so she was not seen. Patrice squatted at the side of the road lowering herself among the tall grasses that edged it. When the tractor-trailer was out of site, she crossed the road and scampered up the hillside.

Patrice knew she had to time this visit perfectly in order to be back on time to make the bus. She had forty minutes. This wasn't much time, but she wanted to see the site she had visited so long ago as a Camp Fire Girl. She felt drawn to the site as if the pull of gravity, itself, was at work.

CHAPTER 9

The hill was steep, and Patrice focused her eyes on the grasses at her feet. She glimpsed upward to see how far she had ascended and caught a glimpse of the ice house which was still standing. Patrice scurried toward the door but found it locked. She had expected it to be open. Across from the ice house was the mansion, and Patrice abandoned the locked structure for it. The remains of the first floor of the mansion were still there but gone was the outline of the fireplace. She found the cemented front steps leading up to the mansion, but they had cracked from the lack of care over the years. The last remaining pedestal with the stone fruit basket had been removed. What a great souvenir that had been for someone she thought.

Patrice walked to the east crest of the hill like she had done with her Camp Fire friend, Carrie. Now there were tall honeysuckle bushes outlining the mansion's east lawn. Patrice assumed it was so tourists couldn't see the mansion as the bushes hid the remains of it from the road below. The bushes also hid her view of Stone City. She turned toward what was left of the mansion and carefully climbed the stairs. She stretched her arms and legs and looked around. The grasses around the buildings had been mowed and the trees outlining the property had grown. She felt protected among the tall and lush foliage. It brought back memories of walking in the grove of trees behind the house on her father's farm. Whether it was winter or summer, Patrice enjoyed the solitude of nature. When she was younger, she would climb and sit in the tree for minutes on time thinking about any problem or concern that she had. It was places like these which gave her the peace and privacy she often craved. She could be whoever she wanted to be with no arguments, no rules, and no one to judge her. Jenny never played in that grove of trees because she had seen an opossum once. The raccoon shape of that opossum, its bland gray color and pointy-shaped nose scared Jenny out of those woods for the rest of her life. Those woods then became Patrice's sanctuary. She felt that same calm on the mansion's grounds today.

In the distance she could barely hear the humming of the tractor-trailer's engine and the voice of Bud, the conductor. Her sense of protection was cut short as she realized she could be arrested for trespassing if anyone caught her there. She reconciled those thoughts with the decision to act as a lost and confused tourist if that happened.

She sat down on the stone remains of the floor and found it hot from direct exposure to the sun. The stillness and sense of solitude she felt were enjoyable, if not a little eerie. She realized she was not used to such stillness, not in New York. New York was perpetually in motion and relentlessly filled with the sounds of humanity. Patrice moved to the edge of the ruins, her feet dangling over the side just three feet above the expanse of the ground. She tilted her head back to let the soft breeze and smells of lilac and grass wash over her. These were scents rarely smelled on the streets of New York, but they were the quintessential fragrance of late spring in Iowa.

An agitated red winged blackbird soared overhead.

"Don't you dare dive bomb me," she admonished. She had many stories of red winged blackbirds dive-bombing her years ago in her parents' garden. It usually meant they were protecting a nest nearby. She placed her hands behind her head and lay back on the warm floor. She thought about Rose's words *a magical place* and let her mind wander to the lyrics of *Blackbird* by The Beatles.

With the lyrics humming in Patrice's mind, she smelled sulfur, a scent so reminiscent of eastern Iowa well water. She remembered the overpowering smell of water flowing from her Aunt Patsy's kitchen and bathroom pipes. Patrice had always refused a drink of water when offered. She wondered how her aunt tolerated the sulfurous water, yet her aunt swore she could not tell the difference in the taste and smell of it. The water on Patrice's parents' farm had been pure and clean—or at least that is how she thought of it in contrast to her aunt's well water. There seemed to be a vast difference between the water sources only thirty miles apart from one another.

Sulfur made her think about the color blue, like the blue you see at the base of a gas flame on a gas stove or the color of the cloudless sky overhead. Patrice continued to picture this in her mind and saw other colors from her mother's kitchen, native colors, olive greens, antique golds, bittersweet oranges, and brown. The colors formed into shapes and curves, silhouettes and shadow, canvas and light.

And then her inner visions shifted, and she saw her feet walking by rows and rows of easels. Her eyes were drawn upward, and she saw paintings on the easels. Very few were plain white. The majority had recognizable drawings. If Patrice looked long enough, the endless rows of canvas took on a stream of color.

Across from every canvas was a person pressing, dotting, or swishing a paintbrush across the canvas before them.

Where did all these artists come from? Patrice scanned the horizon and there were artists and easels as far as the eye could see.

More artists could be found on the slopes of the hill to the west and to the south. None of them were talking; they were all immersed in the enjoyment of painting.

The artists appeared to be different ages, some as young as five and some as old as Patrice's grandmother Marie. Their clothing was not clothing of the present but of the past. The women and girls had dresses and stockings that appeared to be from the 1920s and 1930s, or even earlier. The boys and men were wearing overalls or pants with shirts. The younger boys did not wear shirts underneath their overalls, as if they were anticipating continuous hot weather.

Patrice was in a field of artists. As she drifted by, they acknowledged her with a smile or nod, but none muttered a word. Patrice felt welcomed; her body felt at peace.

This artists' field appeared to be a symphony in itself, a harmony of mutual understanding and diligence. Their purpose was to create, and Patrice could feel this. It was a masterful showing, their paint brushes stroking the canvas in a cadence, a cadence of time. Time was a relevant factor here, but Patrice could not figure out why. She listened for a melody, but she sensed this song could not be heard with the human ear.

The colors in their paintings were magnificent, even more magnificent than what one saw in nature. The colors also gave off a radiance that could only be described as emotional. Patrice could feel it; her arms tingled from it. The yellows were bursting with joy, the reds piercing passion, the browns crisp and fragile expressed vulnerability. The blues were courageous and greens permeated tranquility. Each artist seemed to instinctively know what colors to bring forth.

Still lost in this other world vision, Patrice continued to walk through the field of artists, listening, absorbing. As she passed a young man of about eighteen wearing a straw hat, she turned back to see what he had painted. She saw a painting of forest and field, streams, rock, sand, and people. Every sense seemed to come alive from his painting. She could smell the rain coming off the field, she could hear the running stream, and she could feel the sand under her feet. Could that be?

She turned away and was startled by a youthful face looking up at her. Patrice did not recognize the girl with long flowing brown hair and freckles that hugged a long, straight nose. She wore a lavender dress dotted with small pink and white flowers. An ivory apron covered her from neck to toe, only revealing the tips of her shoes. The girl's dainty fingers pointed to her painting, a country lane that followed a dark blue winding river. She had started to paint birds perching on the fence beside the lane. Her painting was almost complete.

"Hello," Patrice said and offered a smile.

Patrice heard the little girl say hello but never saw her open her lips.

"Tell me, what is everyone doing here?"

"We're imprinting."

Once again Patrice heard the answer but did not see the girl part her lips and form the words. Patrice stepped back, as if trying to understand where the voice came from. The pre-teen girl caught Patrice's gaze and locked eyes with her.

Patrice faltered. "What do you mean ... imprinting?"

"The creator is preparing us for birth," the young girl said, nodding toward her painting. "Before we are born, we design the imprint that will be on our soul as we enter into life." She paused, as if allowing Patrice to absorb all she was saying. "The imprint includes our earthly gifts, our offerings, the emotions we will carry with us for those things that forever direct our destiny while we are on the earthly plane. It's up to us to remember and bring forth these imprints."

The young girl's gaze at Patrice continued, "The moment we add the last brush stroke to this imprint, we are born."

Patrice watched as this brown-eyed artist turned and lifted her paint brush. She stroked the birds with a brilliant blue, so blue that Patrice put her hands over her eyes to shield them from the brightness. When Patrice looked down at the girl, she was now visually younger. She had appeared to be ten or twelve, but now seemed to be seven or eight.

Patrice was perplexed, if not a little scared and curious. "What just happened? How old are you?"

"I'm getting closer to my birth age. All I need to do is complete the horizon on my imprint and I will enter the earth plane."

Patrice stepped between the girl and the canvas, gesturing for her to stop the process. "Before you do, I'd like to ask a few more questions."

The girl considered the request for a moment then nodded.

"Why are all these artists here in this place?"

"We choose the place to recognize our imprint. For it is in this place that our great teacher will arrive to teach us how to apply our gifts on the earthly plane."

"What about those untouched canvases over there, the ones without an artist?"

"Those canvases are waiting for others who have not yet arrived. Souls are given numerous opportunities to return to learn new things."

Patrice had one last question. "What year is it?"

The young girl shook her head and Patrice felt tears on her face. The question echoed and its reverberation became the screeching of tractor brakes just over the hillside. Patrice remembered the tractor-trailer. It must be returning from its tour. The tears she wiped away were raindrops falling from the sky. It was beginning to sprinkle. She sat up and looked around. Voices in the distance reminded her of where she was, and she checked her watch. She had exactly ten minutes to get back to the bus before her tour left.

She grabbed her purse and pushed off the mansion flooring onto the ground below, and dashed toward the hill where she carefully scampered down to the road, careful to avoid slipping and falling. She turned back to look at the mansion ruins and its surroundings. It shimmered in the heat, but there were no people there or artists to be found. She had been alone, or had she? What had she seen? Who were those people and where had they all gone? *Where had they gone?* Maybe she was lost in a vision and stuck between realities--the ordinary one in which she usually lived and this surreal dream she had been under.

She turned and continued down the hill dazed, perplexed, losing her footing on a slick slope of grass. She caught herself with her hands before she fell. *God help me!* At the bottom of the hill, she turned eastward toward the parking lot where the bus sat waiting. She jogged the best she could in the heat of the noon hour, panting like a thirsty dog as she approached the bus. The driver was standing next to the bus looking casual and at peace.

"Were you afraid we were taking off without you?" he asked.

Patrice bent over to catch her breath and nodded in agreement.

"We still have a few minutes. Take your time."

Patrice slowly walked in a circle near the bus, stretching her legs and attempting to regain her composure. She was trying to make sense of what she saw on the mansion grounds. Did she dream this? *It seemed so real!* Had the fumes from the tractor-trailer messed with her mind? *I'm losing it,* she thought. *It's a magical place.* Rose's words rang in her ears.

"What's that mean?" she said.

"What did you say?" the bus driver droned as he leaned on the bus looking in her direction.

"Sorry, just thinking out loud," Patrice said.

She had to remove her thoughts from that vision, or she'd go mad. She started to look around the valley imagining what this place looked like when Grant and Nan were here.

Her eyes followed the hasty river just beyond the parking lot, until she caught sight of what was left of a rusty old railroad bridge. This bridge once hovered over the river about 100 yards south of the main road's bridge. The railroad bridge was a long-standing relic in town. It had been put to rest once the trains stopped coming through this part of Iowa, but the locals sat on top of it to fish lowering their fishing lines the length of a two storied building. That was a faint memory now as the only part left of it existed on the western bluff. The track over the river had been removed. The image of the iron overpass from long ago evoked a memory that Patrice wished she could soon forget. As the trains in the area started to subside, more and more people used the railroad bridge for recreation. Some walked across the bridge, others biked or motorcycled their way from end to end. Others fished from it.

Sitting in the back seat of her family's light blue 1966 Galaxy 500, a young Patrice listened to Martin and Renee Powell discuss a bad accident that had taken place the week before on the bridge. An elderly man and his two grandchildren had been fishing on that bridge when an unexpected train rounded the tracks. The man grabbed his grandchildren and made a run for the far side of the bridge but could not out run the fast pace of the train. All three were killed on that track over the river.

Patrice pressed her eyes shut at the thought of the tragedy. When situations like this happened in their small community everyone knew about it, everyone talked about it, and everyone felt the pain. She placed the back of her hand against her mouth, swallowing repeatedly to keep the erupting acids in her stomach at bay. She recalled having this same reaction as a little girl, wondering why her dad slowed the car down as they neared the bridge versus speeding up to get away from the scene. She remembered her parents expressed their sadness but only in words. She had never seen her parents cry. She assumed that was what it was like to be an adult. They could handle things she couldn't. In the parking lot, she regained her composure thankful for the sunglasses that hid her tears. So many tears since she had flown in from New York. Anger started to seep in for feeling so vulnerable about these memories.

She fixated her moist eyes on the general store in front of her. Its claim to fame was being in Grant Wood's painting: *Stone City*. In all the years that had passed it was still the same. Structurally sound, it was made from the same pale golden limestone that was carved from the quarries across the road. Two-storied, with numerous front windows on the second and first floors, Patrice could not help but admire the stone architecture. The laid stone had been cut into varying shapes which created a pattern of sorts up against the four-foot-tall windows. At the top, the building had its own tiara—a stone piece that gave the original date of the building as 1873. Patrice was giving the building its own persona and her heart felt nothing but respect for this old building that had stood the test of time mainly thanks to Grant Wood's painting.

Lost in thought about the old post office-general store she heard the sound of the other tourists talking to the bus driver and making their climb into the bus. She got in line and followed the others into the bus until she found the first empty seat which was toward the back. The temperature inside of the bus was cooling down and her body took the coolness in, like a salve intended to soothe the confusing thoughts on the other side of her skin.

A woman across the aisle watched Patrice take her lunch out of her purse and waited until Patrice noticed her. "What did you like best about Stone City?" she asked.

Patrice was ready for a distraction. "I have to say I like its remoteness. It's like a treasure that very few people are aware of."

Patrice popped a potato chip in her mouth. The salt would help her rumbling stomach in this heat. She left her comment hanging, not adding that she was glad that Stone City was still pristine, not like most sites overrun by tourists.

"I was hoping it'd be more commercialized," came the answer from across the aisle, you know with little boutiques and restaurants."

Patrice knew the locals would never go for that. They had a keepsake and were not going to exploit it any more than they had to. The only allowance and trace of commercialization was for the annual *Grant Wood Art Festival.*

"I heard that Nan Wood died recently," she said, deliberately sidestepping the issue.

"Yes, wasn't that a pity? By the way I'm Barbara Behrens. I'm a school teacher in the Cedar Rapids School District," she said as she extended her hand across the aisle.

"Hi. I'm Patrice Powell," Patrice said as she shook the woman's hand. "I'm originally from this area, but I live in New York now. I'm just here visiting."

"Welcome home," Barbara said. "I teach sixth grade and my goal is to focus on Iowa artists and writers for our students this year as part of Iowa history curriculum."

"I remember learning about Iowa history in sixth grade. I made a scrapbook for my class project and still have it."

"We still focus on Iowa history as a general theme in sixth grade, but I like to modify it every year. The class coming in this year shows quite an aptitude for music, art and writing, so I'm hoping to bridge that with the Iowa history piece."

"That's great."

The bus started to pull away from the parking lot. Barbara focused on her lunch and Patrice smiled over at her and fixated on her own. She thought again about what had happened up on the hill. The vision had been so vivid. *Should she go back?*

The bus made its way up the steep hill leaving behind the Stone City valley making its way eastward to the west side of Anamosa. The passengers were absorbed in small conversations or eating their lunch. Soon the bus turned onto Anamosa's main street. Natalie announced that the next stop was the Grant Wood Store. The bus turned up Booth Street to park in a lot just a block from the store. The tourists stepped off the cool bus into the hot muggy air and diligently followed Natalie to the store. Patrice spotted the familiar phone booth and thought this would be a good time to call Glenn. She had already been to the store and had no desire to accompany the other tourists as they elbowed their way through the displays of memorabilia and gifts.

She was about to enter the phone booth when she heard a familiar voice say, "Patrice is that you?" She turned to find her Uncle Gary and quickly grabbed him around the shoulders, drawing him in with a big hug, she smelled pipe smoke on his short-sleeved shirt.

"What are you doing here?" she asked, holding him in her embrace.

"Hey I live here. The better question is what are *you* doing here? I didn't know you were back."

"Actually, work brought me home. They asked me to write a story on Nan Wood Graham's death. You know, hometown girl should know about home town legends. I have to admit I'm somewhat lost on how to approach this story, so I'm still in research mode. I thought I'd take this tour in the hope of some inspiration."

Patrice was beaming. Uncle Gary was the reason she had taken up writing. He had been the local newspaper editor for the *Anamosa Journal-Eureka* most of his adult life. While her father had chosen the family business of farming, her uncle had ventured out, gotten a college degree and came home to run the local newspaper. Now he was standing in front of her dressed in dark blue pants, a white and blue summer striped shirt and a straw hat whose brim was shaped to hover over his right eye.

"So, what are you up to?" she asked.

"I'm retired now. I retired about three years ago, and I volunteer at the Grant Wood Store. I come and say a few words now and then when the tours come through town. I've written so much about Grant Wood, his art and the art colony over the years, they think I'm the expert."

Patrice didn't hesitate, "Did you ever meet Grant or Nan?"

"I knew of Grant and yes, I met Nan a few times. In fact, you'll hear me talk about that in a few minutes. Follow me into the store. I don't want to be late."

Patrice and her uncle crossed the street toward the store. She noticed her uncle's stride had slowed and she paced herself with him like she had as a little girl when visiting him at the newspaper office. He was always excited to see her when she entered the office and was never too busy to take her out for a cherry coke or down the street to treat her to lunch at a nearby cafe. She was glad her uncle was keeping busy as she knew her Aunt Patsy's death had left him with a terrible void in his heart. The Powell men were family men centering their existence on those they loved, neighbors and friends too. Both her uncle and her father rarely invested time into hobbies and vacations, but they always had time for others. This thought tugged at her heart. She wanted to reach for her uncle's hand but tucked it away in her pocket like everything else she tucked away when she packed for New York.

Patrice waited until they were near the store before she asked the next question, "How did you meet Nan?"

"She came back for the Grant Wood art festivals and was the Grand Marshal of the first festival and parade. I often interviewed her for the paper."

"What was she like?"

"She was a nice lady. She was very proud of her brother, and fiercely protective of his art and reputation; down to earth, forthright and likeable." Her uncle opened the door for her. "Thanks, you helped me prepare for the little speech I'm about to give. Wish me luck."

He didn't need luck, she knew that much. He was easy to like and down to earth with people. He looked like a younger version of her dad except he didn't wear glasses and was shorter than her father which made Gary Powell look ten pounds heavier. He had a slight German accent but not as much as her father's.

As her uncle gathered the tour group toward a small corner of the store, his voice commanded their attention. Patrice noted he had dropped his German accent. Odd. Patrice leaned against the wall to listen closer. After introducing himself, he told them about his years growing up in Anamosa and described the town and the citizens as unchanged since the time that Grant and Nan were growing up here. Listening to her uncle's words, she learned she came from a very creative community of people who had migrated to Anamosa from Germany, Ireland and Denmark, all seeking freedom to express themselves through work and leisure. He talked about the dozens of painters, writers, and musicians who were from the area or currently lived in the area and how they had made a difference.

Patrice smiled at the thought that her Uncle Gary and Grant Wood were among those who had made a difference in this small town, but her smile faded when Patrice thought about her father, who had stayed in the area to farm. She had been judgmental of her father for this. Why did some people want more, and others did not? Grant had gone to school in Europe and at *The Art Institute of Chicago*, living away from home to study his craft. He had known the importance of learning in different environments and from great teachers. Her Uncle Gary did as well, earning his Journalism degree at Northwestern.

"So, we invite you to join us here for the *Grant Wood Art Festival*, which is in a couple of weeks. Come back and enjoy the festivities. Folks, thank you for coming and until next time."

Gary Powell's signature saying *Until Next Time.* Those familiar words ended every editorial her uncle had ever written for his newspaper.

Patrice edged toward her uncle who was surrounded by four tourists asking questions. The other tourists were making purchases of prints, postcards and calendars. Now it was making sense why her Aunt Patsy took up painting. There was an undercurrent of creative interest in this area. Jenny had been right; Aunt Patsy was the inspired artist in the family and Uncle Gary was the writer. She hoped she could be as good as him someday. Running a small-town newspaper for forty years wasn't an easy thing to do.

Patrice strolled around the store, thinking about Rose Boston and the art colony. The little store was somewhat of a shrine to the art colony and Patrice couldn't help but think so much more could be done with the place. An article on the wall caught her eye and she began to read it. Her uncle walked up behind her and said, "Do you know about Jay Sigmund?"

"Actually, I do," Patrice said reading off the article, "it says right here he was often the master of ceremonies at the art colony on Saturday nights when the art faculty held dances to raise money for the colony. Uh, the students would display their artwork, hoping for a sale. I stopped at the *Davenport Museum of Art* and learned about him. Is he still alive?"

"No, unfortunately he died in a hunting accident only a few years after the art colony closed."

Patrice turned to her uncle with a frown on her face. "Sorry to hear that."

Her uncle nodded his head and looked around at the tourists who were now scattered about the store. "Well, this worked out great. I have about five minutes before my day is over here."

"Uncle Gary, I would love to have you come along with us on this tour. We still have a few local stops to make, and I bet I could talk the tour guide into letting you join us for the remainder of the tour. I'm sure there are details you could add that even Natalie, our tour guide doesn't know. This would give us time to catch up and I'll give you a ride home afterward."

Her uncle looked hesitant but finally surrendered on the condition that it was okay with the tour guide. Patrice found Natalie and offered to pay for her uncle's participation in the tour. Natalie rejected her offer. She knew the value of having Gary Powell along for the tour.

CHAPTER 10

A sking her uncle to join the tour proved to be a brilliant idea. What he had to offer was more than facts. He added color and depth to the information he provided, giving those on the tour the chance to feel like insiders instead of just tourists.

Patrice and her uncle sat toward the front of the bus so everyone could hear him. They traveled to Grant and Nan's birthplace and the cemetery where they were laid to rest. As the bus drove toward the late afternoon sun, he shared the story of John Steuart Curry's visit to Iowa.

Patrice looked behind her at the other passengers wondering if they knew who John Steuart Curry was. She couldn't tell. She turned back around in her seat surprised that any nationally renowned artist had ever visited the art colony. She pulled her small notebook from her purse and jotted down some ideas for her article.

When the tour pulled in front of the *Cedar Rapids Museum of Art*, she and her uncle found her car and made the forty-minute journey back to Anamosa.

"Tell me more about John Steuart Curry's visit to Iowa."

"Well as I said earlier, John Steuart Curry, Thomas Hart-Benton, and Grant Wood had befriended one another. They were known as Regional artists, a term coined during the time-period in which they painted. Up until that time, portraits of people, you know portraits of people posing for the painter, constituted much of what was thought of as American art." Patrice nodded in understanding. "These Regionalists didn't want to spend their time on portraits and during the Great Depression, many people couldn't afford them."

"Hey why am I telling you this, you're the art expert."

"You're doing a great job, continue on. I might learn something from you that I didn't learn in the classroom!" Patrice teased.

"As you know these artists couldn't afford to travel abroad, so they painted what they found in their own backyards. This has great significance—more than people realize. It was the beginning of acknowledgement for American art."

Patrice nodded in agreement.

"John Steuart Curry was from northeast Kansas and his painting reflected his roots -- Kansas history, religious groups, and a focus on the Kansas countryside were all among the themes found in his art. Grant was doing something similar in Iowa, painting local landscapes and painting laboring farm folk, as well as a few portraits. Wood was popular in Iowa, but Curry was not popular in Kansas."

"From what I remember Grant Wood wasn't popular in Anamosa at the time he was painting here, or those were the stories I remember as a little girl."

"You're right. A lot of people around here thought he was a vagabond of sorts, not paying his bills, only painting and not doing a real day's work," her uncle laughed. "That changed over time when Anamosa realized that the rest of the world believed Grant was a big deal and enjoyed his work."

"Going back to Curry, you're right that the people of Kansas did not appreciate his artwork. They felt Curry's paintings of tornados on the Kansas prairie brought down the price of land, and they felt he was making fun of his people, their religion and homeland," Patrice shared.

"That was not his intent and it bothered him greatly. He wondered how Grant was beloved in Iowa and decided to travel to Iowa to find out."

"So, he came to the art colony?"

"Yes, the second summer."

"I didn't know that," Patrice said with amazement in her voice. "I thought Grant's paintings were child-like, almost too perfect, especially the painting of *Stone City*. I remember thinking that I—a non-artist—could paint trees that look like round spheres, and I could paint curvy hillsides. That's why I'm not so impressed with his work."

"You and Curry have something in common. Curry felt that Grant's work was very naive until he came to this area of Iowa and saw the landscape for himself. People often believe Iowa is flat and unassuming, when in fact it has rolling hills and fertile soil that grows any color or shape of plant life one can imagine. Until people visited this area, they often thought Wood was being too idealistic but that's the point of the painting."

Her uncle was silent for a moment, looking at her intently before continuing. "And even though you grew up here, you probably took the pristine quality of our state's natural beauty for granted."

Patrice raised her eyebrows as if she was caught guilty as charged.

"If you look closely at the painting, *Stone City*, you will see two words on a small billboard depicting a cigarette ad that says, 'It satisfies.' The painting of *Stone City* was Grant's dream, his ideal of the perfect landscape. That ideal was not far from the reality of the Stone City countryside, wouldn't you agree?"

"The more I travel, the more unique I find this area of the country," she admitted.

"Yes, he gave it an even more perfect appeal by the way he drew it. The locals seemed to understand this when they saw the painting at the Iowa State Fair in Des Moines. Curry finally understood this when he came to Iowa and saw the area."

"And, yet, I had to leave and return to even begin to see it myself," Patrice said with a sigh.

"Did you know that Grant Wood offered Curry a position at the art colony to teach the third summer," her uncle asked. "Unfortunately, under financial constraints, the third summer was never to be."

"Is there a photo of Wood and Curry at the mansion?" Patrice said, turning from the road to give her uncle a quick glance. He was looking out the window.

"Yes, there should be a picture in the Grant Wood Store of the two men wearing overalls at the mansion, unless someone took it down."

"I must have missed that."

"Curry was so impressed with the art colony that he ended up staying for two weeks. Grant even let him stay in his ice wagon."

"I can't image sleeping in an ice wagon on a hot, muggy Iowa night," Patrice said grimacing. "I wonder where Grant slept."

"Either in the mansion or outside on the ground."

Patrice laughed. "I remember growing up on the farm with no air conditioning. Sometimes I slept outside just to get a good night's sleep. I'd make a tent of blankets over the clothesline or sleep outside on a chaise lounge. I still wonder how we survived that! By the way, Natalie, our tour guide talked about the art students painting near Stone City and even Viola, and possible near our farm."

"Then she told you about *Seed Time and Harvest*."

"She did."

"Yes, it's true. Grant and the students used to jump in their cars and roam the countryside around Stone City looking for just the right landscapes to paint. People in these parts knew of the colony and were obliging with the students, even if they didn't agree this was the best use of their time and money. The farm wasn't owned by your dad at that time of course, we were just schoolboys."

"Did dad know this at the time he bought our farm?"

"No. That information wasn't easy to find. I only heard about it through some of the artists in the area and I believe I once wrote a story about it. The print shows your dad's barn which was actually more of a small storage building...."

"Which he tore down soon after he bought the farm," Patrice

retorted. "Who owns the rights to this work?"

"I'm not sure, I don't believe someone locally owns it or has the rights to it."

"Uncle Gary do you find drawings and paintings of farmland interesting or eye catching?"

"Think about it: thick rows of corn, fencing, ditches, and a large span of horizon. A lot of detail is required to do a painting like that. That takes a meticulous artist and Wood was excellent at meticulous."

Patrice shook her head.

"Why are you shaking your head?"

"I can't believe all this was taking place here, where I grew up and I'm learning about it now."

"What? A national art movement whose grass roots sprung from the Midwest, mainly in your own backyard?" her uncle laughed good naturedly. "Hmmm, now where did you get your love of art?"

"I know where I got my love of writing from too," Patrice glanced at her uncle and couldn't help but giggle at him. He was right, it all began right here, and she had missed some of those obvious signs. She realized she captured a passion of her uncle's too as he continued to talk non-stop. He probably didn't have a lot of people to talk with now that her Aunt Patsy was gone. She found the conversation soothing, just like her mother's chatter. The more they talked the less she had to.

The late afternoon sun was settling low in the western sky behind them casting shadows of the moving car onto the highway. Patrice noticed similar shadows cast from the farm houses, barns and shrubbery they passed along the highway. She thought about the contrast of light in Grant Wood's painting, *Stone City*. Her uncle interrupted her thoughts.

"He did capture the total essence of his environment," Gary Powell said.

"Who?" Patrice asked, unnerved a bit because it was as if her uncle had been reading her mind.

"Grant Wood."

Patrice nodded. It was so easy to get distracted by today's focus on Grant Wood that she had to remember she was writing the story about Nan Wood Graham.

"So how do I find out information about Nan? There's not a lot published about her, just what she says about her brother and his work."

"I think that tells you something about the person. You just need to find people like me who knew her."

"Do you know of any stories?"

"She always stayed with a woman when she was here by the name of Mrs. Bray, but she is now in a nursing home and not doing very well I'm afraid. There's a woman in Davenport who attended the art colony and has a store ... "

"I actually met her, Rose Boston?"

"Yes, how did you know about her?"

"Anna at the Grant Wood Store told me about her."

"Well, good. Rose used to come to the art festival with her husband, Ben. How are they and what did you learn?"

"Not a whole lot. They're not in the best of health, either one of them. I guess I'm just struggling with this whole thing."

"Writer's block?"

"You could call it that. Uncle Gary, I've always wanted to ask you," Patrice turned to look quickly at her uncle before fixing her eyes on the road again, "why did you come back to Anamosa?"

He looked pensive for a moment and then a small smile crossed his face.

"It had everything I needed ... your Aunt Patsy for one. I came back to family and four thousand familiar faces, and the town was prosperous at the time. I had a chance to be a part of that. I also think that familiarity draws out the best in a person."

Patrice caught sight of Anamosa in the distance. "How so? Tell me more about that."

"It has personal meaning. You also understand your part of a collective life force. You understand its existence and how it thinks. You have shared purpose and clarity about what matters. That's familiarity. Those on the outside do not see this or understand this until you share it with them. That's what I think Wood was trying to do. He was giving outsiders a glimpse into our world here, our values, our pride and what we wanted out of life. If you remember, the farmers around here are very skilled about how they manage their farms and raise their crops. What word did we use before to describe Grant? Ahhh...... meticulous. That's right. He had the same skills and used it to depict the area, the people, what's familiar. Nan must have had similar values because she worked hard to preserve that legacy. That's genius."

"Dad ran his farm like that."

"Absolutely. And that's why I admire him."

"You do?"

"Yes, he personifies what is good about the people here: hard-working, honest, hardy, and creating life off the land. That's what we have in common, at the root—we are creators. Just like the Grand Creator. I create through words; your dad created things from the earth by growing crops and raising animals."

The word creator took Patrice's breath away as she thought about the vision she had seen early at the mansion. Didn't the little girl in the lavender dress talk about a creator or was it about a great teacher? *Focus* she told herself trying to get her mind centered, *focus*.

Her uncle was peering out the window at a local fruit stand but continued the conversation. "Did you know that your grandfather was a farmer and your grandmother was a writer?"

"My grandmother was a writer?"

"She often submitted articles to the local newspaper about things that mattered to rural farm women, such as how to raise chickens, how to garden, and how to can fruits and vegetables."

Patrice giggled at the thought of her grandmother writing about raising chickens.

"Don't laugh," Gary Powell admonished.

"I'm sorry."

"That had an impact on women who did not innately know

how to do those things. Your grandmother was a great help to them, and she was a pretty good writer too. You could say your dad and I each took up the work of one of our parents—he took up farming and I took up writing. So, you come by your writing career honestly. It's in your blood."

"I used to wish, sometimes, that you were my dad because you understood my need to go to school out-of-state, getting a change of scenery, writing about topics such as art, living in New York—I always thought you understood this more than my parents who seem to think all of this has been outlandish."

"Now you know how Grant felt; a farmer's son with creative abilities who enjoyed drawing and writing over farm chores. He left home to learn his craft, had different standards of dress than those at home, didn't have what others felt was a solid, secure job, and came home still not feeling like he fit in."

"Is that why he wore overalls?"

"Yes, I suppose so. He was trying to reconnect with his roots."

Her uncle drew in a long breath and stretched his arms, "You were meant to write this story on Nan. These things just don't happen randomly you know. Like Grant, you'll probably find that your best work will come now that you're home to write. You're on the inside more than you know, but you can also provide a different point of view from the eyes of those on the outside."

Gary Powell turned to look at Patrice.

"I don't know what to say," Patrice loosened the tight grip she had on the steering wheel as they stopped at the first red stop light in Anamosa.

"I guess I identify with Grant and Nan; like the painting *Appraisal*, I too dislike snobbery and I find humor in the oddest of places like *Daughters of the American Revolution*. I like real people with ethics and grounded values, not those that are contrived."

"Exactly. This is what the Regionalists were trying to convey. All of this is in the world as well as our own backyards. We just need to recognize it and draw upon it for what it is. What makes life unique is that we can all express it in many different ways."

Patrice pulled onto her uncle's street and soon turned into his driveway. She turned to hide the tear intended for their short time together.

Gary Powell held out his arms to give her a hug. She hugged him back and held onto him tightly.

"So, to answer your question earlier, why did I stay? Overall, I felt like Grant Wood did about this area, it satisfies."

Patrice smiled at her uncle.

"How long are you here?"

"Just until the weekend."

"Okay, come home when you can and don't be a stranger!"

He stepped out of the car and peeked his head through the window, "Oh, one other thing." He grabbed a newspaper clipping from his front shirt pocket. "The Paint 'n Palette Art Club has an exhibit coming up. I thought you might be interested in seeing some local art. Go if it interests you. Until next time!" and he slammed the car door shut.

Patrice lowered her window. "Thank you. It was great seeing you, uncle!"

Already at the door he called, "Keep in touch and say hi to your folks and your sister."

"I will."

Patrice waited until he was safely in the house. She rested her forehead on the steering wheel of the car and thought of her uncle's words. *It satisfies*. Patrice wondered why it had not satisfied her and headed back to Cedar Rapids.

CHAPTER 11

L aughter was pouring out the front door of her parents' home as she pulled into the driveway and the glow from the living room lights lit the sidewalk before her. It had been a long day full of surprises. She had a good deal to think about and was beginning to get a feel for how to approach the story. Her eyes had focused on the light of the sidewalk and she was startled by what she saw when she looked up. Through the living room windows, she saw Glenn and her parents talking and laughing.

What is he doing here?

She took a few steps back, straightened her clothing and pulled her lip gloss from her purse. She didn't want to look like a wilted plant. She was putting on her lip gloss when they seemed to notice her presence.

Her mother came to the front door, "We thought we heard you pull up!"

"Sorry I'm late. I hope you didn't wait on me for dinner."

"We did, but then we went ahead and ate."

"I spent a little more time on the tour then I expected to," Patrice said. She peered over at Mrs. Kroft's house. It wouldn't surprise Patrice if the prying neighbor was outside in the dark watering wild gooseberries. She walked by her mother glad she didn't see the nosy neighbor.

"Surprised?" Glenn beamed as he walked toward her to give her a quick hug.

Patrice froze. *This is awkward.* The look on her face told Glenn the same thing. She never expected to see Glenn Collier in her parents' home. She didn't know if he'd told them he was her boyfriend or if he'd represented himself as her boss. She assumed she would find out soon enough. Glenn held his own under the circumstances.

"Yes, what are you doing here? Aren't you needed in New York?"

"I decided to come to Iowa to see if I could help you with the story," he winked at her.

Glenn was impeccable as always. He was wearing dark navy-blue dress pants, and a white dress shirt. He smelled of cologne, a brand that Patrice didn't recognize. He brushed his locks aside with his fingers. A habit he had when he was very attentive.

"Great."

Patrice looked at her parents and they looked right back at her with approval on their faces.

Oh, God no! What had he told them? Surely Glenn is not here to ask them for my hand in marriage.

She hoped not. They had a lot to work through if they were going to make a life together.

"Glenn tells us you two have worked together for a while," her mother announced, taking a seat on the sofa.

"Yes. He's actually the one who gave me this assignment." Patrice consciously did not say Glenn was her boss, still trying to figure out where this was all going.

"Who was more perfect to do this story than someone from the local area?" Glenn said, as if the answer was evident. "Nan Wood Graham's death is a sad story for our readers."

"Do you really think our readers care about who she is?" Patrice shot back.

"If they don't, they soon will," Glenn volleyed.

Patrice sat down next to her mother. She felt smothered by Glenn's unexpected presence. She glared at him from the sofa and he sat down in her mother's La-Z-Boy, ignoring her gaze. He turned to Patrice's father.

"So, Martin, continue the story about Patrice and that rooster."

"Oh, no! You didn't tell him that story," Patrice wailed.

Martin Powell focused on Glenn and said, "Patti was four years old and learning to ride her trike. She loved that tricycle and rode on the sidewalk between the front door to the back door of our farm house. Back and forth, back and forth, every day. Well, that old bird took notice and one day he started running across the gravel driveway toward her—."

Renee interrupted. "That wasn't the first time that rooster picked on her. There were other instances where he tried to torment her, but we told her to ignore him, and if he didn't quit picking on her to just show him who was in charge and to ride her trike straight for him."

Patrice put her head in her hands, mortified that her parents were sharing this childhood story with her boss.

Renee looked over at her husband and he continued.

"Well, that bird crossed our driveway and came right at little Patti. And she did what we told her. She peddled as hard as she could toward that old bird, and as she did, that bird became agitated, started flapping his wings, and flew toward her face," Martin Powell was making gestures of a flapping bird. *When did her father become so talkative and animated?*

Renee chimed in again. "She ran from her trike and came screaming into the house!"

Glenn was looking from Martin to Renee and back again. Then he glanced over at Patrice, the smile on his face was a cross between a smirk and a dopey grin.

Patrice got up off the couch and headed into the kitchen to grab something to eat. "Mother, please continue on at my expense," she said as she left the room.

Her parents were laughing as they shared the memory with Glenn.

"From that day on, we knew we couldn't keep that old rooster," Renee said, shaking her head.

"What did you do with him?"

"He became dinner."

"Ohhhhhhh, did you have to share that part?" Patrice bellowed from the kitchen as she heard the others laughing.

"I wonder if that's why Patrice is now a vegetarian?" Glenn questioned hoping Patrice would hear him.

Patrice heard continued laughter by the three of them as she unscrewed the lid to the peanut butter jar.

Glenn got up and met Patrice in the kitchen. "How's the story coming?"

"Good. I have a little more research to do, but I think I have some very good content," Patrice replied as she dabbed peanut butter onto a slice of bread.

"Your dad mentioned you were on an art museum trip today?"

"Yes, the *Cedar Rapids Museum of Art* offers a two-day tour of the Grant Wood and Marvin Cone sites. We visited Grant Wood's birthplace, and Nan's as well as the site of the art colony. Tomorrow is day two of two, and we visit the Cedar Rapids sites where he and Marvin lived and painted," she reported.

"Did you eat?" she asked. That question sounded like something her mother would say.

Glenn's intent gaze told her he liked the question. "Yes, your mother was kind enough to fix me a sandwich."

Patrice grabbed a glass of iced tea and with her sandwich in one hand and the iced tea in the other, she headed back into the living room with Glenn behind her. She reclaimed her place on the sofa.

"Guess who I saw today?"

"Who?" her parents chimed at the same time.

"Uncle Gary at the Grant Wood Store in Anamosa."

"We knew he was a volunteer there, but I didn't think about you running into him today," her mother said, stifling a yawn.

"Yes, and he told me to tell you both hello. He gave a talk to the tourists. He had some great stories, and, in fact, he told me that Grant Wood once painted a building that was on our farm," Patrice said.

Patrice's dad nodded his head. "Yes, somewhere I think I have a print or postcard of it."

"If you find it, I would like to see it."

"I heard the county was thinking of buying the farm next to ours and making it into a landfill," her father added, "yet the Wood Foundation argued the historical significance of that area and the county did not proceed."

"Our neighbor's farm, a landfill? That area is too beautiful for that."

Patrice's parents looked at each other.

"What?" Patrice inquired between bites of her sandwich.

"We're glad you think that area is beautiful. We often thought you didn't like it."

Patrice knew her mother was speaking for both of them. Her dad did not comment but Patrice assumed he did not want to start a familiar argument with Patrice. They had covered that ground many times in the past.

"Maybe I'm finally learning to appreciate it." She looked at both her parents with a small smile.

"Tell me more about this tour, this trip?" Glenn asked, missing the moment between Patrice and her parents.

"Tomorrow is only a half day. Afterwards, I was hoping to do some more research at the museum and then head off to Anamosa to go to the Paint'n Palette where they have some art on display by local artists." Patrice was reminded of her uncle's recommendation knowing the Paint'n Palette Art Club reminded him of his deceased wife.

"Overall, this is giving me some background for my story and the people here." Patrice did not want to give away anymore about her research because she often liked to surprise Glenn. "I bet you could go with me tomorrow." Anything to keep him occupied and away from her parents.

"Glenn, where are you staying?" her mother asked.

"I'm downtown at The Grand."

Patrice knew this would impress her parents. The Grand was the nicest hotel in Cedar Rapids.

"I'll fly out on Monday."

"That's when I fly out, too," she said.

"So soon?" her mother said with disappointment in her voice.

"Yes, we'll have Monday morning together, though." Renee Powell grabbed Patrice's hand and held it.

Patrice was looking at her mother when she heard Glenn say he should probably call it a day. She hadn't noticed a car out front so he must have taken a cab.

"Do you need a lift?"

"I do."

After saying good night to her parents, she drove Glenn to his hotel and parked the car in the hotel's parking lot. She turned off the motor. She could feel her anger amplify as she thought about her deadline and the distraction that Glenn brought. She suspected that he was there because he wanted some answers about their future.

"What?" Glenn said. Patrice thought she detected irritation in his voice.

"You know what?" Patrice said staring straight ahead at the street light in the distance.

"Talk to me," Glenn insisted.

"Why are you here? And what did you tell the employees back in the office about coming to Iowa. Did you tell them you were spending the company's precious money to fly out here to help poor Patrice get her story finished?"

"No."

"Then?" Patrice glared at him her arms now crossed over her chest.

"Actually, I told them I was taking a vacation day or two. I didn't tell them I was coming out here. I'm paying for this myself."

"You didn't answer my question. Why did you come?"

"Patrice, why won't you share this with me?" Glenn pleaded.

"Because we are so different Glenn," Patrice blurted. "We have such different backgrounds. You're from a wealthy area of Long Island and I'm from Green Acres, Iowa. My roots, relative to yours, are basic and simple. Maybe I'm afraid ... you'll judge that."

"Give me a chance."

"Okay, what did you think when the cab took you to the suburb where my parents live and what did you think when you met them?" Patrice was accusatory and defensive.

"I admit it. I *whawted* you to do this story so you would come home and come to terms with who you are because it seems to be the thing that holds our relationship back. You've been pushing the notion of marriage away whether you *wannt* to admit it or not. This is *whawt* that is about? You have concerns about where you're from? *So whawt?* We all do in some way. What I know is that I love you and you wouldn't be the person I love if this wasn't a part of you. Let me share this experience with you, Patrice."

Glenn's Long Island accent became prevalent whenever he became stressed or upset. Patrice could see the pain in Glenn's eyes, but she couldn't convince herself of feeling anything but anger for his surprise visit.

Glenn obediently opened the car door. Patrice knew he had had enough for the night.

"Here's the deal. In the next two days, you'll walk in my shoes in the area and with the people I grew up with. You'll get a glimpse into my world. *If* we get married and have children, this will be part of their heritage and we'll be bringing them home to know this side of their family. It will not be compromised in any way. Understand?"

"Yes," Glenn replied looking back at her. "What time are you picking me up in the morning?"

"Seven and we'll grab some breakfast and then be on the tour at eight."

"I'll be waiting." Glenn reached over to squeeze her shoulder and got out of the car and shut the door.

Patrice watched as Glenn walked into the hotel. She couldn't let go of the anger and pounded both fists against the steering wheel. He had confirmed her thoughts. He was here about their future.

CHAPTER 12

When Patrice returned home, her mother was still up watching television. Patrice was relieved. She wanted someone to talk to and she wanted that someone to be her mother.

"Mom, I hope you didn't wait up for me?"

"No, I usually stay up late on Friday and Saturday nights. Old habit."

"I remember. You looked tired earlier tonight, so I thought you might be in bed."

"I got my second wind. Your dad was tired though and went off to bed. He sure liked Glenn."

Patrice sat in her dad's recliner, next to her mother's. She kicked off her shoes and pulled the recliner's handle, drawing up the foot rest just like she always did when she was a little girl only now her legs were longer, so the chair was more comfortable. Her father's chair had been a forbidden place to sit unless he was at work or had gone to bed. She no longer felt the childhood angst of sitting in his chair.

"I'm sorry for the unexpected visit from Glenn. I didn't realize he was coming, and if I had, I would have told you."

"Your father and I were glad to meet him. Seems like a nice man."

"Yes, he is a nice man. Um, did he tell you he's my boss?" Patrice said pulling her hair behind her ear like a guilty child.

"No, just that he worked with you and was responsible for giving you this assignment."

"Then he also didn't tell you we're dating."

Renee Powell turned to her daughter with raised eyebrows. "No, but when I saw how happy he was to see you, I wondered."

"He . . . uh . . . used to be my peer but was promoted recently. Now he's our editor, which complicates our four-year relationship."

Renee Powell remained quiet and did not remove her gaze from her daughter. Patrice saw her mother's thumb tracing her left palm, knowing her mother was concentrating on her. Patrice looked at her feet because she was ashamed that she had not told her family about dating Glenn and dating him going on five years.

"I'm still trying to figure out how to deal with this. I like my work and he likes his promotion," Patrice said like she was confessing her sins to a priest. "It isn't fair to those we work with, either. I just don't know what to do, and neither does he. One of us has to compromise."

Renee listened but offered no advice. She wasn't like most mothers. She didn't pry and she didn't admonish her daughters about their personal matters.

"Part of his visit here will be a test of our relationship. I want to know if I'm ready to take the next step. He seems ready but I want to know how we are going to resolve our career issues. What if we have a family, what do we expect from one another? There are so many things we haven't talked about."

Patrice caught her mother's smile and returned a smile.

"I just wish he would have told me he was coming." Patrice looked down at her folded hands in her lap then looked up again at her mother. She shared Glenn's Long Island upbringing, his graduation from Columbia University, and how they had met at the magazine.

"He's very driven, very serious about his career. He works a lot of hours and I'm probably his only diversion outside of work. Our relationship has gotten complicated since he's become my editor. Sometimes I struggle with when to treat him like my boss and when to treat him as my boyfriend. I guess what I'm really questioning if he can make time for us in a marriage."

"He's here isn't he?"

Patrice was relieved to hear the understanding in her mother's voice.

"I guess. I hope he's here for the right reasons."

"What do you mean?"

"I haven't told him much about all this," Patrice said, looking around the room. "I haven't told him about my family or my up-bringing. Not really."

Patrice saw her mother's face shift and thought she detected hurt on it.

"Oh, I see," Renee said.

Patrice thought about the glimpse of hurt she thought she saw on her mother's face. She wanted to tell her mother that the gesture of clasping her hand earlier tonight had touched her. She wanted to tell her that it started to dissolve something in her heart; something she had justified for years but what that was she didn't specifically know at the moment. The hallway clock struck a chord that said it was at the half hour. Every tick that followed reminded her of the number of times she had hurt those she loved. She seemed so hell bent on hurting everyone around her. Somehow, she had felt warranted when she rarely wrote home, rarely called, or traveled home. Her parents had wanted to visit her, but she found a way to push their trip away saying she had too much work to do or it was too hot or too cold to visit New York. With every surmounting tick of the clock her heart felt heavier. Maybe Glenn sensed this heavy heart long before she did. That's why he was promoted to editor. He established rapport with people just like her Uncle Gary. Glenn seemed to know what stories motivated his employee's minds and their hearts. She thought about the hurt in his face tonight as he got out of the car. She had made sure he knew she was angry, and he'd gotten the message. He also looked tired of it and could resign from it. No one other than Jenny had really confronted Patrice about her actions. Even when Jenny had confronted her, Patrice knew Jenny could have said so much more, but she relented. Why was she so angry? This wasn't about just coming home for this assignment? This anger had been a long time in the making.

"Do you love him?" Her mother's voice seemed to have come from across the room.

"Yes." Patrice said meekly.

"Do you love him enough to accept him and accept his world?"

"I need to know that Glenn accepts mine. I need to know that he accepts me. Does that make sense? Did you ever feel that way when you met dad?" Patrice said feeling confused yet relieved to have these thoughts out in the open.

"Yes. When I met your father, his plans were to become a farmer, and Iowa farmers were revered across the Midwest as being some of the best and wealthiest men around. Your grandfather was so excited to learn I had met your dad. He knew I could have a secure life if I were to fall in love and marry your father, something he felt I wouldn't have if I married and stayed in Missouri."

"I didn't know that about grandpa."

"That he had a concern for my security?"

Patrice nodded.

"Oh yes. We had just come out of the Depression and it was war-time. People had such concerns on their minds. I knew your father would be a great catch, but I couldn't understand what your father could possibly see in me. My family wasn't financially well off, and I was probably just a stop on the road for your dad. I know I've told you this story a dozen times before, but I don't mind repeating it again," Renee Powell chuckled.

Patrice placed her fist under her chin, leaning her elbow on the arm of the chair listening to her mother. She remembered many late nights returning home from a date or a school activity to find her mother still awake. They had some of their best conversations late at night when the day was over, and they were alone.

"Your father came to Missouri to visit a friend of his from the service, Joe Tibble. They went to a dance that I attended with my girlfriend, Millie. He asked me to dance and we just seemed to hit it off. Joe cornered me later and told me not to get my hopes up because Martin had someone at home, he was getting serious with. Yet, I knew that I had had an effect on your father."

"How so?"

"He was curious about me. He wanted to know everything about me, my family, my favorite color, what I wanted to do in the future. He told Joe he was going to give me a ride home and he was ever the gentleman. Your dad was very respectful. The next morning, I thought about what Joe had said and realized that your father might just be a nice man just being nice to a young girl from Missouri. Yet, that afternoon he stopped by to say hello and introduced himself to my parents. They liked him immediately, but I told them he was smitten with someone at home. My own mother said, 'Don't be so sure.' Isn't it funny that other people can see things before we do?" Patrice's mother looked over at her daughter who gave a nod of agreement.

"Later, when we were engaged, I asked your father why he had not chosen someone else. He told me he had not met anyone like me before. He liked my spunk; I was lively and fun. He said I found pleasure in the simple things he did for me. He liked that." Renee was smiling. "I complemented him and as you know, your father is quiet. Yet loves a good laugh . . . and takes life seriously, too. My guess is that you give Glenn something he needs, something he's been looking for in his life."

"That's what I'm worried about. He knows the New York Patrice; he doesn't know much of this Patrice. Will he accept me and all I bring to the marriage or don't bring to the marriage?"

"Honey, you two have more in common than you're giving the situation credit for. Your varied background is what makes you an interesting couple. The fact that he has interest in Grant and Nan Wood tells me he's appreciative of different people and backgrounds. Give him the benefit of the doubt. Is it possible this isn't so much about Glenn as it is about you?"

"What do you mean?" Patrice's interest was piqued.

"You're asking for Glenn's acceptance of you—unconditionally. How can he give it to you if you haven't accepted yourself?"

Patrice's mind clouded in hearing those words.

"Honey, you just said you've been showing him a New York Patrice. Why is that? Why not just be you, wonderful you?"

Tears started to roll down Patrice's face. As much as she wanted to hide them, she could not. It had been a long time since she cried in front of her mother and she covered her face with her hands to muffle the sobs. Her mother walked over to hug her, and she felt comforted in her warm embrace. She had forgotten the safety she felt in her mother's presence. Her mother had never judged her, only provided advice, asked those key questions, the kind that you're afraid to hear but when you do, they release the pent-up feelings inside yourself that need to move on. Patrice felt better in her mother's presence because Renee Powell possessed a calm, quiet strength that radiated into her daughter's soul.

"I know you're right, Mom," Patrice finally said. I just don't know why I struggle with this so." She returned her mother's hug.

"Patrice," her mother said as she cupped Patrice's face in her hands, "all your life it seems you have defined your life by following the culture defined by the media—what was trendy, what was hip and socially acceptable."

Patrice giggled when she heard her mother say the word hip.

"But I think by doing that you always felt something was missing from your life or passing you by."

Patrice nodded with her face still cupped in her mother's hands.

"It's what took you to New York and what helped you find Glenn. But now, find your life with your heart and find out what matters most. Don't let the world define what is real and true for you. You decide that. And whoever said that two people from different backgrounds can't fall in love? It happens every day. If you love Glenn, that's all that matters."

"Thanks, Mom," Patrice said, wiping away tears as her mother removed her hands from her cheeks.

As Patrice composed herself, she thought about what her mother said. It'd been a long time since she asked her heart what she truly wanted; she had only asked her head all these years. By asking her head she was mostly reacting to situations and things in front of her. She decided tomorrow she would take her mother's advice and lead with her heart.

"It's been a long day, hasn't it?" her mother said.

"Yes, a long but good day." Patrice was feeling tired until she remembered the vision at the mansion. Like her mother, she then found her second wind.

"Mom, there's something else I wanted to talk with you about. Something happened today while I was at the art colony site in Stone City."

"The tour allowed you to visit the actual site?" Renee asked in surprise.

"No, I was actually trespassing on private property. I snuck away from the tour group to go up to the site. It wasn't fenced off from the north; just like always."

"What happened?"

"I was enjoying the time alone and decided to lay down on the warm foundation of the mansion floor, and I just inhaled its presence. I guess my senses got the best of me and I fell asleep, or I went into a dream. I can't explain it. What happened to me was very different, vivid. It felt like a dream came to me versus me going into the dream. It was just odd." Patrice shyly peered at her mother.

"Keep going."

"Well, I found myself walking through rows of artists painting. They were each painting on canvas propped on easels. There were rows and rows of easels and artists far as the eye could see. They were working intently, and they didn't really pay much attention to me, so I was able to observe them. They were dressed as if they were from another time—say, early twentieth century. When I turned to see what they were painting, the colors and shapes were incredible. I've never seen anything like it. I could even smell the paint on the canvas. Then a young girl approached me, but she sounded like she was 40 and explained what I was seeing. She said that before people come to Earth, they imprint their worldly gifts onto their soul and they do this by painting, um, uh, some representation of that feeling, or maybe it's just the act of painting, I don't know? The girl continued to say this was the site that recognized their imprints and it was the site where we were standing."

"The art colony."

"That's what I thought, too even though the site felt more open in this vision, trees and bushes were missing. Once their paintings were completed, they would be born into this world, waiting for the time their gifts in life would be self-recognized. That's the sense I got. She said her gifts would be revealed to her by a great teacher."

"Grant Wood."

"That's how I interpreted it, too. When the young girl turned to her own painting and added some brush strokes, her physical appearance started to change. She appeared younger, she went from looking thirteen to seven or something like that. Evidently, she was nearing her birth. When I asked her what year it was, I came out of the dream and almost missed my tour bus."

"Do you remember what the little girl was painting?"

"It felt familiar. She was painting a lane that followed a river. The lane had a fence where bluebirds perched. All she had to do was finish the birds, and like she said, she would be born."

"Bluebird Lane."

"Yes, that would have been a great name for her painting," Patrice said.

"I don't consider myself psychic or mystical, but I have a feeling you talked with your Aunt Patsy."

"What?"

"Yes, your Aunt Patsy grew up on a farm southeast of Anamosa, and their front lane followed the Wapsipinicon River. She wrote a poem entitled "Bluebird Lane" describing bluebirds perching on a river road fence."

"I remember that she liked bluebirds because she had bird figurines around her house," Patrice admitted. "I didn't associate her with my experience this afternoon, and I had no idea she'd written that poem."

"When Aunt Patsy was a little girl, she'd get up before dawn to join her father on his milk route in Anamosa. She often recalled the artists she saw painting, sitting or standing along the sidewalks of Anamosa with their easels in front of them in the early hours of a warm summer morning. Her father told her they were students from the art colony. They'd be scattered up and down the sidewalks of downtown Anamosa and side streets. I'm sure that is how she found her love of art. She would find time to paint after she married your Uncle Gary."

"Do you think she destined herself to grow up in this area just to learn about painting?"

"Sounds like it. It's possible you did, too. Why else would you have a very famous brooch in your possession?"

Patrice reassembled the recliner and stood up to walk over to the *American Gothic* print and pondered her mother's words. The brooch had been a remarkable gift, and one she had only recently come to appreciate fully. The same could be said for her mother's thoughts, words, and support. Patrice said good night to her mother, but before she went to bed, contemplating all the gifts of the day, she walked toward where her mother was sitting and bent over and kissed her mother good night.

CHAPTER 13

Patrice picked up Glenn at the hotel and took him to breakfast at a busy local diner in downtown Cedar Rapids. The June morning was cool and bright. It wouldn't be long until the haze of the day transformed into an oppressive heat.

"It's nice that we're both away from the office. We don't have that opportunity very often," Patrice said after they'd given the waitress their order. She felt revived from the conversation she had with her mother and a good night's sleep.

"To your point, this will be good for us, seeing if we have more in common than just the daily work grind." Glenn folded the newspaper he was peering at and set it aside.

With her chin resting on the palm of her hand, Patrice watched this man across the table from her. He looked striking in his Ralph Lauren tan slacks and striped blue and tan knit shirt. The shirt brought out the flecks of blue in his brown eyes. His slightly gelled brown hair had one curl that wanted to fall across his left eyebrow. The curl he liked to brush with his fingers made her want to kiss him.

"You're staring," Glenn said, lifting the coffee cup to his lips.

"Yes, I am."

Glenn looked up at Patrice and held her eyes for a moment. "Are you finally glad to see me?"

Patrice raised her eyebrows and gave him her best guilty-as-charged look in acknowledgment that she had been less than fully welcoming to him the night before.

"Yes. It unnerved me to see you sitting in my parents' living room. I wanted to be the one that introduced you to them."

"I liked talking with them. They're good people, Patrice."

"How did you introduce yourself to them?"

"I gave them my name and told them that I worked with you at the magazine and had just arrived in Iowa to help with your story. I also handed them my business card to show I was legit. They didn't even look at it. They invited me in like I was a neighbor."

"Welcome to Iowa," Patrice said, sitting up in her seat, "the home of two million friendly and trusting people."

"I'm not used to it, but I like it."

The waitress brought their food and Glenn concentrated on his food in silence. Patrice knew he was cautious to not get into another argument with her. How could she sincerely tell him she was seeing things differently this morning. He might not buy it knowing they had been down this path before. She swallowed a mouthful of oatmeal, sipped her orange juice, and decided she would continue to break the ice until she could win his trust again. Maybe he was just tired last night but she sensed he was close to a breaking point with their relationship.

Feeling very awkward in this moment, she reverted to work talk, "Here's what our day will look like: we'll finish the Marvin Cone, Grant Wood tour around noon, grab some lunch, and then head into Anamosa to the Paint 'n Palette. I'd also like to —."

"Sounds good. Tell me, how much of your story is done?" Glenn continued to focus on the food in front of him.

"There's not as much written information on Nan as I was hoping for. I'm thinking that much of my information will come from the people here who knew Grant and Nan. Yet, I'm finding that not too many of them are still living, or in good health. I did spend some time with an elderly couple, Rose and Ben Boston, who knew Nan and Grant. Rose's art is very popular in this area. I drove to Davenport to meet them both. While I was there, I spent time at the local art museum because both

Nan and Grant's estates were given to this museum."

"What other research have you done?"

"Some with the *Cedar Rapids Museum of Art*, and there's a Grant Wood store in Anamosa that has some information and photos that are local to the area. I also had a chance to talk with a retired Anamosa newspaper editor who knew the Woods and shared some of his stories."

"Good. So today will include more research to include a visit to Stone City?" Glenn asked as he motioned to the waitress for their check.

"Someone has been doing his homework."

Glenn grinned. Patrice could tell he was starting to relax his editor mode.

"Yes, we'll do that today too, but you're on vacation? Are you sure you want to go?" Patrice said with a wink.

"I just want to be with you."

Patrice grabbed one last sip of her orange juice, grabbed her purse and slid out of the booth.

"Great! Then let's get started!"

◆ ◆ ◆

Glenn and Patrice stood in the museum's atrium with fifteen minutes to spare before the tour. Barely talking to the tourists yesterday that she traveled with, today Patrice found herself greeting them good morning and trading small talk and pleasantries. Patrice was pleased that Glenn had shown some interest in the story. She did not know why she had questioned that he wouldn't. After all, they shared an interest in twentieth century art. It was more than that. She liked that he had taken an interest in this particular story—*her* story, a story about artists from the part of the country in which she had grown up.

Her thoughts were interrupted by the arrival of the tour guide.

"Welcome back to day two of the Marvin Cone, Grant Wood

Trail Tour. My name is Anne Kirkpatrick and I'll be your tour guide for the morning. You all got to meet Natalie yesterday and now it's my pleasure to tour you around the Cedar Rapids area. We'll spend the morning showing you where the two artists lived as boys and grown men as well as the schools they attended and the numerous places where they left their imprint."

Anne's choice of words made Patrice's mouth drop open.

"We'll end back here at the museum around the noon hour. After that we invite you to visit the *Cedar Rapids Museum of Art* where we have some of Grant Wood's work on display today and some Marvin Cone paintings which are on loan this summer. Are there any questions before we leave on the tour?"

A few hands shot up, mostly from those who wanted to know the length of time at each destination.

Patrice eyed Anne Kirkpatrick. Her name badge showed she was a curator. Patrice's mind started to spin with all the questions she wanted to ask Anne about the art collection at the museum. Glenn would kill her if he knew she had not scheduled a formal meeting with Anne. Patrice cringed at the thought that she had not really taken this story more seriously.

As the tour group walked outside to board the bus, Patrice noticed Anne's shoes: Naturalizers, with a slight heel. Clearly, the woman was ready for some walking. Patrice realized she should have worn shoes more sensible than the black dress sandals on her feet, but they looked stylish with the white slacks and black top, chosen more for the Paint 'n Palette show than this tour. Besides, Glenn liked black on her because it brought out her blonde hair. She would just have to minimize the walking. Overall, she was feeling good.

They boarded the small travel bus for the tour. Patrice grabbed one of the front seats for her and Glenn so they could be near Anne. The light coming through the bus windows was bright and Patrice donned her sunglasses. Glenn mimicked her and put his on.

"Our first site will be just a few blocks from here on Second Avenue. It's a historic residence here in Cedar Rapids, the former residence of a well-known entrepreneur, George B. Douglas, who founded an oatmeal and cereal business that would later merge with other companies to become Quaker Oats."

"Ah, the home of the world's largest cereal company," Glenn leaned toward Patrice.

Patrice nodded.

"The home was later owned by the Sinclair family, who had the largest meat packing company west of the Mississippi," Anne continued. "You may be asking what that has to do with Grant Wood and Marvin Cone?"

The bus pulled into a parking spot across from a large two-story brick home over a century old.

"This is the site where Grant Wood painted some of his most famous paintings and Marvin Cone was a frequent visitor. At that time, the home was owned by its third owners, the Turner family, who made this residence into their family business—a mortuary. Grant was friends with the Turner family, and they offered the free use of an apartment just above their carriage house. The carriage house, which you can see near the north-west side of the house, was Grant's studio. He lived there for eleven years with his mother and sister, Nan. Here he painted *Daughters of the Revolution, The Midnight Ride of Paul Revere,* and *Dinner for Threshers.* The living quarters were cramped, but the Wood family was just happy to be together. The loft of this carriage house had no address, so it was Grant who coined it *No. 5 Turner Alley.* Grant paid his landlord in paintings and those paintings now reside with the *Cedar Rapids Museum of Art,* thanks to the Turner family. Upon the death of Grant Wood in February 1942, his funeral was held here at Turner Mortuary."

The bus started to pull away from the parking lot. Patrice looked away from the Turner home and caught Anne looking at Glenn. Anne seemed to catch herself in the act of staring and quickly turned to speak to the bus driver. Patrice smiled at Anne's awkwardness in Glenn's presence. Patrice still felt that way in his presence. He was very modest about his good looks and often didn't notice when others gave him extra attention.

As Anne promised, the tour progressed throughout the city, taking the expectant tourists to all points relating to Grant Wood and Marvin Cone.

"Tell me more about Marvin Cone," Glenn whispered to Patrice.

"As you probably know, he was an artist from Cedar Rapids who went to high school with Grant Wood. They also studied together in Paris. Like Grant, Marvin attended *The Art Institute of Chicago*. Marvin became a professor at Coe College, here in Cedar Rapids, and most of his paintings are there," she whispered back.

The most impressive stop for Patrice and Glenn was Veteran's Memorial Building in downtown Cedar Rapids. Patrice was glad to get out of the bus and stretch her legs. They were on a bridge looking out across the wide expanse of the Cedar River. Patrice motioned Glenn to walk over to the bridge's railing and take in the view. In the far distance, it was one large river. As it approached the island that held Veteran's Memorial Building, the island split the river in two, but only for a short distance, less than three city blocks. There were numerous bridges crossing the river from the city into the downtown district.

Anne gathered the group near the front of the building and spoke above the traffic noise. "Veteran's Memorial Building, City Hall, and Linn County Courthouse are all located here on May's Island. Cedar Rapids is the only city in the world whose municipal government is on an island. We're standing in front of Veteran's Memorial Building, which houses many tributes to American Veterans. The stained-glass window in front of us, we'll see it better from inside, depicts U.S. soldiers from the Revolutionary War through WWI as a memorial to their sacrifices. Let's go inside."

Patrice was beginning to feel just a little soggy and lifted her hair off her neck. Even though the lecture in front of the building had been brief, she was happy to step into the air-conditioned building. Glenn looked unaffected by the heat and humidity. She wondered how he managed to look so good across so many variable circumstances.

Once everyone was inside and gathered around Anne, she began the guided tour of the building.

"This twenty-four-foot high by twenty-foot wide stained-glass window was etched by Grant Wood. The cost was $9,000 at that time. It took Grant Wood two years to design, build, and install this stained-glass window to honor our veterans of war. It was completed on March 9, 1929, and there are over 10,000 pieces of stained-glass fitted together with lead. There's nothing else like it in the world."

Patrice and Glenn looked up at a sixteen-foot tall woman within the dome-shaped window, wearing a Grecian robe and floating in the clouds. A blue mourning veil was draped over her head. In her right hand, she held a palm branch and in her left hand, a wreath.

As if reading their minds, Anne said, "the lady in mourning at the center was modeled by Nan Wood Graham, Grant Wood's sister. As you can see, she has a palm in her right hand, which represents peace, and her left hand holds a laurel wreath of victory."

Patrice turned to Glenn and whispered, "Nan continues to be present in so much of his life—two paintings and this stained-glass window."

Anne continued, "also, note at the bottom on the window there are six figures in uniforms representing six wars. Can you name them?" The tour group mumbled their way through naming each war as Anne walked past each six-foot figure individually.

"That's right: The Revolutionary War, The War of 1812, The Mexican War, The Civil War, Spanish American War, and the First World War."

The tourists were given fifteen minutes to walk around the inside of the building. Glenn and Patrice continued to look at the stained-glass window.

"You said that Grant had honored his sister in two paintings," Glenn said. "I know that one was *American Gothic*. What was the other?"

"It's called a *Portrait of Nan*," Patrice replied. "He painted it after *American Gothic*. You could say it was a portrait *for* Nan vs. *of* Nan. She took so much ridicule from the public for her somber look in *American Gothic* that he painted a lovely portrait of her just to make it up to her."

"That's pretty considerate."

"That's what I thought," Patrice admitted.

"I knew Grant Wood had painted quite a few paintings, but I didn't know of the various murals he did across the state of Iowa, and all the other local work he did—book covers, pamphlets, teaching at the University of Iowa ..." Glenn stated looking through the tour brochure and brushing his hair aside with his fingers.

"There was quite an artists' community in the Cedar Rapids area, especially in the 1920's, '30s and '40s. That's how the *Stone City Art Colony* originated."

Anne heard them talking and walked up to the couple. "I overheard you talking about the *Stone City Art Colony*. Did you enjoy yesterday's tour of Stone City and Anamosa?"

"I got to go on the tour yesterday, but he wasn't able to," Patrice said nodding at Glenn. "But, yes, I enjoyed it very much."

Anne continued, "Were you aware that Edward Rowan, Grant Wood, and Adrian Dornbush were the ones who created the blueprint for the art colony in Stone City? Edward Rowan was an art director at a gallery here in Cedar Rapids. Adrian Dornbush had been a director at the *Flint Institute of Art* in Michigan before moving here to Iowa. It was actually Edward Rowan who secured the startup money through the Carnegie Foundation."

"Anne?" one of the tourists said approaching the threesome, "I have a question for you about the Tomb of the Unknown Soldier that sits on the top of this building."

"Sure." Anne Kirkpatrick's attention was swept away with that question.

Glenn turned and quizzed Patrice. "So how much do you know about the *Stone City Art Colony*?"

"I've completed some research, but there's more to do. When we head toward Anamosa, I'll tell you all about it."

CHAPTER 14

As the tour bus pulled up in front of the *Cedar Rapids Museum of Art*, Patrice knew she needed to spend some time with Anne and followed her as she stepped off the tour bus.

"Anne? Hi. My name is Patrice Powell. I meant to formally introduce myself back at the Veteran's Memorial Building when we started to talk about the *Stone City Art Colony*. I work for *European Art* magazine out of New York. I'm originally from this area of Iowa and would like to talk with you about an article I'm writing. Would you have time to join us for lunch?"

The curator turned her attention away from Patrice for a moment. "Bye," she said to one of the people stepping off the bus. She was still saying goodbye to the tourists but turned her attention back to Patrice when the last one walked away.

"I think I could fit that into my schedule today. Would you mind if I ran up to my office to check my calendar to make sure I'm not overcommitting?"

"Sure."

"I'll be right back."

"What's going on?" Glenn asked.

"I'd like to take Anne to lunch with us if that's alright with you. I think we could learn a lot from her."

"You haven't talked to her yet?"

"She's been on my list!" Patrice replied to her boss.

"Patrice," Glenn said with some admonishment in his voice.

"Things have a way of working out, don't they?" she wasn't going to let this situation become a tiff between her and Glenn.

The door to the museum opened, "My schedule is open for the next two hours if you want to go for some lunch," Anne chorused as she stepped down the museum stairs.

"Wonderful. Is there a good restaurant within walking distance?"

"There is and it's not far. I know a great café a few blocks from here."

"Anne, I don't think I've introduced Glenn Collier. He's my editor at the magazine."

"Nice to meet you," Anne said cordially. "Wow, two of you here to do the story, that's impressive. I can't wait to hear about your story. Let's walk this way."

They followed Anne as if they were still on the tour, letting her lead the way.

"What brings you two on the tour?"

"I'm doing a story on Nan Wood Graham's recent death for the magazine," Patrice replied. "Even though I'm from this area of Iowa, I must admit, I don't know much about the Woods, other than just Grant's work and artistic style. We were hoping to learn more about them today. After the tour I realized I have more questions."

"Ask away."

"How many works of art does Cedar Rapids have compared to the *Davenport Museum of Art*?"

"I would say our collection here in Cedar Rapids is unrivaled in quantity and quality. We have about 108 works. The museum bought two of those directly from Grant, *Woman with Plants* and *The Doorway, Perigueux*. Much of our collection came from the Turner family who you heard about today. Davenport owns fifty-five works of art, fourteen of which are paintings, about thirty-two works on paper, and nine works in other media. Most of their collection came from Nan."

"I'm curious how the *Davenport Museum of Art* received Grant's estate. I would have assumed Cedar Rapids would have received all of it?"

"Nan actually inherited his estate first. At the point of Grant's death, he was divorced so he left everything to his little sister. I believe Nan had some connection with the *Davenport Museum of Art* over time and left his estate with them and I believe will be leaving any remains of her estate with Davenport as well."

"I also learned that when Nan lived at No. 5 Turner Alley with her brother and mother, she was married to Edward Graham. Why was she living with Grant and her mother?"

"Edward actually came down with tuberculosis and was staying at a health clinic in the local area to recover. It was at that time that Nan lived with her family at No. 5 Turner Alley. She lived with them for about a year until her husband recovered from his illness. Here's the café I was talking about." Anne held the door for Patrice and Glenn. It was called *The Eclectic Café* and they could see why. The café's surroundings included paintings by what appeared to be local artists. The art included paintings, quilts, sculptures, and ceramics. Anne explained that if they were to look closely, they would see that all the art was for sale.

"There are two owners: one is a local artist and the other a local chef. The café not only offers local art, but a menu of fresh foods that are local to the area."

They sat at a table near a window looking out over a garden. Glenn held the chairs for both women.

"What would you ladies recommend?" Glenn said taking his own seat.

"Patrice probably knows what you like best Glenn. I'll let her do the recommending. Menus are here on the table, so take a look," Anne said handing the menus to Glenn and Patrice.

Patrice scanned the menu, "Oh, I would recommend the breaded pork tenderloin sandwich because I don't believe you've ever had one, Glenn."

"That's true, is it good?"

"It's the best! It's one of the things I miss about being vegetarian," Patrice replied.

"Add some sweet corn, which I'm surprised is on the menu because it's too early for sweet corn."

"It's possible it's sweet corn that they harvested last year and froze," Anne offered.

"Okay, then add the sweet corn and save room for dessert from the Amana Colonies."

"What are the Amana Colonies?" Glenn asked, looking from Patrice to Anne.

"It's a settlement of seven German colonies southwest of here about ten miles that historically has had some of the best food in the world," Patrice said.

"Trust her on that," Anne agreed with a nod.

Patrice and Anne set down the menu, but Glenn was still reviewing it as their waiter came over to the table to take their order.

"Hello. I'm Bryn. Thanks for dining with us today. Do you have any questions about the menu?" he asked.

"Yes, what are koo la chez?" Glenn stammered.

"Kolaches," the other three echoed.

Patrice smiled, bemused. "Said like 'coal lot cheese.'"

"I don't know what they are."

Bryn helped him out. "They are round sweet rolls with a fruit filling placed in the middle and some icing drizzled over the roll. They're made here by local bakeries, and the fruit fillings today are peach and cherry."

"I'll try one of those for dessert—a peach one—along with the pork tenderloin sandwich and a side of sweet corn."

"Good choice, and for you ladies?"

"I'm going to have the chicken salad on a croissant and some iced tea," Anne responded.

"I'll have the Caesar salad, no chicken added please. Water is fine for me," said Patrice.

"I'll have water too," Glenn added.

"Very good." And with that, Bryn turned to place their order with the kitchen staff.

"I'm looking forward to this breaded pork tenderloin sandwich," Glenn said. "I don't think I've seen those in New York."

"When I was growing up, I thought I'd always find a pork tenderloin sandwich wherever I went in the United States. It didn't take long to know these hot sandwiches can only be found in Iowa."

"Is that so? I assumed we could find them anywhere too," Anne said with surprise in her voice.

"Unfortunately, not. I do a lot of traveling and I think I saw one once on a menu in Colorado. Anne, did you grow up in Iowa?"

"Just up the road in Alburnett. I went to school at the University of Iowa. How about you, Patrice, where are you from?"

"I graduated high school in Anamosa and then went to school at Columbia University. I got a scholarship there, which helped immensely. Glenn went there, too."

"Really?"

"Yeah, we didn't know each other until we found ourselves working at the same magazine."

"You both work for *European Art* magazine. What's the reason for doing a story on a Regionalist artist?"

"Great question," Patrice said, then became quiet, awaiting the answer along with Anne.

"For our November issue, we're adding a section about great American art that had its roots in Europe. We're doing 3-4 stories in that space. I had started researching Grant Wood and upon hearing of Nan Wood Graham's death, I got even more diligent about learning about the artist. I know he made three to four trips to study abroad and much of his style is derived from European masters. Overall, I'm interested in his work, and wanted to highlight it and his connection to Europe. When I heard about Nan's death, it became important to me to honor this famous face in what I consider his best work of art." Glenn ended his commentary by staring into Patrice's eyes.

Bryn arrived with the iced tea and waters and Anne thanked him as Patrice and Glenn gazed upon one another.

"Yes, I wish we had that piece here in Cedar Rapids, but it gets a lot of attention being in Chicago. What did you think about the stained-glass window?"

"Beautiful," Glenn said still gazing at Patrice.

"That's a good example of Grant working with European experts," Anne explained. "He worked on that with a group out of Munich. He became familiar with that area when he traveled there in the late 1920s to study. In fact, there's a well-known quote from Grant Wood about the fact that U.S. art critics and art dealers didn't recognize or want American art in those days. That great art was only in Europe. He learned from them, but he made his work his own. By doing that, the Regionalists started to change those attitudes. This is why we're proud of what we have in our museum and in the local area."

Patrice deep in thought, turned to Anne.

"I grew up with the same attitudes of those art dealers and critics. Even though my schooling was in the U.S., my major was writing, with an emphasis in European art. I turned my back on a lot of American art adopting those attitudes."

"You're not the first, and you won't be the last," Anne assured her. "I hope you'll have a chance to learn more about it while you're here, while you're writing this piece on Nan. She was definitely part of the Regionalist movement."

Patrice took a sip of her water thinking about all this. The Regionalists were serious about their art, and what Patrice liked about them is that they persevered despite the critics and the attitudes about their art. She looked at Glenn with a knowing appreciation now for this assignment to discover Iowa and its native art--art with morals, values, meaning and wit about people with a work ethic.

"That's a large sandwich!" Glenn said, eyeing the plate set before him.

"Enjoy your food," Bryn said, and he placed lunch on the table, "and let me know if I can get you all anything else."

The hungry three dived into their food. Patrice watched as Glenn took a bite of the tenderloin sandwich, nodding his approval of the savory taste in his mouth.

"Do you like it?"

"Mmm...," he said, too busy chewing to give a proper answer.

"It's delicious," he finally said after two additional bites.

"Anne, can you share what you know about the *Stone City Art Colony*?" Glenn asked before taking another bite.

Yes," Patrice said. "Natalie did a great job yesterday, but I sense you have more to share?"

"I do, and it will bring in more information about the Regionalist movement as well."

"Good, we'd like to hear it," Glenn said.

"I believe Natalie gave some of the basics yesterday, and usually the Grant Wood Store fills in the rest of the information, but there's so much more. Grant started the colony with his good friend Edward Rowan and it was Rowan who knew Adrian Dornbush and invited him into the idea. As I mentioned earlier, those three were responsible for the art colony of 1932 and 1933. As they pondered what the colony would offer, they began to recruit some of their friends. Many of those friends were educated at *The Art Institute of Chicago* or at local universities, and most had studied art abroad. This group of friends and artists became the *Stone City Art Colony* faculty. For example, Grant invited his high school friend and art colleague Marvin Cone who, as you know from today's tour, was a well-known figure drawer from Cedar Rapids. He also invited Francis Chapin, an instructor from *The Art Institute in Chicago*, to teach lithography. Grant would teach advanced painting. Arnold Pyle, a protégé of Grant Wood's, would teach framing, which was extremely popular at the time. Florence Sprague Smith was asked to teach sculpture. She was an instructor at Drake University in Des Moines. David McCosh was asked to teach painting and lithography."

Patrice had pulled a notebook from her purse and was taking notes.

"Also interesting is the fact that they had John Steuart Curry during the second summer. He was a Regionalist from Kansas and very famous."

"We're familiar with John Steuart Curry," Glenn inserted. "I've seen his work at The Metropolitan, along with Wood's, Benton's, and Hopper's."

"Yes, well John Steuart Curry hadn't sold a painting to any native Kansan at that time because his local paintings showed what Kansan's felt was a darker side to their state. Wood was so beloved in Iowa. It's said that when Curry saw the painting of *Stone City*, he thought it was too perfect. He doubted there was anywhere on earth where a landscape that pristine could be found. It was Curry's curiosity about both matters that brought him to the colony. Curry ended up staying for a while and taught a class or two of his own."

Glenn looked at Patrice, who was squirming in her chair.

"Yes?" he questioned with a smile looking at Patrice again. He was clearly amused by Patrice's behavior.

"Glenn, the retired newspaper editor I talked with from Anamosa shared the same story about John Steuart Curry's visit, but he hadn't mentioned that Curry actually taught some classes there. This is new information."

"Did you talk to Gary Powell?" Anne inquired.

"Yes."

"We love Gary. He's been a great support for our tours when they come through Anamosa."

"He's my uncle." Patrice kept her focus on Anne's face, knowing Glenn's face now held a look of surprise.

"You have a great source there with Gary."

"I do. Anne, when I was growing up, everyone in the county had a print of *Stone City* in their house, including my parents when we were out on the farm. I agreed with Curry in many ways. I didn't care for the painting. I was only ten at the time—so take it with a grain of salt—but I thought paintings of cornfields and quarries were boring. I grew up around it; I didn't need to see it in a painting. That's why I never wanted to learn about it. I just didn't think it was sophisticated or intriguing."

"I think I appreciated it more when I learned about Grant Wood the artist. His greatness came when he started to paint from his Iowa surroundings plus his paintings speak to the kind of man he was —his sense of humor in *Daughters of the American Revolution*. *Stone City* shows his eye for beauty, and his admiration for hard working people can be seen in *Dinner with Threshers. Appraisal* shows his dismay over bigotry."

Anne paused and looked from Patrice to Glenn, as if to see if they were following her. They nodded encouraging her to continue. "Sorry I get carried away. Stop me if this gets too much. It's what the Regionalists were about. They cared about what was around them and they captured that in their art. We take that for granted today, I guess because we're so used to keeping busy and not thinking about what's around us. Back then this was new. Up to that time, art in the United States mainly consisted of portraits. The Regionalists brought the environment to their work: landscapes, people, and attitude into the forefront of art. What people don't realize today is that the Regionalists broke a glass ceiling of sorts. For the first time American art and artists were taken seriously."

"Part of that was because they had all traveled and worked with the great masters abroad," Patrice said.

"Yes, but they Americanized all of that by painting most of their work here at home," Glenn added.

"What also intrigues me about the art colony is this all happened during the Depression. What did I learn . . . that they expected something like thirty students and ninety came?"

"Yes," Anne agreed with Patrice's statement. "And the students paid for their classes and their supplies, but if someone was in need, Grant and the faculty found a way to help. For instance, on the weekends they held events: a Saturday night dance and on Sunday evening chicken dinner. Both were open to the public."

"I've heard about that," Patrice said. "I know they charged for them, apparently with the hopes of making some additional money."

"I don't think they did," Anne replied. "In fact, I think the opposite happened."

"Can I get you anything else today?" Bryn had appeared from nowhere.

"The lunch was very good, even the kolache," Glenn said to

Bryn with a smile.

"Good. Do you care for coffee?" he asked.

"This was wonderful, but nothing else for me," Patrice replied.

"Me either," added Anne.

"Great, I'm glad you enjoyed it. Now here's the bad news. Here's the check."

"I'll take that, thank you," said Glenn, quickly scooping up the check.

"Sold!" Bryn laughed. "I'll be right back."

"Anne, I meant to ask what kind of classes they offered in 1932 and 1933. I know you mentioned general painting and figure drawing," Glenn said grabbing his billfold from his pant pocket.

"Well, as I mentioned, framing was also very popular. Lithography was a popular form of printing in the Depression era. Grant took his students around the countryside to paint landscapes using oils and paints, and they also learned sculpting. There was also life drawing, nudes ... that sort of thing."

"Nudes?" Patrice said.

"That's really fascinating," Glenn exclaimed, "I can't wait to see the site."

Anne looked at her watch. "I should get back to work. I don't know if I helped you much with your story."

"Thank you. You did, actually," Patrice replied. She wanted to tell Anne about the brooch, but she hesitated and said, "Did you ever have the opportunity to meet Nan Wood Graham?"

"Actually, I did. It was a long time ago, but I had just started my career at the museum, and she stopped in to see Grant's paintings. She enjoyed seeing *Woman with Plants* because it was a portrait of her mother, Hattie. As with all Grant's paintings, there's so much meaning in that one. For example, the plant Hattie is holding is the snake plant. These plants are hardy, strong houseplants. This same plant can also be found in the painting *American Gothic* on the porch of the house. I like the inference. From what I have heard, Nan could be a tough lady much like her mother."

"I believe that hardy symbolism is a representation for Iowans too."

"Yes. Overall, Nan was a very sweet lady and so proud of her brother and all that he accomplished. She was very protective of him and his legacy. He came under such scrutiny when the war was about to break out because Regional art was being ignored for European art. Abstract art was finding its way into the world. It's like a lot of things today, the work became obsolete. Times had changed. What I really want you to walk away with from this conversation is this: Grant Wood is considered by many to be truly the first *American* artist. Those artists before him were considered imitators of Europe. Time has shown that *American Gothic* is the most famous and recognizable painting of the 20th century. That's quite a legacy to leave behind and Nan ensured people did not forget that."

They left the restaurant in silence and walked back to the museum. The afternoon sun was blistering and the air was thick. Patrice looked across the street to a city park that was void of people. Even though it was shaded with large elm trees, the muggy air was too much for people to be out in. Anne invited them into the museum to take a look at the art on display. They took her up on the offer.

"Thank you for lunch. It was great to meet the both of you," Anne said, shaking hands with each of them in turn. "I'm sorry I won't be able to walk you through the gallery, but please take your time as my guests. When you enter the gallery, you will see four of Grant Wood's paintings currently on display: *Young Corn, Woman with Plants, Portrait of John B. Turner,* and *Overmantel Decoration.* Here's my card if you ever need anything."

Glenn and Patrice both thanked Anne for her generosity, as well as the invitation to walk around the museum.

Patrice opened the door to the gallery and spotted *Woman with Plants* just to her right. Glenn followed her to the painting.

"This is his mother?" Glenn asked.

"Yes, after talking with Anne, I'd like to continue research on the symbolism of Wood's paintings. I overheard her say on the tour today that Grant Wood added a windmill to almost every painting; that he had grown up with them and added them to his paintings as a personal trademark. See, he added a windmill to *Woman with Plants*. She's right, there is a lot of symbolism. In this painting, you have the apron with the rickrack border, which depicts this era. The plant she is holding describes the woman who is his mother and notice the cameo she is wearing. It's the same piece that Nan wore in *American Gothic*. Remind me to tell you more about this brooch."

"Okay, so do you see his work differently now?"

"I do actually."

Glenn walked over to *Young Corn*. "I really like the colors in this painting."

"I agree. It looks great under this lighting and really draws your eye." Patrice walked up behind Glenn and put her hand on his shoulder. "Glenn, this is what the countryside will look like when we drive into Jones County this afternoon."

"This looks contained."

"What do you mean?" Patrice said.

"The shape of the trees and plants are painted with a lot of control. Nothing is out of place or appears loose or flowing. It's an interesting way to depict a landscape. It's as if there's no air current or hope for wind," Glenn grinned.

"He probably painted it on a day like today when it's hot and humid and a person would give anything for a little breeze."

"I thought Wood had studied impressionism in Paris at the *Academie Dianen*."

"Yes," Patrice admitted, "and some of his paintings from the 1920s depict that style, but when he came home and matured, his work moved away from that training. Do you remember when we were at the Veterans Memorial Building today and learned that he went to Munich to supervise the fabrication of the glass? When he was in Munich, that's when he saw some of the Northern Renaissance, Gothic artwork. One of the artists he was most impressed by was Jan van Eyck and the way he used oils in painting. Wood's work after that trip was definitely influenced by van Eyck."

"Where did you find that information?"

"I heard it in the ladies' restroom at the Veterans Memorial Building today. Don't worry, I'll double check that."

"Please do." Glenn replied with a serious tone. Patrice was reminded that he didn't like teasing when it came to work but she was enjoying working with him on this project. Their passion for art, reading each other's minds, and getting excited about what they were learning gave her the urge to kiss him, but she stuffed her feelings away and decided she would hold that thought for later.

Glenn found the *Portrait of John B. Turner*. "So, this is the guy from the mortuary family who funded Wood's living space."

"Yes, and was given a lot of Grant's work in exchange for that support. It's a testament to the family for giving this work to the museum."

"I love the county map behind John's portrait detailing his life. Wood liked the details."

"For sure. I heard Anne say today it often took Wood two years to complete a painting. He had his photo taken with his art so no one could ever say it wasn't an original piece of his. That was a pretty smart way to validate the authenticity of his work in those days. He often did this at the time he lived at No. 5 Turner Alley. It's interesting to have not only the painting on film, but also the space where he painted."

The couple moved on to the *Overmantel Decoration*.

"Another painting he completed at No. 5 Turner Alley. You see more motion in this painting with the willows showing some swaying next to the house and the horseman on the road in front of the house," Patrice said.

"Yes, this portrait was translated from a Willow Ware fine china pattern," Glenn said thoughtfully.

Patrice was both impressed and surprised by this tidbit from him. "Is this part of your homework?"

Glenn ignored the remark, "Think about that, Patrice. In 1930 he would have had to have seen or heard about this fine china company out of England and some of their patterns. Makes you wonder if the Turners had such china."

"You're right," she replied. Patrice looked at her watch. "We should probably get on the road. I'm going to call my parents from the pay phone at the entrance of the museum. I'll tell them where we are and what time they can expect us home for dinner." She thought about dinner with her parents. With Glenn there, it would be different somehow. She was no longer threatened about seeing them through Glenn's eyes. In the last twenty-four hours she knew it would be alright. Her perspective was changing, and she liked that.

CHAPTER 15

Seeing her family through Glenn's eyes wasn't the only thing Patrice liked about now having Glenn in Iowa with her. The more involved Glenn was with the story, the more Patrice realized she enjoyed his collaboration on it. It wasn't just his knowledge of and interest in art, though Patrice had to admit to herself that there was something exciting about sleuthing into the lives of Grant and Nan with a colleague. She and Glenn had never worked on a project like this together and she found she liked his company very much. Working together was giving them a chance to know one another in a new way.

As they were heading toward Anamosa, Patrice leaned over and gave him a kiss. "No kissing a co-worker while on the job," Glenn teased.

"Hey, you can say boss." She said with respect in her voice.

The smile on his face told her that meant a lot to him.

"Okay back to business, here's the itinerary for the day. As we leave the Cedar Rapids-Marion area, we'll be heading east to the area where I grew up. We'll head to Anamosa first, because I don't want to miss the local art show at Paint 'n Palette, and then we'll stop by the Grant Wood Store, drive to Stone City, and then go past the farm where I grew up. This loop will bring us back on the highway to Cedar Rapids."

"Good. I meant to ask you, where was *American Gothic* painted?"

"At Stone City and finished in Cedar Rapids, in 1934."

"Have you ever seen the original painting?"

"No, I'd like to, though."

"I guess more people will see it in Chicago. There is something to be said for it being at a prestigious place like *The Art Institute of Chicago.*"

They had left the city and were now in farm country. Glenn looked from left to right, taking it all in.

"Are those cornfields?"

"Yes, you'll see a lot of those between here and Anamosa. The corn isn't very high yet."

"There's so much land and openness."

"As far as the eye can see."

"The farms are nicely mowed and well kept."

"People take great pride in their farms. My dad was one of those farmers; he was scrupulous. Dad landscaped our yard, kept the ditches mowed and spread new gravel on the driveway almost every year. Mom worked hard, too, keeping a very large garden. It was impeccably cared for, but it took a lot of work. Our place looked nice."

"Why are they now living in town?"

"Dad couldn't make a living on the farm, especially when the economy took a toll on farmers in the early 1980s. They made a decision to move into town, and Dad is semi-retired and works part-time at the grain elevator just outside of town."

"Does he miss it?"

"I think so. He doesn't talk very much about it, but I think he misses having all that land. He grew up on a farm, so that's really been all he's known."

They crossed the county line into Jones County.

"We're in Grant Wood Country and Stone City is about two miles to our left, to the north," Patrice said. "Our farm is in this area too. I haven't mentioned this to you, but the painting of *Stone City* illustrates part of my bus route to school when I was growing up. We'd pick up about five or six families of kids in that community. I can look at that painting and remember who lived in those houses when I was going to school."

"That's cool. I'm finding out all kind of things about you," Glenn said, caressing her shoulder. "And, hey, I thought Iowa was flat," Glenn teased.

"And I think New Jersey smells good," Patrice smirked.

"This is beautiful country, and my baby came from here." Glenn stroked Patrice's hair.

"I love you too." Patrice said her eyes misting as she finally realized the depth of her true feelings for Glenn. He grabbed her hand and squeezed it.

Patrice had taken the 151 bypass and they approached the east side of Anamosa. The hills surrounding Anamosa were abundantly green, with wildflowers and trees. Mother Nature had been good to Iowa.

Patrice made a right turn on Highway 64.

"You still know your way around."

"Some things have changed but for the most part, things have remained pretty consistent."

"So, what are you hoping to see, or learn, at this art show?"

"Paint 'n Palette is actually the name of an art club that has existed here as long as I can remember. When I was growing up, my family never went to one of these art shows, but my Aunt Patsy was part of this club. I'm curious to go and see my hometown from a different point of view—a creative one. The building is up here on the left, and on the same site is the one-room schoolhouse that Grant Wood attended when he was a small boy, as well as the Antioch Church. We drove by this area many times when we visited friends and family who lived out this way."

"Wow, there are a lot of people here. Where are we going to park?"

"Probably along the highway somewhere."

"That's legal?"

"Around here it is." Patrice pulled in behind other cars lining the highway.

"Watch your step as you get out of the car. There's a pretty steep ditch there."

"You're not kidding," Glenn said trying to place his foot on the ground.

Patrice and Glenn carefully stepped out of the car and stood on the edge of the highway.

Glenn pointed to two structures on the east side of the acreage. "Is the brick structure the church and the white wooded building the school house?"

"Yes." Patrice realized the two structures were not well marked and because they were so simple and plain, it was probably hard to tell which was which. "Nan would have just been a baby when they lived near here, so she didn't attend the school. The Wood family had lived just about a mile north from here. The family moved to Cedar Rapids after Francis Wood died in 1901. Just think, that's ninety years ago."

"That means these buildings are over one hundred years old and they are in great condition."

Glenn and Patrice carefully crossed the highway and saw a sign that said *Grant Wood Memorial Park*.

"Interesting that the Paint 'n Palette building is made to look like a long, narrow log cabin," Glenn pointed out.

"You'll find the log cabin *look* across many homes and some businesses in the area."

Once inside, they saw numerous paintings displayed around the room. Glenn and Patrice walked slowly up and down the aisles, peering at each painting.

"Do you notice anything area-specific in these paintings?" Patrice asked.

"That's a good question," Glenn replied. "Let me continue to look."

Glenn was leading the way, peering from painting to painting.

"Is the Antioch School open?"

"Usually it's locked. When I was growing up, they were still using the building for special occasions."

"It's so small, they couldn't have had too many events," Glenn added, surprised by how the building had been used.

"Well, most of those events were held in summer, so they

often extended outside to the lawn," Patrice pointed out.

"I never knew much about the church. The name 'Antioch' is biblical, so I'm sure they meant there to be a biblical reference to the name. The only thing I ever knew about this location was that it marked the area where Grant Wood was born and first started school."

"Okay, I'm ready to answer your question," Glenn said, clearly into the challenge. "You asked if I noticed anything area-specific to these paintings. I'm assuming you were asking if I saw anything in common to them, as a group, even though they are painted by several artists. So, that is how I'm going to answer it."

"The artists appear to use the same type of canvas and paints. They seem to use the same style in their landscapes that Grant Wood used. There's a roundness to the shape of their trees, flowers, and even vases; large use of landscape, physical environment, and still life."

"No one seems to use dark colors," Patrice added, "except in contrast."

"Yes, I would agree," said Glenn. "I don't see a lot of abstract in any of them. They were definitely created with the eye versus the mind."

Patrice saw some names familiar to the Anamosa area on the paintings: Brown, Carpenter, Zimmerman, and Hall. She did not see any familiar faces, but she enjoyed the vibe of the environment.

"I wanted to see this show because I remembered talking to a graphic designer in New York that worked with a group from Cedar Rapids. I remember him saying that their designs looked like a Grant Wood painting. I wanted to get a sense if this was true even for local painters."

"Possibly."

"Wood was criticized at the art colony for producing clones of his work versus encouraging the student's own expression."

"Who cares as long as they enjoy what they're doing."

Once they left Paint 'n Palette, Patrice drove Glenn through downtown Anamosa, pointing out the various points of interest. They stopped at her Uncle Gary's house, but he was not home, so Patrice left a note. They stopped at the Grant Wood Store and Riverside Cemetery. She showed him Nan and Grant's burial place and she stopped by to pay her respects at her Aunt Patsy's grave. Patrice explained to Glenn how close she felt to her aunt and uncle and that, unfortunately, her Aunt Patsy had died about six years earlier of cancer.

"My Aunt Patsy was too young to attend the art colony, but she saw the art colony students painting on the streets of town. I think that's why it was important for me to go to the Paint 'n Palette today."

"Why's that?"

"My Aunt Patsy belonged to that organization. She was an artist and poet, and the Paint 'n Palette was probably one of the few social environments where she could express her artistic side. And…" with emotion in her voice Patrice struggled to finish the sentence, "I didn't come home for her funeral."

Glenn leaned in so he could hear the last part of her comment. He nodded in understanding and took her hand for a moment. "It's like this place was its own little Paris."

"All this history happened here, and I didn't have a clue," Patrice whispered softly.

"If neither your parents nor your sister were into Regional art, it only makes sense you wouldn't be. What *is* interesting is that you came to an interest in art at all," Glenn added.

"When I hear about the Depression, I just hear my parents recalling their early youth and how much families struggled. If I asked my dad what he remembers about Grant Wood during that time, he remembers the struggling artist who lived in a shack by the quarry not paying his bills."

"How did your dad know that?"

"Small community, local gossip."

"I'm sure there were people in the area who felt that attending an art colony was a waste of time and money during the Depression," Glenn said.

"In my research I have gotten a sense of two different perspectives. The art colony actually drew many people who needed that communal feeling during the Depression and inspiration. Then there is this other side my parents depict—a time of required hard work and struggle. Both sides just dealt with the Depression the best way they could."

"I think you're fortunate to know the different viewpoints shared in this area of the country, because it provides a richer, fuller perspective of that time period."

"How close are we to Stone City?"

"We're probably a mile or two at this point. We'd best be going if we're going to be home for dinner in time." Patrice found the Ridge Road and Glenn noticed the street sign.

"The Ridge Road as in *Death on the Ridge Road?*"

Patrice nodded.

"I see why they call this the Ridge Road. I can see valleys to the left and to the right."

"Stone City is the valley to your left. We'll go down this hill," Patrice said as she made a left turn with the car, "and you'll see one of the quarries to your right. The other quarries are tucked away around the bends of the river. If you were to place yourself in the painting of *Stone City*, right now you'd be in the upper right quarter of the painting."

The car came to the bottom of the hill and followed the curve of the road to the west. Patrice pulled the car over to the side of the road, reached into the backseat, and grabbed a tube. From it she pulled out the print of *Stone City*.

"I bought this print at the Grant Wood Store in Anamosa and I'm taking it home." She unrolled the print and pointed to the part of the painting where the two were parked.

"Like in a mall, where the mall directory says, 'You are Here,' this is where we're at on this painting."

She handed the 16" x 20" print over to Glenn and he examined it.

"So, the river is before us and the church is on the hill," he said as he looked up and caught a glimpse of the church.

"Yes, that's St. Joseph's."

"That's a beautiful church. I'm assuming it's Catholic. Is that right?"

"Yes, it's very natural in Iowa to find Catholic churches, not only in towns and cities, but in rural settings. We also have some monasteries between here and Dubuque on the top of some beautiful river bluffs. The location of the art colony is across the road from the church and out of view. So, basically, he painted this landscape from up there on the hill," Patrice said pointing to the *Stone City* print and then out her window toward a field that crested above the river.

"So, tell me how this town got its name. I guess it's obvious with the quarries here."

"There were originally about five limestone quarries at the turn of the twentieth century here and one has survived. The quarries had a booming business going until cement was introduced in the early 1900s. Weber Stone, which is to our right, is still in business. The signs at Anamosa's high school, the library, and other places around the area are made from this stone, as well as some of the fences. You'll be able to see the quarry better from on top of the hill to our left."

Patrice edged the car back onto the paved road. They crossed the Wapsipinicon River and continued west.

"Now, this is the same river that we saw at the cemetery in Anamosa?" Glenn asked.

"Yes, and we call it the Wapsi for short."

"Ah, you're letting me in on local-speak," Glenn said in mock seriousness.

"Yes, I've decided you'll become a native son, especially since you've revised our November issue to celebrate some of this."

"I stand behind what I said at lunch today. You even heard Anne say it: European art had an impact on the Regionalist's style of art. They knew they'd needed that experience on their résumés."

"I would agree with that," Patrice said.

"Now, the property which the mansion's foundation sits on is private property. There is a way up to the site if you want to take it. We're not really dressed to climb the hill, but I'm game if you are? It's worth it once we get up there."

"You promise we won't get arrested? That will be hard to explain on Monday afternoon at work."

Patrice gave Glenn a look of feigned disgust.

"Well, I didn't expect my boss to show up this week, and I also didn't expect my boyfriend to show up either." Patrice grinned at Glenn.

"Are you leaving yourself enough time to make this deadline?"

"I'll make it." Patrice was half convincing herself.

Patrice parked in the parking lot near St. Joseph's. "We'll have to do a little walking and I'm sure the locals will be wondering what's up with the two people walking along the side of the road, but when we get to the path up the hill, it's not near anyone's home."

"Okay, I'm trusting you."

Glenn looked out the window at St. Joseph's Roman Catholic Church. "This is really a beautiful church. It's made of the stone that was mined here in Stone City?"

Patrice nodded.

The church appeared to be one story but hidden against the hillside was a lower story that could only be seen from the valley road and river to the east. The church had an additional structure on the road- side, about four stories high, that served as a steeple. It had small architectural adornments dotting the top of its flat top. All the windows on the main floor and steeple were stained glass, the majority of them gothic in shape, except for the lower storied windows, which were rectangular and smaller.

"Have you ever been in this church?" Glenn asked.

"No. I don't think I even knew anyone who attended services here."

They got out of the car and Glenn walked toward the church.

Patrice was already crossing the road to what looked to be a fenced-in area of electrical lines.

"Glenn, the church is locked," Patrice yelled and gestured for Glenn to cross the road.

"I could really use some *cawffey* right now." Glenn called back.

Patrice heard the accent and even though Glenn was being a good sport, she was sure this had been a long day for him being part boss, part boyfriend.

"This probably seems strange, but at one time, a large opulent hotel with all the modern conveniences stood here. It was Columbia Hall." Patrice stood with her arms spread wide trying to give some lightness in the muggy heat of the late afternoon. "Stone City was like a mining town where the workers had everything they needed at their disposal: hotels, post office, stores, etc. I didn't know this until I started to do my research *and I grew up two miles from here!*"

"I think you're ready to give the tours for the art museum."

"Thank you," she mocked. "You wanted to get the gist of what this article could look like. Bear with me here."

"At this point, I truly think you have enough information for a book."

Patrice didn't hear Glenn's response as she was looking for a clearing in the tall grasses and started to ascend the hilly path.

"Wait up! How did you know this was here?" Glenn called now amazed to see a path before him. The path had been invisible from the road.

"From childhood."

"Now, who could have written this story any better than you?" Glenn was beginning to sweat. His knit shirt was not appropriate for this climb on a hot afternoon and Patrice had sympathy for him but knew he would rather have the chance to see the mansion ruins that remain sweat-free.

Patrice stopped to catch her breath and Glenn caught up with her. "We're on the grounds of what was Green Mansion. John Green was a quarry owner and built this house at the end of the 1800s. You can see remnants of his carriage house and servant quarters." Patrice pointed at various sections of the property. She pointed to two stone buildings that were barely standing.

She turned and continued the climb. The stone water tower was in view.

"What does Green Mansion have to do with the art colony?" Glenn asked.

"The art colony was on the grounds of John Green's property, and the classes were in the mansion. We're nearing the mansion now," she said over her shoulder. "That cylindrical building up at the crown of the hill was the water tower on site, and at the time of the art colony, the top of the water tower was an apartment for Adrian Dornbush. He climbed up to it using a ladder. The lower part of the water tower was where the students gathered. It was like a little bar and eatery where they'd hang out," Patrice said talking a mile a minute.

Patrice continued to climb until the land finally leveled out and the foundation of the mansion was in front of them.

Glenn walked up to the foundation and put his hand against the stone. "Where's the mansion?"

"Your hand is on what's left of it."

"So, I'm confused. This quarry guy's former house and farm was where the art colony was?"

"Yes, when his business collapsed at the turn of the century, he sold his land and the current owner only used the property as a summer home. That owner rented the land to Grant Wood and the other art directors for the art colony."

"Got it."

"I came up here with my Camp Fire Troop when I was about eleven years old. We had hiked from the neighboring town of Viola and followed the railroad tracks to get here. I think by following the railroad tracks we probably cut that trip down by half. That was my earliest memory of Stone City, and it also led to a chance meeting with Nan Wood Graham."

"You met her?" Glenn stared at her with this news.

"Yes."

"And you didn't tell me?"

"I was mad that you gave me this story."

"I could tell that you were skeptical about doing the story, but

173

I guess I didn't know you were that upset. You didn't say anything to me directly."

"I just felt this was a story for a junior writer because, as you now know, I undervalued this art." Patrice was tracing her fingers along the foundation.

"I gave you this story because you were the best one to write it!"

"And?"

Glenn approached Patrice. "And like I said the other night, I wanted to know more about who you are. My trip here was more spontaneous. I didn't plan that." Glenn paused. "We've been seeing one another for four years, yet I don't know a lot about your parents or your sister . . . or even about you—not this side of you, anyway. I like it."

He bent forward and grabbed both of her hands. He leaned forward and kissed her softly.

When their lips parted Glenn said, "I do love you and I do want a future with you."

"I want a future with you, too, Glenn. I just think there's a lot to work through."

"Where is this hesitancy coming from?"

"Think about it Glenn, you're my boss right now. We haven't shared that with very many people. Think of the office politics when we do. We need to resolve this. We've both been so busy we haven't really dealt with it."

"I think we're doing some of that now." Glenn let go of Patrice's hands.

"I know I haven't really shared any information about my past or my family with you, Glenn. I guess I didn't want to be judged on any of it." Patrice said putting her hands in her pockets.

"Coming back here was hard on me because I've always had to defend who I am, what I wanted and where I came from. That might be hard for you to understand. You grew up very differently. Do you know when I was about twelve years old, I found a pen pal in one of those kid's magazines. On the back of the magazine, kids would list their names and addresses offering to be someone's pen pal. I wrote to a girl on Long Island. After two letters she dropped me saying she didn't want a boring pen pal from a farm in Iowa. That's one of the many examples where I was made to feel ashamed of where I'm from. I was just a kid and somehow, I decided they were right so when I left here, I didn't want to look back. I didn't think I could handle it, if you judged me too."

Glenn turned and walked toward the decaying steps, which looked as if they might crumble at any moment and sat down carefully. "You know, I have some of the same worries you have."

Patrice walked toward him and sat down next to him. "What worries are those?"

"If you'll accept me," Glenn said looking at her matter-of-factly. "I'm not perfect. I know I work too much and get caught up in it all. But I think I want the same things as you," he said grabbing her hand in his. "I'd like to settle down, raise some kids, and still feel as if I'm doing something with my life. I wonder, too, if you'll embrace my family and their ways. I think about all that stuff."

"I'm glad you do because you're right, those are the things I worry about too. I often think I'll need to get a different job, and will you allow me to work if we get married and have kids. My career is important to me. I also struggle with knowing when to treat you as the editor and when to treat you as my boyfriend, and it seems strange to go home with *my superior* sometimes during the week night," Patrice broke the tension laughing.

Glenn hugged her and kissed her on the forehead, then pulled back to look at her directly. "So, can we work on this future of ours? Can we keep talking and sharing these types of things?"

"Yes, boss!" Patrice teased and hugged him back with a sense of relief. She had underestimated Glenn. He loved her unconditionally. Rose was right. This was a magical place.

CHAPTER 16

"You still haven't told me how you met Nan Wood Graham," Glenn inquired in his management-like tone.

"It was after my Camp Fire Girl walk to this location. Our leader asked us to make some drawings from our hike. There was a pedestal that stood right here." Patrice stood up and marked the spot with her foot. "On the top of this stone pedestal was a basket of fruit made from the same stone as the house, from the quarry below this hill. The pedestal was standing here all by itself. It seemed out of place and I connected to that. Well, that's one of the things I drew, and I entered those drawings in the *Grant Wood Art Festival* for my age division. It was the first year of the festival and Nan Wood Graham was back from California. She had been asked to be the Grand Marshal of the parade. I remember watching the parade from the sidewalk in Anamosa and seeing her in the Grand Marshall's convertible. She was waving to the crowd. I don't think I was clear about who Grant Wood was or who Nan was. I was eleven and the festival had a carnival in Anamosa and that's all I cared about. Anyway, our Camp Fire troop was required to meet back at the pavilion to see if we'd won any prizes. None of my drawings won a prize, but I saw Nan holding the drawing of the pedestal. My troop leader, Ellen, saw Nan holding my work and told me to walk up to her and ask if she liked my drawing. So, I did, and that's when Nan asked me how I came up with that drawing of the stone fruit pedestal. I told her about the hike to Green Mansion. I didn't know that the Green Mansion represented the *Stone City Art Colony* to her. I just remember she clasped her hand against her chest and complimented me on that drawing. My mother had walked up behind me, probably sensing her young daughter had no clue who she was talking to . . . and that's when Nan took a small item from her purse and placed that small gift in my hand and closed my fingers around that gift." Patrice was closing her hand with her fingers mimicking the gesture of that memory.

"What was it?"

"A brooch with a cameo face on it. I remember that Nan looked at my mother as if to say, 'Take good care of it,' because I remember looking up at my mother, who was nodding in understanding. I'd forgotten this until I came back, and my parents reminded me of this gift."

"You have a brooch from a very famous lady."

"I have *the* brooch that was in a very famous painting and used again in another painting."

"What?"

"I have the brooch that Nan wore in *American Gothic*. I have the brooch that Grant Wood's mother wore in *Woman with Plants*."

"Are you sure?" Glenn asked as if he could hardly believe what she was saying.

"As Anne mentioned today, Nan's estate went to the *Davenport Museum of Art*. I went to the museum on Thursday and asked if they had the brooch. They did not, and they are still waiting for the rest of her belongings to arrive at the museum. I'll follow up with them to see if they received one, but I don't believe they will. My brooch looks exactly like the brooch in those paintings."

"Why do you think she would part with that brooch?"

"I don't know. Maybe there are numerous reasons. Maybe my drawing made her think fondly of her brother. Maybe it made her reminisce about the art colony and a brief but very special time in her life. Or maybe she didn't have a female friend or relative to share something like that with." Patrice looked from the ground to Glenn, "Maybe . . . she was missing home."

"Wow. When did you realize you might have the brooch from *American Gothic*?"

"Not until this trip. My mother reminded me that I had the brooch. Then, when I was at the Grant Wood Store, they said the brooch should be with Nan's estate. When I asked about it at the *Davenport Museum of Art*, they believed it should be coming with her final things, but they hadn't seen it yet. They know it exists."

"That would be a wise thing to do," Glenn said pacing in front of her.

"What?"

"Double checking if they received it with her final belongings."

"I will, I promise."

"If it is the real deal, what are you going to do with it?"

"I haven't thought that far ahead, but let's keep it between us for now until we can figure this all out. I'll show it to you when we're at my parents' house. We should head back. We are trespassing you know?"

"This should be a state historical site, but until it is, let's get out of here." Glenn ushered Patrice down the hill.

Patrice and Glenn got back in the car and entered the road to leave Stone City.

"If you look behind you Glenn, out the back of the car's window, you will see your own rendition of *Stone City*. Grant painted it from the field that is to our left."

"Doesn't quite look the same but I get the gist of it."

"There's a lot of information about Grant Wood but not so much about Nan. What's your angle going to be for the story?"

"That's been the big struggle for me. That's why I've started to learn more about Grant's life. It gives me some insight into Nan's life. I've learned she was very dependent on him financially, even after she married, and because of that she became fiercely loyal to him, his work and his legacy."

Patrice made a right turn and headed west toward Viola. Both she and Glenn pulled down the window shades of the car defusing the bright sun from the western sky.

"If you look off toward the horizon, our farm is in view," Patrice said, pointing. "Can you imagine? I lived that close to Stone City growing up, and I never really thought anything about it."

"I like some of the terms I hear you say like *horizon*. I don't hear that word often in New York."

"Or cornfields. Or gravel roads."

"True."

"Actually, this used to be a gravel road. I'm enjoying the pavement. And see this hill we're descending? I saw a charcoal on brown paper tracing of this hill at the *Davenport Museum of Art*."

"Grant Wood's work?"

"Yes. I don't think I would have recognized it if he hadn't called it *Hill Near Viola*. I used to ride my bike on it."

"That's why you have great legs."

"Why, thank you," Patrice replied. "Glad you like my legs ... and other assets. Thanks for noticing," she teased.

"You're welcome. And, yes, I *have* noticed , repeatedly." Glenn shifted in his seat and pulled his damp shirt from his skin. "But if I don't stop thinking about your legs, I'll be even more overheated than I am now. As it is, I'd like to take a shower before we have dinner with your parents. That is, if there's time. I'm pretty sweaty from our little hike and the rest of the day's activities."

Glenn paused for only a moment before switching gears. "And speaking of today's activities, I'm still trying to grasp the fact that you are in possession of the brooch. Let's talk about that some more."

"Well, it's something that needs to be shared with others. I should probably give it to a museum. I have thought about loaning it to the *Cedar Rapids Museum of Art*."

"Why not Davenport?"

"Well, if I gave it to Cedar Rapids, it could be displayed near *Woman with Plants*, or I could give it to *The Art Institute of Chi-*

cago so it's near *American Gothic*. I'd like it to stay close to its original locale. I think Hattie and Nan would have liked that."

"Good."

"Viola is ahead, but it's hard to see through all the trees. Grant Wood brought his art colony students here to paint. They'd just pull over and enter someone's field with their paints and easels or sit on someone's front yard. I'm hoping he got permission from the farmers whose land they invaded, but I don't know that he did."

"Where did you find that out?"

"In Nan's scrapbooks at Davenport."

Patrice turned left, heading south on a gravel road. The car swayed across the loose gravel.

"Hey, stay on the road!" Glenn called out.

Patrice gave him a curious look. "You've never driven on a gravel road before have you?"

"No, this is my first time," Glenn said grabbing the door handle.

"Loose gravel does that. I'll slow down. Look at the dust the car is generating behind us."

Glenn looked in the side mirror toward the cloud of dust behind them that covered the view at the rear of the car.

"That's enough to force anyone off the road."

"Our farm is up here on the right." Patrice slowly drove past the sixty acres that her father had once owned.

"Your parents actually owned a level piece of property?"

"We did, and this was our house. This place was my dad's dream. He loved the hard work; I didn't," Patrice said as she slowed the car down further and came to a stop at the edge of the road.

They sat in silence. The farmhouse had been kept white with black shutters, just as it had been when Patrice was growing up. Flowers were planted along the driveway, which told Patrice that the current owners cared about their home. They still took care of the garden that her mother had nurtured.

"Remind me again, why did your parents move?" Glenn finally

asked.

"They planned to retire in town. When Jenny and I grew up and left home, there wasn't anyone here to really help them take care of it."

"Will I get to meet Jenny while I'm here?"

"I don't think so. She was just here this past week. She lives in Davenport, and that's about two hours away from here."

Patrice started the car and slowly pulled away from the side of the road. She came to a stop again pulling the car into a narrow strip of ground that served as the entrance to a cornfield.

"This will only take a minute," she said.

"What are we doing?" Glenn asked as Patrice slid out of the car, walked around it, and opened his door, motioning him to get out.

"Come on," Patrice coaxed.

Glenn got out of the car reluctantly.

"Are you wanting a picture or something?" he asked.

"That's actually a good idea. Come on."

Patrice grabbed his hand and pulled him into the cornfield.

"Now, take off your shoes and socks and take a walk into this cornfield."

Patrice was already pulling off her sandals. "Oh, this feels great!" she moaned in relief.

Glenn watched as Patrice sank her feet into the soft Iowa dirt.

"There's nothing like this black soil—anywhere." She said. "This is why Iowa can easily be the world's largest producer of food. It's this black soil and the humid climate."

"It feels like a *greenhouse* here," Glenn said, his voice lacking the deep appreciation that Patrice was hoping for.

"I know. Come on, take off your shoes."

"Okay, okay," Glenn said as he hesitantly removed his shoes and socks. Like a cautious child he dipped his foot onto the soil until he felt comfortable.

"Step out toward me. Give it a chance."

"More trespassing. Won't the neighbors shoot us for this?"

"What is it with you and trespassing?" Patrice volleyed.

"Well, among other things, it's against the law!"

"They'll remember me around here. It's all right," Patrice soothed.

"They'll remember you, but that doesn't mean there won't be consequences."

Patrice stepped toward Glenn. "Now, feel this corn leaf. You've never felt one before, right?"

"Right." Glenn appeased Patrice and bent over to feel the corn leaf and rubbed it between his fingers. "I wouldn't have guessed it has a scratchy feeling to it. I assumed it would feel more like plastic. Like the plants I know back in New York.

"This is the real deal!" Patrice chirped as she continued to stomp her feet in the dirt.

"Let's head to Cedar Rapids, Miss Lady of the Corn Cob. We're going to be late."

They both rubbed the dirt off the bottom of their feet.

"Here, wipe your feet in the grass." Patrice demonstrated what she meant. "It will wipe the dirt off."

Glenn mimicked Patrice.

From a distance, the landowner watched the couple in his field. He was relieved when they jumped back in the car and drove away. "Damn tourists," he muttered.

◆ ◆ ◆

Patrice called her mother from Glenn's hotel room as she waited for him to finish his shower.

"Patrice, you got a phone call late this afternoon. Someone named Dora called from Davenport and wants you to call her this evening if you could."

Patrice's mother rattled off the telephone number and Patrice scrambled to find a pen and paper to write it down.

"She said this is her personal number. I told her you wouldn't be back until this evening."

"Thanks, Mom. I'll call her from here, and we'll see you at

seven o'clock."

"What's going on?" Glenn asked.

Patrice turned to see him step out of the bathroom. One towel was draped around his hips and he was drying his hair with another.

"I got a call from Rose Boston's housekeeper."

"The artist in Davenport? You were supposed to tell me more about her."

"Another part of my research I need to share with you," Patrice replied. "I'll explain after I make this call to Dora." Looking him up and down, she raised her eyebrows and added, "But get into some clothes, will you, please . . . before I ask *you* to share more with *me*."

CHAPTER 17

Dora answered on the first ring.

"Patrice, thank you for returning my call so promptly. Rose would like to talk with you. She hopes you can return to Davenport tomorrow."

"Do you know what this is about?"

"Yes and no. All I know is that she urgently wants to talk with you, in person."

"I'll be there. What time?" Patrice replied.

"Will 9:00 a.m. work for you?"

"I'll make that work. And I'll see you then. Thank you."

Now Patrice was intrigued and turned to Glenn.

"I need to be in Davenport tomorrow. I'll have to fly back to New York on Tuesday."

"Patrice, your draft is due."

"I know. I'll stay up tonight and finish the draft. You can read it on the plane tomorrow."

"You're going to be up awfully late, so we'll make this time with your parents special, but we're going to have to make it an early night."

◆ ◆ ◆

They might have intended an early night, but Patrice had her doubts when she saw her sister's car in her parents' driveway. Her reaction was immediate and paradoxical. On the one hand, she was elated that her sister—and probably her sister's entire family—would be able to meet Glenn. On the other hand, it was going to be difficult to break away and work under the circumstances.

"We're here," she called as she opened the front door.

"Come on in," Martin Powell called from the living room.

Patrice and Glenn stepped in to see her nephew and brother-in-law approaching them.

"Hi, Tom. Hi, Mitch. Good to see you!"

Mitch walked over to his aunt and grabbed her hand. "We're here for dinner so we could see you."

Patrice bent down and gave him a hug. "That's so nice! Glenn, I want you to meet my nephew, Mitch, and my brother-in-law, Tom."

Glenn shook Tom's hand and then extended his hand to Mitch who grabbed it readily and shook it hard.

"How do you know my aunt?"

"We work together in New York," Glenn replied.

"And he's my boyfriend," Patrice added.

"Wow, that's cool. Mom, Aunt Patti is here," Mitch shouted not thinking about what his aunt had just told him.

The group left the entry and headed for the living room. Jenny and Renee joined them just as Martin was offering his hellos.

Patrice introduced Glenn to Jenny, and they exchanged greetings.

"The two of you look a lot alike," Glenn remarked.

"I'll take that as a compliment," Jenny said, eyeing Patrice.

"Mom, this is Aunt Patti's boyfriend!" Mitch exclaimed with the kind of glee reserved for those who believe they are divulging something surprising and wonderful.

"I'm aware of that," Jenny replied.

Mitch was undaunted and grinned up at her.

"All right, everybody, dinner is ready. Come into the dining room," Renee announced.

"Do I get a hug?" Tom said to Patrice.

"Of course."

As they hugged, Tom said, "Long time no see."

"I know."

"Can I sit by you Aunt Patrice?" Andrea asked.

"Yes, I would like that very much," Patrice answered.

The family headed for the dining room, but Patrice lingered to accompany her father, who was in the process of lifting himself out of his recliner.

She extended her hand to help him up and he accepted. He was still stronger than her and she planted her feet solidly on the floor for additional leverage. They giggled as he pulled himself up.

Patrice looked her father in the eye. "I love you, Dad."

"I love *you*, honey," he replied. He pulled her next to his chest and gave her a hug.

Patrice struggled to keep from crying as waves of emotion came to the surface. "Next time, it won't be so long between trips," she whispered.

"I'd like that." He gave his youngest daughter a big squeeze and released her.

Patrice wiped her eyes and the two joined the others in the dining room.

"Glenn, we hope you like steak," Jenny said as she brought out the main course. "This is some of the best there is in the country, good Iowa corn feed beef."

"I love steak."

"Well you get to pick the first piece," Jenny replied as she brought the platter of steak over to where Glenn was sitting.

Patrice watched as Glenn took the largest piece of steak from the platter. She noticed the grins on her family's faces as they watched his confidence in taking the largest piece. Glenn looked at Martin Powell to ensure it was okay to take the largest piece from the head of the family. Martin Powell grinned and nodded at Glenn to continue. Glenn beamed when he placed the juicy steak on his plate. Patrice realized that Glenn had paid her family the biggest compliment by accepting their hospitality and enjoying their company. Patrice squeezed Glenn's leg under the table and smiled at him. Glenn brought out the best in everyone and she was forever grateful.

"For dessert we have gooseberry pie, compliments of our neighbor Mrs. Kroft!" her mother beamed, and Patrice busted out laughing.

◆ ◆ ◆

True to her word, Patrice stayed up half the night to produce the first draft. She knocked on Glenn's hotel room door at 7:00 a.m. and handed him the paperwork.

"How late were you up?"

"Till about 3:00 a.m. I called the airlines this morning and changed my flight. Can we meet in the office tomorrow around 5:00 to finalize the story?"

"Sure, my flight isn't until 1:00 today, so I'll read your draft, add my notes, and drop this off at your parents' house before I head to the airport. You still haven't told me about Rose Boston and her husband."

"I've tracked down the last living students who attended the art colony. They are a married couple who met there. Her name is Rose Boston, and she's a well-known sculptress. Her husband, Ben, is one of the very last known Regionalists. They both knew Grant and Nan. Unfortunately, they are in poor health. I met them on Friday and talked mainly to Rose. She wasn't feeling very well, so I got what information I could. They've asked me back today. I don't know what it's about, but I'm going to find out."

"That's great. Is some of that conversation from Friday captured in this draft?"

"Yes."

"I look forward to reading it. By the way, I enjoyed dinner with your family last night."

"I could tell they enjoyed having dinner with you, too, *and* my sister seemed relieved that there's a man in my life."

Glenn laughed. "She took good care of me last night, making sure I had enough of that delicious steak and gooseberry pie."

"She knows a good man when she sees one," Patrice said with admiration.

Glenn gave Patrice a hug. "Don't stress too much over this story. You've got a very good basis to write from."

"Thanks honey." Patrice pulled back and put her hands on Glenn's face. She gave him an open-mouthed kiss that conveyed how much she would miss him even if it was for a day.

"Thank you!" Glenn said giving her one last kiss while dipping her dramatically toward the floor. She pulled away from the soulful kiss and said, "Walk me to the car?"

"Oh, you're so romantic." Glenn brought her back to her feet and opened the door to the hotel room. "After you my dear."

Patrice walked toward the door and affectionately slapped his buttocks and darted out the door.

CHAPTER 18

Patrice was in front of Rose's house at 8:55 a.m. The morning sun shone brightly on the door as she knocked, and Patrice saw the park reflected on the glass of the front door. She turned to look at the park. The bright morning sun found her eyes and she held her hand up to shield them. Past the park, in the distance, was the Mississippi River. It sparkled in the morning light like a diamond bracelet proudly casting its glimmer.

Dora opened the door, gave her a quick smile, and invited her in. Rose was sitting in the front sun room with the sun streaming through the windows and stopping at her feet. Patrice scanned the room but did not see any sign of Ben. Dora walked her over to where Rose was sitting. Rose extended her hand toward the small chair with the white seat cushion that was embroidered with red roses and Patrice sat down.

"Rose, it's lovely to see you again. Thank you for inviting me back. How are you?"

"I'm in better health this weekend. I thought this would be a good day to continue our conversation. How's your story coming?"

"I finished the first draft last night."

Patrice looked at Rose's frail body, her hands clasped in front of her and her head tremor subtle but apparent.

Rose asked, "Who did you say you write for?"

"I write for *European Art* magazine in New York City. I was given the assignment to come home and write about Nan Wood Graham's death. Even though I grew up here, I didn't know very much about Grant or Nan. If you don't mind, I'll take notes. Is that all right with you?"

Dora was standing behind Patrice and Patrice turned to see Dora's nod of approval when Rose answered, "Yes."

"When I talked with you the other day, I didn't know whether to trust you," Rose admitted. "I wanted to understand what your intent was. Dora assures me your intent is honest and true."

"I can understand why. My notification and request were very last minute." Patrice realized that if she had asked to tape the conversation during her first visit, she probably would have been turned down. "You must have many people wanting to interview you and learn about your life." Patrice said. "I can understand how tiring that might be. I'm appreciative that you took the time to see me and called me here today."

It struck Patrice that an interview style of questions and answers might not be appropriate. She had a hunch that Rose wanted to share something with her. Patrice forfeited the idea of a tape recorder. It just didn't seem appropriate.

"Shall we get started?" Patrice looked from Dora to Rose. Both nodded their heads. Before she could write down the name of the interview and purpose, Rose began to talk.

"I told you that I went to the art colony, thanks to my father, who encouraged my art. The first summer there I often went to the quarry like the rest of the students, to ask for limestone to carve from. The men at the quarry were nice and helped me carry that heavy limestone up the hill to the mansion grounds. I'd sit outside, usually on the north side of the mansion in the shade, chiseling away at that limestone. This was during the Depression and my father was making good money working at a foundry here in Davenport. I wanted to return the next summer and made plans."

Rose concentrated on her breathing before moving on.

"I was fortunate that my father funded many of my interests.

I was also enrolled at St. Ambrose College for the fall. I wanted to be an art teacher. The next year the economy continued to take a toll in Davenport. My father lost his job and my parents were struggling to make ends meet. I knew if I wanted to return to the art colony, I was going to have to come up with that money myself. I had heard about an art professor at St. Ambrose College, Dr. Gray, who was a friend of Grant's and a supporter of the art colony. I contacted him and asked about ways to earn money for my attendance. I had remembered that Grant had given Ben a job in exchange for his attendance and I asked about something similar for me. Dr. Gray thought they could work something out. In fact, he was asked to teach at the colony. He said he would personally pay my wages in return for some work. It wasn't until later that I realized that he wanted me to model nude for his figure drawing class at the colony."

Rose paused and studied Patrice's face before continuing.

"I knew that the great artists in Europe painted nudes and thought nothing of it. I wanted to go to college and complete my teaching certificate, so I decided to do it."

"Did you tell your parents?" Patrice asked.

"All they knew was that I had a job as a teacher's assistant that summer in return for the cost of attending the colony."

Patrice wondered why Rose was going into this private detail.

"The first year of the colony was the first time I had met Grant. I was in awe of him. This colony was his dream. Grant was regionally known at the time, and as we know today, he completed his best work when he returned home from Europe and people started to take notice."

Rose slowly started to reach for her water. Dora helped her tuck the glass in her hand and watched as she swallowed the cool liquid.

"When I first saw Grant that summer, he was wearing his signature overalls. This surprised me. When I had seen him before, he had worn clothes purchased while studying in Europe and usually looked quite dapper. He was quiet and didn't say much. He was like a father figure to all of us, though, and ensured we all had a safe place to learn and sleep."

Patrice glanced at Dora, who seemed captivated by a story she had evidently never heard.

"Where did the students stay?" asked Patrice.

"Some women lived at the home of a quarry magnate by the name of Bryce Ronen. They were a nice Irish family and wanted to bring culture to the area. Others stayed on the top floor of the mansion."

"Where did the male students live?"

"It was the Depression and Grant was looking for ways to help these artists afford the colony's tuition. He got the idea to order ice wagons from an ice company in Cedar Rapids. The men lived in them and camped near the river by Ronen's quarry. That worked quite well. Ben's sleeping quarters were in Grant's ice wagon."

Patrice smiled at the thought of the two men sleeping bunk over bunk in a narrow ice wagon.

"What kind of classes did the art colony offer?" Patrice asked. She knew the answer but wanted to understand if Rose had anything different to offer.

"Grant taught advanced painting and if I remember correctly, there were classes in frame making, drawing, sculpture, along with lectures on art. Both Grant or Marvin Cone would take the students out for the day and they would comb the countryside for different settings to paint or draw."

"Why Stone City?" Patrice asked.

Rose grew starry eyed. "It was a magical place, Patrice. It had a feeling of past grandeur, a lingering sense of opulence that the Depression was stripping from us."

"How did the local people hear about the colony and what did they think about it?"

"They heard about it in the newspapers and through word of mouth. Some were excited about it and some thought it was a waste of time. Come to think of it, that's probably why Grant wore overalls. He was trying to help the locals feel at ease."

"Did you ever meet his sister Nan?"

"I was waiting for this question."

Patrice was surprised at Rose's response. Rose was looking at her squarely in the eye.

"Yes, she was a lovely girl, and much younger than Grant. She visited her brother often. They were very close." Rose didn't take her eyes off Patrice.

"I read he started painting *American Gothic* at the art colony. Did you see him painting it? Did you see Nan posing?"

Rose became very quiet and looked downward as if deep in thought. She looked up at Patrice, then Dora. She took a slow breath in and said, "Grant wanted to capture the daily struggle of the Depression in his art. He approached me to pose for a portrait. He wanted a portrait of a young girl and her father." Rose slowly lifted her hands to her cheeks as if remembering a younger version of herself. "Grant decided that the face for the father should be another student, Ben Boston."

"Your husband," Patrice said, surprised.

"Yes, but we weren't married then."

Rose folded her hands and placed them back on her lap. Patrice realized these body gestures were signs of Rose's medical condition. She was certain that Dora was alert to the same gestures and movements.

"We posed for that painting over a period of two weeks. Grant usually drew the outline first before he applied paint. He labored over this painting longer than usual." Rose paused and rested. Dora and Patrice remained patient. "Grant had given me a brooch to wear with the dress I wore in the painting. It had been his mother's and it had great value to him."

Patrice grabbed the neckline of her own summer blouse listening intently.

"I think Grant had developed a little crush on me. But by that time, I had fallen for Ben and he had become my lover. Grant found out and near the completion of the portrait, he asked for the brooch back. I knew that was his way of showing his disappointment."

Rose paused again. Patrice waited patiently for her to say

more. "Did you give the brooch back to Grant?"

"I did."

"Did you know what he did with the brooch?"

"No. I assumed he kept it."

Rose hadn't addressed Patrice's question about whether she had seen Nan posing for *American Gothic*. She decided she would come back to that. Patrice was concerned that Rose would grow tired so continued with her list of questions.

"Why did the art colony only last two years?"

"It was the combination of things, financial issues, pressures from local citizens , and finally a fire in the mansion destroyed the vision of this colony."

"There was a fire?"

"Yes." Rose's eyes grew wide with emotion. "I was living in the mansion that summer because Professor Gray had given me a room to myself, something he promised my parents who were concerned about their only daughter living away from home. I was naïve and didn't understand what that implied in the minds of the other women at the colony."

"One night, Ben snuck into my room to see me. We were still awake when we smelled smoke. We opened the door and saw smoke coming from the stairwell. We followed the others to the back stairway, knocking on doors making sure people were awake and getting out of the mansion. I knew that Grant had our completed painting in his office and had stored it behind his desk. I wanted that painting and didn't want to lose it in the fire. I ran into the office and grabbed it. There was so much confusion that night no one knew I even had it in my hand. Grant had been down by the river with some of the students when the fire happened. At first, we thought the fire was started by some of the locals. Some didn't approve of the "shenanigans going on" at the mansion, which included my nude modeling. Tensions over the summer had been building among the faculty too. We couldn't prove anything, though."

"Eventually, we found that the fire started in the fireplace in the first-floor parlor. Grant's office was just behind that fireplace, and the fire destroyed most of the items in his office. It was the beginning of the end for the art colony and it did not open the following summer. I heard later that Grant thought he had lost the painting of Ben and me in the fire. It wasn't until a year later that I realized he had repainted our portrait. Only this time, he had Nan and a dentist friend pose for the painting. As you know, it is a very famous painting today."

Patrice was trying to absorb all that she had just heard. Her voice was soft and low when she said, "And *you* could have been the face that made American history." Patrice looked from Rose to Dora. She could tell that Dora was just as startled as she was.

"It wasn't meant to be," Rose said, breaking the silence, "and I've never told a soul." Her voice drifted off with her thoughts.

"I say this respectfully, Rose, but why should I believe that you and Ben were the original faces in *American Gothic*? And why are you telling this story now?"

Patrice wrung her hands in a state of confusion. If this story was true, how could she prove it? And who would believe this story, coming as it did from an eighty-four-year-old woman who was not in a state of good health?

Rose answered, "Because Nan was my friend, and now that she is gone, Ben and I are the last survivors who attended the colony. We kept in touch with some of the other students until they passed on." Rose studied Patrice's face and said, "Follow me, dear," and asked Dora to push her wheelchair toward the back of the room.

They entered the room where the Russian icons hung and there was a door to the back of the room that Patrice hadn't noticed before. Dora opened the door and pushed Rose's wheelchair through the opening and Patrice followed. The walls in this room were higher and Patrice assumed this was an extension added to the house. The windows were close to the ceiling, so the interior walls were mainly painted dry wall covered with Ben's paintings and shelves holding Rose's sculptures and some of her original casts.

Patrice soaked in all the beauty of this art studio. Then she spotted Ben standing in the corner near his easel. He turned toward them as if finally noticing they were there.

Rose's voice carried great pride as she said, "Ben still paints. He enters local art festivals every year."

On the widest wall was an oblong wood structure with a mural on it. The mural was of snowcapped mountains. Rose nodded toward it. "That mural is what's left of Grant and Ben's ice wagon."

Patrice walked over to it with her mouth gaping open. She recognized it from the photos and article in Nan's scrapbook.

"I can't believe you have this!"

"Grant didn't want it," Ben replied.

"This is so beautiful," Patrice said, keeping her eyes on the mural. "In my research I saw pictures of this ice wagon mural and read this mountain scene was based on Grant's visit to Estes Park, Colorado. Is that accurate?"

Ben nodded.

"Can you bring out the painting, dear?"

Patrice whispered, "What?"

Ben gazed from Rose to Dora to Patrice. Patrice caught his startled look and couldn't quite decipher what it was all about.

"It's time dear," Rose said with a loving smile.

He reached behind the ice wagon mural which appeared to be a false front to another panel right behind it. He carefully pulled out something wrapped in brown paper. Dora went over to help him remove the wrap of paper from what appeared to be a painting. He turned it around for Patrice and Rose to look at. It was a rendition of *American Gothic* with a young Rose and Ben. Rose was wearing the cameo brooch. Patrice stared at the painting. In her own state of disbelief, Dora helped Ben hold the painting.

Rose looked over to Patrice and said, "You see, I didn't want to dishonor Nan. When she visited the art colony, she made an effort to talk with me and the other students. She befriended me at the art colony when other women shunned me and didn't want to talk with someone who modeled without their clothes on. I wanted her to believe that she was the original face in *American Gothic*, not me. I loved her that much."

Patrice grasped the significance of the moment and cupped her mouth. Her heart was racing, and her face was flushing. Dora and Ben placed the sixty-year-old portrait on another wood easel in the room.

Patrice's hand had moved from her mouth to her heart. "Do you know what this means to the art world today?" Patrice said, wide-eyed, looking from Rose to Ben.

"Yes, we do," Rose replied, smiling. "You will write the story about Nan's death, but I also hope you will someday write about *this* story. Who could understand it better than someone who knows art and is a writer from Iowa?"

◆ ◆ ◆

The story of Nan's death was written. Patrice gazed out the airplane window with a heavy heart. Iowa was slipping behind her as the plane made its ascent into the clouds. She thought of the tearful goodbye from her mother. Her father did not shed a tear, but his silence and hunched body told Patrice he was struggling with their goodbye. Patrice had promised to return home for Christmas and she vowed to make that happen.

The Mississippi was now below her and her thoughts raced back to Rose and Ben. Less than twenty-four hours earlier, she had been standing in their studio as they revealed a long-held secret. The painting was pretty good. So good that Patrice knew Grant had intended it to be a masterpiece. His signature "Wood" in the lower right-hand corner and the date appeared to be authentic. The painting of Ben as the farmer with the pitchfork mirrored Dr. Byron McKeeby's expression in *American Gothic.* What was different was Rose's pose. Her face revealed more of a smile than Nan's pout in *American Gothic*. Patrice wondered if Grant had posed Nan that way purposefully, because of his disappointment in Rose for not returning his affection.

◆ ◆ ◆

Patrice was in the office before 5:00 p.m., final copy in hand.

Glenn lit up as she approached.

"Hi, welcome back!"

"Thank you," she replied. "It's good to be back, and I have to say, I enjoyed my time in Iowa. Oh, and I got your mark-ups and implemented those but made some adds to the story. Take a look."

"Let's see what you have here." Glenn took the paper from Patrice's hand and leaned back in his chair and read.

Patrice watched him as he carefully read the words on the page.

"I think this is good to go to print. You bring a Midwestern feel to this story; nice job. Were your parents sad to see you go?"

"Yes. Mom was in tears," Patrice said in a soft voice.

"How about you?"

"I have to admit, I was struggling with saying goodbye," Patrice bit her lip and looked away for the moment.

"Well, go ahead and submit your story. Then go home and get some rest."

"Thanks, Glenn."

Patrice rose from the chair. She had so much more to tell Glenn but knew he had deadlines to grapple with before the night was over. Before she walked out, she turned to him and smiled, "Would you have time for a late-night dinner or drink?"

"I would."

"Then I'll see you at my place at 8:00. I have another story to share with you that will be an exclusive just for *European Art* magazine."

"Don't leave me hanging, tell me now --."

Patrice had already stepped out and shut the door.

◆ ◆ ◆

Fall in New York was beautiful. What it lacked in autumn scents, it always made up for with a pallet of soft rusts, sage greens and deep golds. These were colors she saw on the sidewalks as New Yorkers dressed to the hilt in the latest line-up of fall fashion. Patrice was watching the colorful catwalk from her cab heading to Central Park. When she was three blocks from her destination, she asked the cab driver to pull over and let her out. She wanted to walk. With her jeans tucked into her boots, she wrapped her camel colored jacket around her slim waist and adjusted her scarf. It was cool, but she knew the walk would warm her up. Being near the park, she could see others had the same idea—to feel the sunshine on their backs and enjoy the last days of a warm fall. The walk took away some of the anxiety she was feeling. She stuffed her hands in her pockets and imagined what the afternoon would be like.

She climbed the steps of The *Metropolitan Museum of Art* and slipped into the front doors. She had arrived an hour early. This place had been her New York refuge, a place that provided seclusion from a world that was often hectic and moved so fast. Art was lasting, stable, and durable. It captured moments, people and silhouettes that only the eye could see or hold on to for brief periods of time. When Patrice craved those qualities and circumstances, she found herself in the museum.

Patrice showed her membership card to the staff member behind the desk and was granted entrance. She took a museum map, opened and scanned it quickly to search for an area of the museum she had rarely frequented—the American Artists section—shown on the main floor in the west wing. She felt her adrenalin rise as she walked into the area. She wanted some time alone with it, to reconnect her feelings with the masterpiece, a piece she used to make fun of and laugh at. *Would it be different this time?*

She walked past other American artwork, past *The New Bonnet* by Francis William Edmonds and *Fur Traders Descending the Missouri* by George Caleb Bingham. She continued, rounding a second corner, and then she saw it. It was at the end of the cove opposite her. The cove was dimly lit, and Patrice stopped in her tracks. Those in the cove looked over at her and followed her gaze to *Stone City*, on loan from the *Joslyn Art Museum*.

Patrice stared at the piece. It shimmered under the lighting, much like the shimmer she had seen rise off the Mississippi. She walked toward the painting like a bride walking to the altar. She took in all the familiarity of the painting. She was intimate with this place twenty years ago and now today. For her, *Stone City* was, for the most part, timeless.

She concentrated on the billboard in the lower right-hand corner of the painting. And for the first time, she could read what was printed: *it satisfies*. No print of this painting had ever picked up that inscription on the small billboard. A tear rolled down Patrice's cheek. When the tear reached her chin, more tears followed.

With thoughts of her Uncle Gary, Patrice walked out of the museum and into the fall sunshine, stopping to sit on one of the museum's large steps. She pulled a small compact from her purse and checked her make-up. She had some mascara smudged, but nothing she could not fix with some Kleenex she had stashed in her purse. She had guessed she would feel differently about that painting than she had in the past, and she did. The emotional release of tears told her more--that her love for art actually started when she stared at that print every day in the family's living room back in Iowa.

Patrice peered at her watch. It was 1:50 and she was anxious to get the afternoon on its way. She pulled out her lip gloss and applied the first stroke.

"You're beautiful, just as you are."

There, standing above her, was Jenny, wearing a pair of brown corduroy slacks with a tan raincoat.

"You made it! Welcome to New York." Patrice stood and gave her sister a long hug.

Jenny held on tight and said in Patrice's ear, "I'm overwhelmed by this place, but I love it, all at the same time."

"There's nothing like it! What did Tom and the kids say when you told them you were coming?"

"They were supportive, as always. Mom drove to Davenport to be with the kids and that's helping Tom out. I'm ready if you are. I hope you know what you're doing because I'm going to take your lead," Jenny said giving her sister another half-hug.

"I'm nervous," Patrice confided, "but I'm also excited."

With that, Patrice guided her sister to the front entrance of the museum.

"This museum is one of the main reasons I applied at *European Art* magazine. When I was in school, I'd often spend time here. I didn't grow up thinking I was an art lover, but this place changed me."

Jenny did not comment.

"Our meeting isn't until 3:00, but I asked you to come earlier so we could take some time to walk through the museum."

Patrice ushered Jenny through the entrance desk, paid her fee, showed her membership card again, and led Jenny toward the American Artists wing. She caught the reflection of her sister's face in a glass case, and she could see Jenny taking it all in.

"*George Washington*," Jenny said, her voice a mingling of surprise and awe.

"Yes, by Gilbert Stuart."

"I've seen this picture in books and magazines so many times that I can hardly believe I'm seeing it for real."

Patrice watched Jenny as she moved in to get a closer look at the painting.

"Make sure you don't touch anything. You'll have guards pulling you away before you can say Valley Forge."

"I know, I know," Jenny said in a distinct voice. "Wow."

"You sound the way I did ten years ago."

"To know this actually exists . . . well, it's mind-boggling . . .

and so beautiful."

"It is."

Jenny turned and caught her breath. She looked at Patrice and then moved toward a display. "Hey, *The Midnight Ride of Paul Revere*. They own a Grant Wood painting?"

"Yes. He did pretty well, don't you think?" Patrice whispered and walked toward Jenny.

"Sorry, I'm getting loud, aren't I?"

Patrice nodded, but also gave her sister a smile to let her know she understood.

"Oh, look Patrice," Jenny whispered. "This is a dedication to the four Regionalists." Jenny was moving from painting to painting like a point guard in a basketball game. "Here are paintings by John Steuart Curry, Thomas Hart Benton, and Edward Hopper. I love Benton's *July Hay*."

"Did you know, Curry, Benton, and Wood all studied at *The Art Institute of Chicago*?"

"I didn't know that; I'm learning a lot from you."

The sisters stood in front of the display commenting on all they had learned since the previous June.

"I guess we're not laughing anymore?"

"I think the laugh is on us," Patrice replied.

"Is this what you wanted me to see?"

"Actually, follow me."

Jenny followed Patrice, weaving in and around the numerous visitors to the museum. Patrice summoned her sister into the cove of the American Artists.

"Look."

Jenny followed Patrice's pointed finger and placed her eyes on *Stone City*.

"Oh, Patrice. It's the real deal isn't it? Not a print like we see back home?"

"The real deal."

Jenny stood transfixed while Patrice spoke to the detail and meaning behind the painting. Others began to edge closer to them, listening to Patrice's monologue about the work.

"Just think, Patrice, this is where we're from and it's displayed in a New York museum!"

"I know. Pretty wonderful, isn't it?"

"Did you say it's on loan from the *Joslyn Art Museum*? Where's that?"

"Omaha."

"Oh, not in Iowa?" Jenny asked.

"No."

"I guess I always thought it was in Cedar Rapids or Des Moines."

"The *Joslyn Art Museum* in Omaha is highly respected, and they know a great painting when they see one," Patrice said expecting Jenny to laugh but she didn't.

"So, we're talking to the experts today?"

"Yes, it's about 3:00. We should head to our meeting," Patrice declared.

"Lead the way!"

Patrice led Jenny to an elevator. "We're heading to the ground floor. By the way, how was your flight?"

"Flying through Chicago was a zoo, but other than that, it was fine. I had my overnight bag shipped to your workplace, just like you said so I can meet you here at the museum. Did you get it?"

"I did, and it's back at my apartment," Patrice replied. "Based on your schedule, my schedule, and this meeting, I didn't want you to worry about it. Here we are."

"Who are we going to see?" Jenny asked.

"A conservationist of sorts." Patrice found the room and knocked on the door. A woman in a white lab coat appeared. Patrice guessed her age to be about 25 years old.

"Can I help you?"

"Hello, I'm Patrice Powell and this is my sister, Jenny Coulson. We have a meeting with David Brooks."

"Yes, follow me."

Patrice and Jenny followed the small woman toward the back of the room and saw an office sign near the door that read "David Brooks."

The woman knocked on the open door and said, "David, you

have someone here to see you."

"Hi," Patrice said poking her head into his open office, "I'm Patrice Powell."

"Come in," came the reply as a tall and rugged looking man came from around the large oak desk, peeled off a plastic glove, and extended his hand to Patrice. "I'm David Brooks."

"Nice to meet you. This is my sister, Jenny Coulson. She flew here from Iowa to meet with you as well."

"Very nice to meet you, Jenny. Here, take a seat."

David Brooks pulled out a chair for each sister and sat on the edge of his desk. His eyes had creases on the outer corners and his forehead had the start of numerous wrinkles as if he had put considerable time and thought into his life's work.

"Tell me how you came across this painting."

"I work for *European Art* magazine, here in New York, and we were doing a feature on the European influence of American art. About that time, we heard about the death of Nan Wood Graham, and my editor sent me to Iowa to do a story about her. Through my research, I found a couple living in Iowa who knew Nan, and I interviewed them. It was that interview that led to this painting. Before I sent it to you, we secured the permission of the owners to ship it here to authenticate it."

"Where was the painting found? In the owner's attic?"

"Sort of."

"Sort of?"

"Let's say they didn't think about it for a long time, and the opportunity to present it ... well ... presented itself."

"Which is recently? Did they show it to you when you interviewed them?"

"Yes. Of course, you can see that it replicates *American Gothic*," Patrice pushed.

"Yes. It's quite remarkable, actually."

"The owners, a man and wife, knew Grant Wood and posed for this painting in 1932. He painted this prior to the *American Gothic* we know today."

David Brooks stood up, his hand on his chin, and walked to the back of his desk. "Can you prove this painting you shipped to me was finished in 1933?"

"Yes."

"How? It won't be enough for the art community to just see his name on that painting. It will forever be questioned as a forgery."

"Grant Wood always took a picture of himself with his paintings in order to prove he was the artist. It was his way of copyrighting his paintings." Patrice looked at Jenny and back at David Brooks.

"Go on."

"Well, the summer of 1932, he opened an art colony in Stone City, Iowa. He traced the image of his painting in pencil before applying the paint and oils. He finished the penciling of the portrait the first week of July in 1932. He used the drawing as part of an oil painting class he was teaching and began painting it in class that same summer, to showcase his technique. He didn't finish it that summer. The art colony closed mid-August, so he made the decision to complete it the following summer, 1933."

David Brooks took a seat behind his desk and leaned back in his chair. "Even if the owners have the picture of the painting with Grant Wood, the value of the painting would increase if it can be proven it was painted before 1934. Wood only signed his last name to his paintings and even with authenticating the painting it would help an auction house to have additional proof of the timing."

Patrice saw Jenny nervously twisting the strap of her purse and when Jenny looked at Patrice her face read, *I hope to God you have the answer for this.*

"The proof is in where the picture was taken. It was taken in front of the mansion where the art colony classes were held and where some of the students stayed. The mansion is called Green Mansion, and it is well known in that part of Iowa."

"And?"

Patrice knew that David Brooks was a man who had learned to be dubious. She was sure that Jenny sensed it to.

"In the summer of 1933, Grant Wood finished this painting in July, and the picture was taken that same month in front of the mansion. In early August of 1933, that mansion burned to the ground. *American Gothic*, the painting we know today, was finished in 1934, and the picture of Grant in front of *American Gothic* was taken at 5 Turner Alley, his art studio in Cedar Rapids."

"Do you have the picture with you?"

"I have a copy of it." Patrice pulled the picture from her purse and handed it to the conservationist.

David Brooks looked at the picture, unmoved, and handed it back to Patrice.

"Why didn't the painting get damaged in the fire?"

"The painting was in Grant's office the night of the fire. He was preparing to enter it at the Iowa State Fair. After the fair, he planned to give it to the woman that posed for it."

"How do you know that?"

"This is what the owners shared with me."

"He was just going to *give* it to the woman?"

"Yes."

"I don't believe that. A starving artist during the Depression wouldn't just give his paintings away."

"Grant often gave his paintings away or gave them away in return for his own room and board. This was not an uncommon practice of his," Patrice said firmly.

"Who rescued the painting from his office so it wouldn't burn in the fire?"

"The current owners."

"Did they tell Grant Wood that they had the painting?"

"No."

"Why not?"

Patrice remained calm. "It's a private matter."

"A private matter?"

"Yes, and it's not for me to tell."

David Brooks got up from his chair and looked out the window.

"The point is, the painting was saved from the fire," Patrice added. "Grant Wood did not know it was saved and, therefore repainted it—only this time, Nan Wood Graham and Dr. B.H. McKeeby were his chosen subjects for *American Gothic*."

"And I assume the owners didn't say anything because they had *stolen* the painting."

"It's not like that."

The conservationist turned toward Patrice. "So why did the owners feel the need to share this with you, and why did they allow you to ship something like this, thousands of miles to New York?"

"Because they trust my sister," Jenny retorted.

Patrice said, "Both are artists and they are entering their nineties. Time is precious. I offered to bring it to The Metropolitan partly because I live in New York and, partly, because I know your background."

"You know my background."

"I know you come from a family of conservationists who have restored great art and your family owns an auction house here in New York. You were a guest lecturer in one of my art history classes at Columbia. You talked about your family and some of your favorite American artists, and one of them was Grant Wood."

"You remembered all that?"

"Yes, *Dr.* Brooks."

"You took a great chance to have this painting shipped here. What if something had happened?" he scolded.

"Well, we insured it for the trip and my sister," Patrice looked at Jenny, "made sure it got here safely."

"That's never enough for something like this."

"And I left collateral."

"What do you mean?"

"Yes, what do you mean?" Jenny echoed and shot Patrice a quizzical look.

"Let's just say I have something valuable that the owners have access to in case something happens to this painting."

Dr. Brooks sat down and put his elbows on the desk, his head now in his hands.

Patrice asked, "So can I ask your help in authenticating this painting? You know the auction house world here in New York and I know you're well connected."

"Yes."

"When can we start?"

"In the next couple of weeks."

"Thank you, Dr. Brooks. Can we see the painting before we go?" Patrice asked.

"Thank you for keeping it for us. Will you keep it locked up, so nothing happens to it?" Jenny chimed in.

"Yes, it's in the lab next door and this lab is secured. Only three of us have permission and access to work with it. I need you to wear gloves and a mask over your mouth. Please do not touch the painting. The gloves will keep the oils from your hands away from it."

Brooks handed Jenny and Patrice each a pair of gloves and a mask while escorting them to the painting. It was on a table, covered with a light cream-colored dust cloth. The other conservationist standing near the table took her cue from Dr. Brooks and lifted the dust cloth from the painting. Jenny and Patrice scrutinized the painting carefully.

"Do the faces look familiar?" Patrice asked, smiling at Jenny through the mask.

"Somewhat."

Patrice looked at Dr. Brooks, "Here's my card. I look forward to your call in a couple of weeks."

Dr. Brooks walked Patrice and Jenny to the door. "We'll be in touch."

The sisters thanked their host and left the museum.

"You did great in there. He started drilling you, but you seemed unfazed," Jenny said.

"I'm sure he's worked with all kinds of people making claims that they have some rare painting. That's why I had to pick someone who had some emotional ties to this work. Plus, his reputation precedes him."

"Do you think he believed you?"

"I do. His questions suggested that he is looking for additional ways to authenticate the work. I have a feeling he'll want to come out to Iowa to meet the Bostons. Are you hungry?"

"Famished," Jenny said.

"Let's get a cab and I'll take you out for dinner at one of my favorite spots. We can finish talking there."

"Sounds good," Jenny said eagerly.

Patrice took Jenny to Joey's, an Italian Restaurant in midtown, one of the places that she and Glenn often frequented when they wanted good food and relaxation.

"I love their marinara here," Patrice said, browsing the menu. "Even though I eat here about once a month, I still love to look at all the things on the menu."

"I hope you're buying, these prices are outrageous. I can cook this for one sixth of the price."

"Jenny, it's my treat. I can't thank you and Tom enough for the help with the Bostons. Their housekeeper, Dora, told me how much she enjoyed meeting you."

"They were very nice. Do you know how well known they are in Davenport? I had to pinch myself just to believe I was in their house. I couldn't wait to tell Tom and the kids all about it. Oh, Patrice, I can't decide what to have. Can you just order for me?"

"Sure, I'd like you to try the gnocchi."

"The what?"

"Their potato noodle," Patrice giggled.

"Oh, okay."

"I'll order a sausage for you too; would you like that?"

"It wouldn't offend you to have a sausage at the table?" Jenny teased.

"No, Glenn does it all the time."

Their waiter approached the table with some house wine.

"Yes, thank you," Patrice said with a nod.

"I'll have some too, she's buying," Jenny added.

Patrice ordered the gnocchi for the two of them and the sausage link for her sister, along with house salad.

Patrice held up her wine glass. "To my lovely sister. I couldn't have done it without you!"

"Hear, hear."

They touched wine glasses. Patrice consumed a mouthful, watching her older sister delicately sip hers. Across the room, musicians were pulling their instruments out of their cases. Jenny and Patrice watched as the musicians joked with the wait staff.

"They play music here too?"

"They do. You'll love it. They mainly play string instruments. Between their music and this wine, you'll sleep like a baby tonight."

Jenny grinned, "We'll see about that. Hey, I want to get back to our conversation before we grabbed the cab. I have some of the same questions that Dr. Brooks asked like, why have the Bostons kept this hidden for so long? Does the painting really belong to them?"

"They saved it from Grant Wood's office when the Green Mansion was burning," Patrice replied.

"But isn't that stealing."

"From a certain point of view, I suppose. They did have every intention of giving it back after the fire, but Rose was a little shy to talk to Grant because she didn't return his affections. They both remembered Grant saying that he would give it to Rose eventually. Rose also told me that she overheard Grant saying he was going to paint another one, but this time, Nan would be the one posing as the daughter."

"Why wouldn't Grant just ask Rose and Ben to do it again?"

"This part stays between us Jenny," Patrice said, then took another swallow of wine. "When the Bostons were at the art colony, they were not married. In fact, they were both struggling to make the tuition. Grant invited them to pose for the painting and it took some of the cost off their room and board. Rose was also posing for the life drawing class."

"When you say posing for a life drawing class, what are you

saying?"

"She posed in the nude."

"What?"

"It was the Depression. I'm sure a lot of strange things happened during the Depression in eastern Iowa."

"Oh, my."

"Over the course of time, Rose and Ben fell in love. It was the second summer when they revealed their love affair, and Grant was not pleased."

"Because he liked Rose."

"Yes, and that's why Rose and Ben were afraid to tell him they had the painting. They believed he was going to sell it at the Iowa State Fair. After the fire, when they overheard him say that he was going to repaint it and ask Nan to pose, they decided not to say anything about having the original painting."

"Wow."

"Rose and Ben also decided not to reveal the painting because Rose and Nan were friends. Nan was very accepting of Rose, and that meant a lot to her."

"Nan probably didn't realize what she was in for!"

"I think you're right. She took a lot of flack for being the face that could "sour milk."

"So, all this time, Rose and Ben didn't say a word."

"Well, *American Gothic* became so famous so fast that they didn't want to jeopardize Grant's or Nan's success. They found the experience at the art colony to be one of the best periods of their lives."

"Of course, that's where they met, too."

Patrice nodded, and her attention shifted. "Here comes our food."

The waiter placed a plate in front of Jenny and a plate in front of Patrice. He placed a basket of warm Italian bread between them, a bowl full of salad, and a second bowl full of gnocchi for the women to share. Then he put a small plate containing Jenny's sausage link to the left of her plate.

A second waiter poured more water into their glasses and a

third waiter filled their wine glasses.

"I was hoping for better service and cuter waiters, but I guess this will do," Jenny joked.

"Hey, I'm telling Tom on you!"

"Never mind." Jenny lifted one of the noodles to her mouth. "Oh, this is *good*."

Patrice smiled in response and watched her sister enjoy her dinner for a few moments before digging into her own.

"One last question, and then I'll drill you about Glenn. What was the collateral you left with the Bostons?"

"Mom probably told you about the brooch I have that Nan gave me."

"Yes, she did. I can't tell you how many times I almost removed that from your vest when we were younger. I thought it was so *old* looking."

"I'm glad you didn't because that brooch has been in three paintings, *American Gothic, Woman with Plants,* and now the picture with Rose and Ben."

Jenny stopped, fork in mid-air. "Oh, Patrice," she said as she set down her fork, her mouth gaping.

"I know. Glenn helped me get it insured, as best we could, that is."

"Yeah, how do you insure priceless?" Jenny whispered, looking around to make sure no one heard her.

"The day the Bostons revealed their painting to me, I had the brooch in my jacket pocket, wrapped in bubble wrap. I unwrapped it in front of them and Rose knew right away what it was. Imagine, looking at a piece of jewelry you haven't seen in sixty years."

"Was she upset that you had it; did she wonder *why* you had it?"

"I told her about meeting Nan as a small girl at the first *Grant Wood Art Festival*. It didn't surprise her that Nan gave me the brooch. She said the Woods were so giving."

"Isn't it interesting how life works?"

"It is. I have to say I was actually sad to leave." Patrice downed her second glass of wine and a waiter promptly came to the table to fill her glass again. She nodded her approval while Jenny looked on.

"You were sad?"

"Umm, a mixture of feelings but yes, mainly sadness."

"I never thought I'd hear you say that."

"Why?"

"Why? Hmmm, let's see," Jenny mimicked her comment by putting her finger to her chin, "you've rarely been home across ten years, and when you did come home you were usually on a quick flight back to New York."

"Jenny, I have worked hard since I left home for college, going from one thing to the next. It wasn't easy to just get on a plane and go home. The trip back to Iowa was out of the blue and seemed like an inconvenience with everything I had on my plate. I was actually mad at Glenn for sending me."

"What? Why?"

"Because I thought the story of Nan's death didn't match what *European Art* is about. I thought it was a waste of time, and I didn't want to search for a way to connect the story of her death to our magazine. I blamed Glenn for all those inconveniences."

Jenny's stare unnerved Patrice. That stare went back across three decades. It was the stare that she had always gotten from her older sister whenever she had disappointed her.

"Hear me out, Jenny. When I left the farm, I took that Iowa work ethic to New York with me. It felt extravagant to go to school in New York, and because it did, I felt a lot was expected of me. I worked hard—maybe too hard. All I know is that I never looked back. My work here, the demands on my time, the busy pace of this city."

"I'm not buying it," Jenny cut her off like a New York minute.

"Not buying what?"

"That you've been too busy to come home," Jenny said looking at her straight in the eye. "What's eating at you?"

Oh no, another cross-examination on this topic. *Would this never end?* Patrice closed her eyes and downed her third glass

213

of wine. As the sweet liquid coated her throat, she thought about reacting in anger like a sister does to a vulnerable sibling. That was too easy though and Jenny wasn't that vulnerable person anymore. Instead, a strong, no non-sense kind of woman was sitting across the table from her staring her down. Patrice wanted a relationship with her sister more than she wanted to continue this dance of anger and justification. She knew if she didn't solve for this now, she'd unravel the progress she had made in connecting with her family again.

"It's not that simple Jenny. It's not like I think about this all the time so bare with me."

"Okay, I'm waiting." Jenny finished the last of her sausage peering over at her sister between bites.

"It feels like a multiple list of reasons. I guess I have rationalized it differently over the years, finding reasons not to go back, finding fault with everything and everyone. Very soon it all seemed a world away. I thought I didn't want to go back when really, it was about being afraid to go home and facing all these feelings."

Jenny put her fork down and started on her second glass of wine.

"You know what's really interesting?" Patrice added, pensively. "I thought art and writing about art started in New York, like I had to leave home to find it. I believed it only existed in specific places."

"Like New York?" Jenny answered as she watched the waiter fill Patrice's wine glass.

"But that's where I was wrong. It's all around us, it was all around us growing up, Jenny. I didn't know that, but that's what the Regionalists knew. They connected to something deep within when they were home, some kind of acknowledgement, or acceptance, and when they allowed it in." Patrice froze her hand with the wine glass near her face as if realizing something for the first time.

"What?"

"I never wanted to acknowledge it. Accept it."

"What are you talking about?"

"Shame. The shame I have felt for so long for who I am, where I come from."

"I'm not following you. What shame are you talking about?"

"Jenny, do you remember when I won that state short-story contest and the prize was to travel to Iowa City to the University of Iowa's Writer's Workshop?"

"Yeah, what about it?"

"I was so angry that mom and dad wouldn't let me go. I won first place and I couldn't even present my story. Do you know how embarrassing that was to go back to school and tell Mrs. Levin under no circumstances could I go?"

"I'll admit that sucked," Jenny answered.

Patrice put her wine glass down and pulled her hair back into a ponytail with shaky hands as if she'd just seen a ghost.

"Do you know you pull your hair back when there's something you don't want to do or think about?" Jenny said.

Patrice finished pulling her hair back and grabbed the arms of her chair. She was having an insight and no amount of wine was going to keep it from materializing. She knew if she was truly honest with herself and pass through the pain she was starting to feel in her stomach, she could get to the core of why she didn't want to go home. Her thoughts drifted back to her junior year of high school and her hands clasped tighter around the arms of her chair.

As long as she could remember, she loved to read. She was inspired by her elementary school teachers who read stories out loud to their students such as the *Little House on the Prairie* books by Laura Ingalls Wilder, *Charlotte's Web*, and Beverly Cleary's books like *Mitch and Amy*. When her sixth-grade teacher stopped the cycle of teachers reading to her students, Patrice indulged in books like Nancy Drew and biographies of presidents, athletes, and famous women. By junior high she was scouring the school library for young adult books like *The Outsiders*, and *Where the Red Fern Grows*. She excelled in her English and debate classes. By ninth grade, she was taking English, a creative writing class, and one of her favorite classes, Novel, where the course outline was a semester of reading great classics. This is when she first learned about *Catcher in the Rye* and although they did not read it in class, her curiosity found a copy of it at the public library. She didn't understand the book entirely, but she knew very quickly she had never read anything like it.

Patrice remembered a familiar quote she liked in the book: "What I was really hanging around for, I was trying to feel some goodbye. I mean I've left schools and places I didn't even know I was leaving them. I hate that." Intrigued by the writing, Patrice read that novel every year for the next five years. J.D. Salinger became her idol.

By high school, Patrice signed up for the school newspaper and student yearbook clubs, because she wanted to spend her life writing like J.D. Salinger. She received a journal for her sixteenth birthday, and this began a life-long love affair of writing in journals. She wrote every evening before she went to bed capturing her thoughts of the day and the people she had encountered. Her mind was at ease when she wrote her thoughts down in that journal. Her creative writing teacher at that time, Mrs. Levin, encouraged Patrice and her classmates to write poetry, short stories, and essays. Mrs. Levin was grooming her students for local, state, and regional high school writing contests and often presented topics for the students to write about. Every class was devoted to writing, presenting, and critiquing the student's work. This particular day, Patrice and her classmates were to write about the one living person they wanted to meet. Patrice presented a short story about wanting to meet and interview J.D. Salinger. She remembered the shift on her teacher's face from a look of scrutiny to a look of captivation. Patrice knew at that moment this story had a chance of being entered into a contest. Mrs. Levin worked with her during lunch time on numerous occasions for the purpose of helping her prepare her story for entry into the State of Iowa's High School Student Writer's Contest. The winners would read their stories in front of university faculty, parents and other writers at the world-renowned Writer's Workshop at the University of Iowa in Iowa City. When the story met all requirements, Mrs. Levin helped Patrice fill out the contest application. Patrice licked the envelope and with delight pounded the stamp onto the upper right-hand corner of the envelope. It was late November and they would hear if she had won in four months. That night Patrice proudly shared this with her parents that she had entered a short story to the state writers contest. They shook their heads in approval and said the pleasantries of *good for you* but continued to eat their dinner and did not ask to read the story. Only Jenny remarked, "That's cool." Patrice was on cloud nine not caring what her family thought because she felt for the first time a purpose in her life that was worth pursuing.

February came and went, and school activities kept Patrice so busy that she sometimes forgot about the contest. Diane Johnston, another student in Mrs. Levin's class was an A student. She knew Mrs. Levin had also devoted her time to helping Diane and in Patrice's mind, Diane was sure to win. Yet when Mrs. Levin announced Diane had not won but applauded her for submitting her work, Patrice grew nervous about her short story. Diane was a student that always won at everything she did. Patrice started to feel a small pain deep inside that she had never felt before. The type of pain that tells you that something matters more than you realize. At seventeen, Patrice thought it was nerves and dismissed it.

It was St. Patrick's Day and Patrice wore the customary color for the holiday by putting on a green sweater. She didn't want to be teased and pinched by the other students for not wearing the color of the holiday. When she opened the door to the high school, she saw Mrs. Levin at the top of the steps waiting for her. She too was wearing green, a long-sleeved dress that complemented her golden colored shoulder-length hairdo. In her hand was an envelope. She waved it at Patrice.

"Let's find a room where we can open this letter from the State of Iowa Writer's Contest and talk before classes start." Patrice timidly followed her esteemed teacher to the Guidance Counselor's Office, and they sat down at the nearest table.

Mrs. Levin cautioned, "No matter what news you receive today from this letter, remember, this is the beginning of a life of great things for you because you're willing to put yourself out there and try."

She didn't want to let her teacher down, and those words drew out the pain that Patrice felt in the pit of her stomach.

Patrice carefully opened the envelope, unfolded the letter and read the first two lines. She screamed with excitement.

"What, what is it?" Mrs. Levin said with a bewildered look on her face.

"My story, it placed first and they want me in Iowa City in three weeks to present it!" She stretched out her arm to hand the letter to her teacher and stood up and clasped her hands together like she was praying fervently to God.

Mrs. Levin scanned the letter and then she stood up and grabbed Patrice's hands and together they looked into each other's face with glee and did a happy stomp with their feet.

"What's going on in there?" Mrs. Raines, the guidance counselor, said poking her head out of her office. Her face softened when she saw Mrs. Levin.

"We have cause to celebrate. Patrice Powell just won first place in a state writing contest for her short story!" Mrs. Levin said putting one arm around Patrice and facing her toward Mrs. Raines as if she were presenting her.

"That's quite an accomplishment! Can I see the letter?" Mrs. Raines nodded toward the paperwork in Patrice's grasp.

"Sure," Patrice said dutifully walking the letter over to her guidance counselor who was wearing a green scarf around her neck.

Mrs. Raines scanned the letter and said, "Well, well, I'm impressed. Award winning writers like you can get scholarships to great writing schools you know."

Patrice hadn't even thought that far ahead but now her thoughts were really swirling. Maybe she could get a scholarship at the University of Iowa! She beamed at the thought and the attention she was receiving from these women. She could hardly wait to go home to tell her parents.

The day dragged as Patrice imagined the look on her parents' faces as their youngest daughter shared this news. They knew she had worked very hard on her essays and short-stories and now she had something to show for all that hard work.

It was raining when Patrice stepped off the school bus and walked the driveway toward the house. She was barely aware she was drenched from head to toe when she stepped into the kitchen where her mother was making dinner. Her mother was wearing one of her Julia Child inspired aprons whose apron strings were so long they tied across the front of the apron that clung to her mother's skirt. Her mother had a dish towel tucked just off center from the tied bow of the apron strings. Patrice loved that her mother tried to instill her heritage in these small and subtle ways. Jenny was in the living room preoccupied with after school shows on the television when Patrice shared the award letter with her mother. Her mother hugged her and said her father would be quite proud of her too. When Martin Powell came in for dinner after doing the chores, she shared her award. He nodded in approval and sat down for coffee before his evening meal. That nod of approval was enough from her quiet father as her mother had compensated for the emotions he lacked. With both her parents in the room Patrice talked about the travel to Iowa City to read her award-winning story on a Wednesday afternoon in early April. The look on her parents' faces deteriorated. The first words she heard from her father's mouth was no.

Patrice started to endorse the importance of the occasion and the expectation from her teacher but quickly stopped when her father's index finger gestured for Patrice to stop talking. Patrice looked at her mother's face. Her mother also looked at her sternly to stop.

"We are not driving all the way to Iowa City for an award," were the words that Patrice remembered. Patrice looked behind her and saw Jenny standing in the entrance to the kitchen. Jenny's hands were folded across her chest and looked downward when Patrice glanced at her. Jenny knew that tone too. The tone that echoed *don't talk back.*

Many children would have refused to eat dinner on an evening like this, but Patrice knew better. Her obedience under the tense circumstances would aid her in talking about Iowa City at a later time when her parents were calmer, and the stresses of the day were off their shoulders.

Late in the evening, Patrice entered the living room where her mother sat on the sofa reading. Her father and sister had gone to bed.

Patrice asked softly, "Why can't we travel to Iowa City? This award means a lot to me and my school."

Her mother closed her book and looked at Patrice with weary eyes. "We have a lot to do to get the farm ready for spring. We don't have time to traipse you to Iowa City. Besides, the gas prices are almost seventy cents per gallon right now. That's way too much money for a trip to Iowa City for a writing contest!"

Patrice heard her mother's tone escalating and looked away. "What if my teacher Mrs. Levin drove me there?" Patrice responded trying to keep the conversation civilized yet trying to find a resolution.

"No, we're not going to inconvenience Mrs. Levin. We need you here on the farm to do the spring planting. We have the fields to prepare as well as the garden."

"Isn't April too early to do that? We usually plant in May." Patrice said watching her tone.

"We're to have a warm spring this year so we want to get prepared earlier and plant earlier," her mother responded with a firm sound.

At this point, Patrice couldn't let it go. "Mom, I've decided I want to be a writer someday, so this award means a lot. Maybe I have the talent to get a college scholarship."

Martin Powell entered the room in his pajamas and by the look on his face Patrice knew he had heard the conversation and was fit to be tied. She tried to hide her fear by standing up straighter and looking him in the eye.

"Patrice, enough!" he said sternly. "Your mother and I don't want to hear any more talk about this award, traveling to Iowa City, or your pursuit in writing. That's not a practical occupation for a young woman to have. Writers starve! You're wasting your time thinking about this crazy dream." Her father's head was cocked to the side and that was his look for believing something was stupid. That pain in her gut returned but she ignored it.

"I think I have talent. If you read my stories you would know I could write for a newspaper or . . ." Patrice said knowing this plea would go nowhere.

"Your father is right. You'd be better off doing something practical like getting a business degree, becoming a teacher, or marrying someone from here," her mother said cutting her off.

"Besides, what makes you think you have the talent? This one award has gone to your head young lady. You need to rethink your priorities! Now, go . . . to . . . bed," her father demanded.

Patrice quickly left the conversation and went to bed as she was told. Her parents had been strict with Patrice and Jenny and she knew how far she could challenge them. She fell on her bed with her stomach in knots thinking about their conversation. There had to be a way to go to that award ceremony. She fell into a fitful sleep, her mind unrelenting and the pain in her stomach wanting its time and attention.

Her parents barely talked to her for two days after that conversation. That was usually the penalty in the household when someone was being selfish. She ended up making the decision she had made, she'd shut down and tucked away her feelings. This is how she had learned to survive their anger. Over the years those feelings brought resentment for the farm and its survival that had always come first. Patrice felt the family sacrificed for this way of life.

Jenny sided with her parents and didn't talk to Patrice as well. Patrice understood why Jenny made that decision, but it angered her to have the entire family against her. Her family's anger was further supplemented by her own shame and embarrassment in telling Mrs. Levin the state winner could not attend, read her short-story, and represent her school.

◆ ◆ ◆

Still deep in thought Patrice finished the quote by J.D. Salinger out-loud, "I don't care if it's a sad goodbye or a bad goodbye, but when I leave a place, I like to know I'm leaving it." She finished her wine.

"Hello, what's going on with you?" Jenny was waving her hand in front of Patrice's face. "You've had about ten different looks on your face while you were zoned out."

Patrice looked at Jenny as if recognizing her for the first time. "Jenny, that represented so much more than just a contest to me. That was a future that I wanted, and they accused me of being selfish, and overly proud of myself. I was just a young girl who wanted a dream. I thought people that loved me would want that for me and when they didn't, I thought something was wrong with me!" Patrice folded her arms across her chest, resting the wine glass on her left elbow. She stared at the wine glass instead of looking at her sister.

"Is that why you haven't been home for so long?"

Patrice nodded at her wine glass. "I didn't want to feel that shame again."

"But you ended up going to Columbia University on a writing scholarship. Mom and dad supported that, so I'm still confused about where you're going with all of this."

"I think they let me take that scholarship out of guilt and even though they let me go, they seemed happy about it, like they were glad to see me off. You know, as far away as possible." Patrice's voice drifted as if she was watching herself leave for New York.

Patrice gulped and caught her breath. Gut-wrenching sobs changed the contours of her face.

"Patrice?" Jenny strained a whisper.

Patrice placed her forehead on the wine glass, which rose and fell with her continued sobs. Jenny leaned forward and gently pulled the wine glass from her sister's hand and placed it on the table. She laid her napkin in her sister's open palm.

"Patrice."

Patrice's breath was rapid as she said, "What?"

"Didn't you know that mom and dad talked to Mrs. Levin?"

Patrice didn't respond.

Jenny slid her food aside and looked at Patrice. "Knowing how painful this had been for you, not getting to go to Iowa City to accept your award, mom went to talk to Mrs. Levin." Jenny waited for any utterance from Patrice but did not get one. Mrs. Levin shared your story and some of your other writings with mom who sat in the office and read them. Mrs. Levin confirmed you were a gifted writer. Mom took your work home to dad and he read your work too. Mom returned to Mrs. Levin asking her to help find a writing scholarship for you."

"What? Why didn't they tell me this?" Patrice said, lifting her head.

"You were shut down after that and they saw how it changed you. They were afraid that any help they would offer you would be pushed away, and, in the end, you would not pursue writing. They decided to remain silent about it."

"How did you know about this?" Patrice said, her voice dropping down an octave with emotion.

"I sat on the staircase and listened to them talk about it one night when they thought you and I had gone to bed."

"Since when do you keep secrets?" Patrice joked in a soft voice.

"I tried to tell you a couple of times, but you pushed me away and soon I just forgot about it. I think mom and dad were just afraid when you won that award."

"Afraid of what?"

"That they couldn't afford to send you to college to help you with your aspirations. That was a tough economic time in Iowa especially for farmers. Commodity prices and land prices were down, and mom and dad were having a tough time of making ends meet. Mrs. Levin assured them she could find a scholarship and with the help of student aid that going to college could be affordable. She also showed them what kind of jobs you could get that paid well in writing, especially if you lived in a city. When that great scholarship from Columbia University came along, even though it was hard for mom and dad to see you go, they relented."

"You know what hurt the most, Jenny? They never seemed interested in reading anything I wrote. It took my high school teacher to coax them into being interested in my writing." Patrice couldn't shut off her tears and rearranged the cloth napkin to find a dry spot.

"Yes, it took an experienced writing teacher to help them understand your talent, but they've read everything since."

"What do you mean?" Patrice said finally looking at her sister.

"They've had a subscription to *European Art* ever since the day you started there."

"I've never seen a copy on a table or coffee table?" Patrice said shaking her head refusing to believe what she heard.

"It's true. You probably have never seen a copy on a table or coffee table because number one, mom is a clean freak and puts magazines in the magazine rack next to dad's chair, and number two, she shares them with their next-door neighbor, Mrs. Kroft."

"Mrs. Kroft! Why would she do that?"

"Crazy Mrs. Kroft is Mrs. Levin's aunt and she makes sure Mrs. Levin gets to see every issue."

Patrice broke down in more tears only this time the pain in her stomach was gone and she started to giggle at the thoughts of Mrs. Kroft.

Jenny took one look at her sister, motioned the waiter for the check and said, "Patrice, let's go home."

CHAPTER 19

The next day, Patrice sat down on her sofa and took the November issue of *European Art* from her coffee table. So much had happened before that issue hit the newsstands. She had uncovered a valuable piece of art, she was in contact with her family more than she had been for the past five to ten years, and she had found some peace thanks to the therapy session Jenny had given her the night before.

The New York skyline out her window was bright but there was a chance of rain in the forecast. She knew she had to speak to Glenn about finding another job with another magazine. Patrice was ready for a new challenge in many aspects of her life. She knew Glenn would be very supportive of that decision if not somewhat relieved.

As she thumbed through the magazine, she thought about how helpful he had been to bring the painting to New York and was thankful for a sister who ensured it arrived safely. Patrice guided and organized the process for the Bostons, but Jenny and Glenn were extremely instrumental in making sure everything went smoothly from Iowa to New York. Patrice looked out the window again. She could see a future with Glenn.

"I overslept."

"Oh, you scared me!"

"Sorry," Jenny said pulling her robe tighter around her body.

"Jenny, when was the last time you had a chance to sleep in?"

"It's been a long time. It was all the excitement from last

night," she grinned.

"It's your last full day in town, let's make the best of it. What would you like to do?"

"I'd like to see a day in the life of Patrice Powell."

"What do you mean?" Patrice broke into her own smile.

"Show me your office, your favorite stores. Heck, I've never seen Columbia University. I know that Columbia University is no longer a part of your usual day, but I'd like to see it, too."

"All right. Glenn has invited us to dinner at his place, so you'll get to see where he lives. There's some coffee made in the kitchen and some bagels. If you want something more, just let me know."

"This is perfect." Jenny was already in the small kitchen grabbing a coffee mug. "Thanks for giving up your bed. You must feel cramped with a guest in your apartment."

"I don't mind. It gives me a chance to try out the sofa bed. It's not too bad."

"Don't you wish you had more room than this studio apartment?"

"I'm just thankful to not have a roommate, or two, like I did up until last year. It's nice to have my own space, even if it's limited."

"Patrice, let's not let so much time go by before we see each other again." Jenny looked into her mug as she spoke to her sister. "I miss you."

"Jenny, it's meant a lot to me that you came out to New York."

"Well, you paid for it."

"That's because you did me a big favor. I hope you'll stop by and check in on the Bostons once in a while. They would enjoy getting to know you even more."

"I'd like to get to know them."

"Finish your coffee, and let's get dressed."

Out on the street, the looming Manhattan skyline wasn't enough to shelter the sisters against the dribble of rain. Patrice opened her umbrella extending it over her head and Jenny's.

"Brr, it's getting chilly out here." Patrice said with a shiver,

"We'll catch the subway and it's just two blocks away."

They walked among the Manhattan bustle of people dodging raincoats, hooded sweatshirts, and those with umbrellas in their hands.

"This way," Patrice said as they stepped down the subway steps. Patrice paid for both of them. "We'll probably end up standing."

They boarded the 10:40 subway train and Patrice grabbed a pole to hang on to. She invited Jenny to do the same. "I thought we'd go to the magazine so you can see where I work, but before we do let's do a little shopping."

Jenny nodded, her face looking a bit like a cornered animal.

Patrice realized this trip had been a lot for Jenny. She knew that New York and its crowds must feel overwhelming to her sister, but she didn't want to make Jenny feel worse by being overly solicitous. Instead, Patrice made a face at Jenny.

Jenny gave a grin that turned into giggles. "What was that for?"

"It's just nice to be with you." Patrice said affectionately, bumping her sister with her shoulder.

◆ ◆ ◆

The subway came to the 59th Street and Lexington stop. Coming up to the street level they saw the sign for Bloomingdale's directly in front of them, like a beacon, calling shoppers and tourists into its magnetic embrace.

"Can we go in there?" Jenny asked, almost breathless at the thought.

"Yes. I thought we could start here, see a few shops on Madison Avenue, and have lunch. We'll head back to Lower Manhattan this afternoon."

The rest of the morning flew by quickly as the pair walked the shopping district of Manhattan, mainly window-shopping so Jenny could see the storefronts of famous designers such as Calvin Klein, Boutique Giorgio, and Chanel. It was nearly 2:00 p.m. when their hunger won the battle for their attention.

"I want to take you to Serendipity 3."

"What's that?"

"It's a restaurant, but they also serve some great ice cream specialties. It's a New York favorite."

"Sounds interesting."

The wait outside Serendipity 3 on the Upper East Side was thirty minutes.

"This actually isn't too long of a wait compared to what it could be," Patrice confided.

"I'm just glad I wore some comfortable shoes and a warm coat." The sun was beginning to peer from behind the clouds, but the shade created by the skyline blocked any warmth the sun would provide. "So, what do you like about this place?"

"It's fun and the atmosphere is different. People love the ice cream here, especially the frozen hot chocolate. It's like a frozen chocolate daiquiri with various chocolates blended with ice and cocoa and lots of whipped cream."

"I'll probably need a nap after this."

"No napping. We're going to jump back on the subway after we eat and go to Columbia University and then to the magazine. There is so much to see in New York. I wish we had more time, so I could show you more."

"I've never experienced anything like this."

"It does take some getting used to."

The line was moving, and Jenny and Patrice descended the stairs to the basement restaurant.

"How did you move to such a place when you were only eighteen?"

"I guess I didn't know better at the time. My roommates and I would spend our weekends riding the subway, exploring stores, and once in a while we'd splurge at some restaurant."

When their table was ready, Patrice and Jenny walked through the double doors and into the foyer. They were escorted through a hallway that displayed novelties and gifts of all kinds highlighting the experience at Serendipity 3.

"Oh, I can't wait to check this out," Jenny blurted as she

stopped to look at some t-shirts, but Patrice didn't hear her as she was already in the distance, following the host to a table.

The restaurant was packed with people of all ages, most with shopping bags and umbrellas hanging off the back of their chairs. Patrice and Jenny were seated in a room of numerous Tiffany-style lampshades in reds, greens, golds and oranges. It was also accented with frosted lamps with glowing white light that cast soft lighting around the room.

"Hey, maybe I should switch seats with you so you can do some of the people watching from here," Patrice said, starting to move her things.

"No. Stay put. Looking at the art behind you puts my mind at ease."

"I like the artsy feel to the place, too. Shouldn't surprise you, huh?"

"It's all very funky. I would like to walk around and look at the rest of the place. I looked up the stairs we just passed and saw a pink ceiling."

"Isn't that great? I wish we could have sat upstairs. You should see it at Christmas time."

Patrice and Jenny ordered salads and topped off their lunch sharing a frozen hot chocolate. The waiter brought the decadent dessert and placed it in the center of the table. Chocolate liquid flowed over the side of the large goblet onto a white saucer. Whipped cream sat on top, showered with chocolate shavings. The waitress handed them each a spoon.

Jenny just shook her head.

"Is everything over the top here?"

"Yes, it is. Bon appétit."

"I'm so glad you talked me into ordering salad. Otherwise I would never be able to tackle this!"

Jenny took her first bite. "Is this how you spend most of your days, Patrice?"

"Hardly! I work or I spend quiet weekends with Glenn. I have to save my money for small pleasures such as this."

"This frozen hot chocolate is really good."

"I thought you might like it. Whenever Glenn and I are on this side of town, we try to stop in."

"So, what is Glenn up to today?"

"He was heading to The Metropolitan. He made an appointment to see the painting."

"Is someone there to let him see it?"

"One of the staff members that Dr. Brooks referred to works the weekend so they're expecting him."

"What time was his appointment?"

"4:00."

"And we're due at his house for dinner at what time?"

"8:00."

"Let's meet him. We're not far from the park. How far away do you think we are from The Metropolitan?"

"We're about 20 blocks from here to the museum; sounds far but in New York that equates to a 30-minute walk. What's this about? I thought you wanted to do more sightseeing."

"I do, but I'd like to see the park again, and I need to walk off this dessert. Besides, wouldn't you like to see Glenn's initial reaction to the painting? Let's finish here and meet up with him."

"Okay. We could do that. I admit, I *would* like to see his face when he sees the painting for the first time. Are you sure, Jenn? This is our time together."

"I know but I'd also like to see Glenn. All I need to do is stop by the gift shop before we leave and purchase some of this frozen hot chocolate mix. Tom and the kids will love it."

The cold New York air enveloped them at the door. It was now windy and those waiting in line were huddling together to stay warm.

"We should walk on the sunny side of the street to stay warm, especially after the frozen hot chocolate."

"Yes. I'll follow you."

Patrice stepped out into the crosswalk and Jenny was already falling behind. Patrice slowed a bit and Jenny stepped up her pace. The two were quickly side by side again.

As they stepped into the thin rays of sunlight, Jenny said, "I hope what I shared with you last night you heard in the right way. We all love you."

"You gave me space to let it all out," Patrice said, dodging some of the walkers on the street.

"I still see you as my successful sister, you know, always strong, never yielding. I was taken aback by all your emotion around it."

"It surprised me, too. Here I am, talking about what I learned from the Regionalists, and the next thing I knew I'm having a meltdown with a wine glass in my hand. That was really good wine by the way."

"I never knew you had been dealing with all of that. We should have made an effort to come to New York to see you. Somehow, we got it into our heads that maybe you didn't want us here," Jenny said, looking at Patrice's face for a reaction.

"I'm sure I conveyed that in one way or another."

"Well, we're going to change that. Even though this city intimidates the hell out of me, I would feel comfortable coming back here to visit with you, and I will encourage our parents to come with Tom and me."

"I'd like that."

"You know, New York isn't so different from Iowa," Jenny pointed out.

"So, you say," Patrice replied.

"The people here have been pretty nice—not what I've heard of New Yorkers. I see similar work ethics. Everyone here seems to be serious about their work."

"I would agree with that."

"And, we have the same *chilly* fall weather that requires coats, scarves, and gloves," Jenny added.

"That's for sure, but I don't recall seeing skyscrapers in Iowa," Patrice said, scanning the skyline.

"Maybe one in Des Moines," Jenny countered.

"Or great shopping," Patrice volleyed.

"Kansas City has a Macy's."

"That doesn't count."

"I know. But yesterday when I saw Central Park with its trees dressed for fall and gardens holding on to the last of their blooms, it did give me a sense of home."

Patrice caught sight of The Metropolitan. "Look ahead. We're almost there."

"Do you think they'll call us in a couple of weeks to confirm that the painting is authentic?"

"Dr. Brooks already knows it's the real deal. He just wants to socialize it around town and brag about it."

"Why did you bring it here rather than say, Chicago?"

"The Met may decide to purchase it, and if they do, the painting will stay here. If it were owned by *The Art Institute of Chicago*, I'm afraid it would compete with the *other American Gothic*.

"And if it stays in Cedar Rapids or Davenport?"

"It will be cared for there as well."

"Look at it this way, if the painting stays here, you'll always have a little reminder of home here in New York. If the painting stays in Iowa, you can visit and bring a little bit of New York to Iowa. Either way, you have the best of both worlds."

Patrice locked arms with her sister. "And that's all I've ever wanted."

EPILOGUE

The day was lovely. A cool breeze drifted across Patrice's skin as she ascended the steps with the invitation in her hand. She felt honored by this special summons. She opened one of the double doors and stepped inside.

"Mrs. Collier?"

"Yes."

"Miss Kirkpatrick will be here shortly," said a man in a black suit who gave Patrice a full-length glance.

She caught her reflection in a doorway to the main gallery. She had forsaken her ponytail for curled hair that now cascaded down across her shoulders. She smoothed her pale light blue silk dress and wrap, nodding her approval at her reflection. Her face lit up when she saw Anne Kirkpatrick.

"Patrice, we're glad to see you!"

"Hi, Anne, I'm glad to be here."

"Did Glenn come with you?"

"He did. He's bringing my family with him to the public viewing this evening."

"We have so much to show you all. Follow me upstairs."

"I can't wait to see it."

"Just to let you know, we followed the instructions of our anonymous donor. As I mentioned to you on the phone, the funds came with very specific instructions for how the wing should be constructed, as well as how the money should be spent."

Patrice and Anne reached the top step.

"Here it is. We wanted you to be the first to see it before we opened it up to the public tonight." Anne held open the door to the gallery wing.

Patrice stepped inside and put her hand to her mouth, catching her breath. Anne smiled and slipped quietly from the room.

In front of Patrice were larger than life black and white photos of scenes from the *Stone City Art Colony*. The museum had secured numerous photos of the art colony by publishing requests in the local and national newspapers. They were displayed on large wooden frames hung from the ceiling throughout the gallery in various lengths and sizes. The feel in the gallery was very nostalgic and celebratory.

The first image was Green Mansion and labeled so. The large photo loomed over Patrice as she remembered the day over three years earlier when she fell asleep on the remains of the mansion's floor. She would never fully understand the vision she saw that day other than as a reinforcement of Rose's words, thanks to her Aunt Patsy, about the mansion grounds being a magical place for the people who lived or visited there. She wished she could have seen the mansion in its entire splendor and walked its halls like the art students had.

She followed the image to the next wall photo—the *Stone City Art Colony* faculty sitting in front of the mansion with the stone fruit pedestal. Each faculty member, Patrice had found, went on to make significant contributions to the art world or to society after they each left the art colony. Another testament to the magic of that place Patrice thought. *For a moment in time, 1932 and 1933, they were all together, all connected.*

Beyond that picture, was a clear glass case. Patrice peered downward and saw an original brochure, "Aim of the Colony," from the *Stone City Art Colony and School*. Next to the brochure were paint brushes, used paint tubes, and drafting pencils owned by Grant Wood. There was a brown paper pencil drawing called *Hill Near Viola* on loan from the *Davenport Museum of Art*. Grant's glasses were also in the case. Patrice thought about the curator at the *Davenport Museum of Art*. They still have his collectibles! She wondered if the curator, Sheila, was still employed there.

Next, she saw another life-size photo of those who attended the art colony in 1932 just off to her right. Everyone appeared to be sitting under large shade trees. Grant was in the photo and the Bostons. Patrice wished that Nan somehow could have been in that photo. The students appeared to be dressed in their Sunday best. The women wore dresses and the men were in summer shirts and pants. Grant and another student were in overalls but wore white short-sleeved dress shirts underneath them. Most of the students wore light colored clothing so most stood out in this black and white photo.

She then strolled by the photo of the checkered tablecloth lying over the large picnic table, with students sitting around it, enjoying their Sunday dinner. The atmosphere of the day looked joyous.

The photos continued across the room. There are so many of them she thought. The next photo showed the grounds of the *Stone City Art Colony* with the ice wagons parked sporadically across the lawn. Patrice had seen a similar picture in Nan's scrapbooks but not this one. She studied the detail of the artistic designs on the individual ice wagons, some faint against the dull gray of the picture.

In the adjoining room, the next exhibit stopped Patrice in her tracks. On the wall was a fragile-looking rectangular slab of wood the size of a large picture window. The slab revealed beautiful art work with snowy mountain peaks and evergreens. It was the false front of the ice wagon that had been in the Bostons' home. She had to restrain herself from touching it for this made the entire exhibit feel real. She pulled tissues from her purse and dabbed her eyes. She stepped back and took in the journey of it all.

Next was a framed glass the size of a wall hanging in a living room that held the story of *Gothic*. Through her moist eyes Patrice read the story chronicling *Gothic's* fifty-eight years in storage and its beginnings at the *Stone City Art Colony and School*.

Now in sight was *Gothic* at the far end of the wing. The lighting over the painting gave it special distinction among the black-and-white photos of the past. Rose's mint green smock with small pink flowers and pink bordering overlaid a sky-blue dress that complemented the blue-gray threads of the farmer's overalls standing next to her. Rose's dark flapper hair style nicely framed her porcelain skin. As Patrice drew closer, she observed that the brooch was somewhat lost against the brighter colors of Rose's dress and smock. Ben wore a white shirt with rolled up sleeves under his overalls looking much younger than the farmer in *American Gothic*. He looked handsome Patrice thought. Though he had a pitchfork in his hand, Ben wasn't wearing the jacket that Dr. Byron McKeeby did in *American Gothic*. In fact, the Bostons looked more like a newly married couple as opposed to a farmer and his daughter. Overall, Patrice thought *Gothic* emoted grit and determination on the faces of its characters as opposed to *American Gothic*'s portrayal of a sour and puritan existence.

Patrice bent low and saw underneath the painting a small plaque which read: "On loan from *The Metropolitan Museum of Art*, New York City, New York." Patrice smiled.

The exhibit now took her through two wheat colored limestone boulders, a tad shorter than her own height. She walked up to the wall photo of Florence Sprague Smith, the sculptress from Drake University who posed with students in the quarry. Patrice thought of her conversation with Rose about the quarry: *I went to the quarry as often as I could to choose rock that I could carve. How did I lug that stone up the hill? I had help from the men who worked in the quarry.* Those summer days had been the beginning of Rose's life's work. Patrice smiled as she thought about Rose chiseling away at the stone, sitting on the mansion steps, and making a mess that would begin a conversation with a man who would someday be her husband.

Next Patrice's eyes caught a display of artifacts from those who had attended the *Stone City Art Colony*. Among the artifacts was a Rose Boston sculpture of a young girl with a butterfly in the palm of her hand, made from a concrete mold, hand finished to look like weathered bronze.

Patrice looked around and shook her head, wondering where they had found more pictures of art students standing in a field with Grant Wood painting the Iowa countryside and Grant standing alone in a field with his wooden easel. The same easel was on display and Patrice was now standing beside it. She gently touched the easel, running her fingers down the side of the wood. She quickly pulled her hands away and looked around, slightly admonishing herself for indulging in the moment.

Beyond the easel, another photo showed John Steuart Curry with Grant in front of the mansion, laughing with an inscription that read: "John Steuart Curry comes to Iowa and dons a pair of overalls". Patrice hoped these photos would inspire people to learn more about the art colony and share stories passed down or stories simply known.

The last photo wasn't a wall photo but a life-size five to six-foot tall picture that stood on the floor. It was Nan standing on the mansion grounds talking with a student. The student she was talking to was Rose Boston who had her hands on her hips with sculpting utensils in both palms. Rose looked as if she had just returned from the quarry as dust appeared on her pants and perspiration on her brow. Nan was gazing at Rose with an affectionate look on her face. *Two famous faces now immortalized.* Patrice stood there transfixed looking from one iconic face to the other. Her admiration for these two women washed across her heart and Patrice bent her head downward like a servant expressing her gratitude.

Her heart was pounding when Patrice turned to what was now the end of the exhibit. A narrow wooden case stood before her with the top portion made of glass on all four sides. Resting on a dark blue velvet stand as if it was the hope diamond at the Smithsonian, was the brooch. It looked radiant under the bright light hovering above the case. Patrice's chest rose and fell with the pride she felt in sharing this brooch with those who had interest in this story now and into the future.

Patrice looked around and took it all in. Above her it read, "The *Stone City Art Colony and School, 1932-1933.*" The caption summed up the whole exhibit honoring the spirit and the legacy of the art colony.

Her eyes scanned the exhibit and rested on the stone fruit basket pedestal captured in the photo of the *Stone City Art Faculty*. *This is where it all started.* That hike to Stone City, so long ago, had aroused a life's journey.

The assignment of writing about Nan's death had reconnected Patrice back to that stone fruit pedestal. It hadn't taken her long after she returned to New York from Iowa to understand what they represented to her. That opulent pedestal, rooted in the Midwestern soil, surrounded by distressed prairie grasses and whiffs of distant hog barns, seemed out of place. She had felt that too growing up here: out of place and unaccepted. Yet she had choices that the pedestal did not have, the choice to leave. The choice to try, see and know where she did fit. Like, Grant and Nan, she left to find her life, but by returning to those familiar environments and people, her heart was awakened and when it was, it reacquainted her with what really mattered...*that we do not know how significant the moments in life are until the heart remembers.*

AFTERWORD

The lives of Nan Wood Graham and Grant Wood are very inspiring to me. I grew up in the Anamosa, Iowa area years after they did, not understanding the incredible impact their lives had on our world. To align what I learned about them with my story, I took liberties with the following key information to allow the story of *Stone Fruit* to flow:

American Gothic was painted in 1930 (not 1934) and was constructed and completed at Grant Wood's home, 5 Turner Alley, Cedar Rapids, Iowa.

Green Mansion was not damaged by fire in August of 1933, but in November 1963.

The brooch belongs to the *Figge Art Museum* in Davenport, Iowa.

Nan Wood died December 14, 1990 versus spring of 1990.

The *Grant Wood Art Festival* began in 1973, not 1972.

There is no "original" *American Gothic* (at least that we are aware of).

I share this with the reader because in writing the story, I found how important it was to Nan for the reader to know the accuracy of her story and her brother Grant's.

Made in the USA
Monee, IL
22 June 2020